Late Knight

Late Knight

Laurence Payne

Hodder & Stoughton
LONDON SYDNEY AUCKLAND TORONTO

British Library Cataloguing in Publication Data
Payne, Laurence
  Late knight.
  I. Title
823'.914[F]   PR6066.A93

ISBN 0 340 40928 2

Hodder and Stoughton Editorial Office: 47 Bedford Square, London WC1B 3DP.

For

JAY SWALLOW

A *Steak Diane* in Hunstanton perhaps?

Note to the Reader

For dramatic purposes I have taken certain liberties with the production schedules presently operating at the Royal Shakespeare Theatre, Stratford-upon-Avon.

My thanks are due to Mr Roger Howells, the theatre's Production Manager, for much patient help and friendship; also for allowing me to include him in the telling of the story. Apart from this and the use of the redoubtable name of Mr Trevor Nunn, the Artistic Director of the theatre, all characters are fictional and bear no relation to living persons.

L.P.

When sorrows come, they come not single spies,
But in battalions.

Hamlet

Chapter One

Stratford was a shambles. No wonder the swans left. Their departure was the end of an era, as lamentable as the Tower of London losing its ravens or Gibraltar its Barbary apes.

Hunched over the parapet of old Clopton Bridge I cast a jaundiced eye over the seething clutter of river traffic and the littered green sward of the adjoining Bancroft Gardens strident with blaring radios, day-tripping picnickers and screaming children.

Mid-winter is the time to see Stratford, when the captains and the kings have departed and the town is left to lick its wounds and sink back into the peaceful parochialism of its own people. For the rest of the year, throughout the theatrical season in fact, it has never been anything but messy; if you don't care for Shakespeare, it's hell on wheels, with its chronic parking problems, its plethora of souvenir shops, overcrowded restaurants and countless pubs and inns and hotels, ancient and modern, bursting at the seams with Shakespearean groupies and puzzled visitors from abroad.

Only the parish church rides the storm with any semblance of dignity, the landmark of its elegant spire spearing the surrounding trees. The theatre too, strangely enough, has a kind of contained peace, its weathered bulk moored alongside the river like a landlocked leviathan awaiting sailing orders.

Gloomily I turned away and hoofed it slowly across the bridge and into town. Much had changed since I had last been there, and nothing more so than the general tendency for all to be brasher and louder; it was a holiday resort housing a three-ringed circus. The patina of wonder and respect had gone with the swans. It reminded me of Pompeii where the local youth play football among the ruins.

On a sudden impulse and remembering my need for socks to

9

go with shorts I elbowed my way into Marks and Spencer's housed now in the building which had once been the White Horse Hotel. Sweltering as we were in the midst of an Indian summer the place was steamy with sweating, underclad shoppers, most of them irritable, all of them blazing their own individual trails with elbows and shoulders, some with the aid of shopping trolleys and children's push-chairs. I hadn't been in the place thirty seconds when one of these last, packed with a couple of hideously plain twins, ran over both my feet and sent me cannoning into the arms of a luscious red-head who fielded me with remarkable adroitness and then stood, wide-eyed and open-mouthed, holding on to me with both hands as if the world were about to come to an end.

I too felt my jaw begin to sag as I realised with a jolt that I had once been married to this young person for the best part of a couple of years and hadn't seen her for at least six.

"Mark?" she whispered wonderingly.

"Well, well," was all I could think of, then followed it up with a sharp, "What are you doing here?"

"I work here."

"In Marks and Spencer's?"

That made her laugh, showing her fine teeth and a healthy tongue. "Fool!" she said and was diverted from further intelligence by some idiot of a woman running into her from behind with a shopping-trolley.

"Why don't we get out of here?" I muttered crossly and without further ado took her by the arm and thrust her through the throng like a diminutive ice-breaker. I remember thinking as I deposited her on the baking pavement outside that she hadn't grown an inch in the last six years and still fitted comfortably under my arm.

"It's too hot to stand about here," I said. "Where can we go?"

"The Cobweb's the only place at this time." She slid a familiar arm through mine and drew me away.

The Cobweb had been one of my favourite haunts. I was surprised and gratified to find it had survived the general rearrangement of the town. We found a vacant oak settle upstairs and creaked our way between it and a dangerously rocky table, ordered tea and cakes from a highly bedworthy young waitress, then drew back into our opposing corners and eyed each other critically for the first time in years.

She looked good enough to eat. Pert face, golden satin skin, green eyes, trim boyish figure clad devastatingly in an off-the-shoulder sage green blouse and white linen tennis shorts. The thin gold chain around her throat had been a gift from me; the engagement ring she now wore on her right hand was the one she and I had pondered over for so long in a King's Road jewellers nearly ten years ago. It made me feel old and sad.

"You've changed your hair," I said. "Gone red."

"For the play."

"What play?"

"*Lear.* Tonight. At the theatre."

"You're in *Lear*? I didn't know that."

She pouted a smile. "And here was I thinking you had come all this way to see li'l ol' me."

"I'm here to see the play certainly, but I had no idea li'l ol' you were in it. Sorry. What are you playing?"

"Regan."

I smirked. "That figures."

"Beast."

Tea and cakes saved the day and while they were being set out I was aware of her staring at me with those ever-hungry eyes of hers. When the beddable young wench had departed with her empty tray Sonia said quietly, "You're still pretty ravishing, do you know that?" She smiled slyly. "Remember what Gingold once said about you? That you were a steaming hot dish . . .?"

"You here for the whole season?"

She nodded. "Last season too and probably next."

"I've lost touch with theatrical doings," I admitted. "It's ages since I even went to a theatre."

"Why this one? Why tonight?"

"Grantley. I want to see what he does with Lear. He's one of the last of the few."

"Of course, you did a movie with him, didn't you? I'd forgotten that."

"Two. I thought he was the greatest thing on two legs. So did everyone else; they tried to sign him up for more but he wasn't

11

having any. Thinks movie-making's kid's stuff, silly old bugger." She was stirring her tea, a thoughtful frown on her face. "What's he going to be like as Lear?"

She shrugged. "Rehearsals have been quite frightful – in fact, they broke down altogether at one point. He's scared stiff, but who wouldn't be in that part?"

"Too old for it, perhaps. He must be nearly seventy."

"Sixty-eight," she said almost primly. "Yesterday at the dress-rehearsal he just gave up, didn't even try in the last act, just spoke the lines. Still, that's nothing to go by, is it? He'll probably be okay on the night, as they say. He's the type that thrives on first nights."

"Nobody thrives on first nights."

"I bet he does." She gave a wan little laugh. "Unlike me. Look at me, will you?" She held out her hands. "I'm already on the tremble and there's three hours to go yet. Let's change the subject, shall we? How have things been with you?"

I shrugged, registering as I did so the plain gold ring on her left hand. "Mustn't grumble."

"Have you packed up acting altogether?"

"I opted out. I was junkie of the year – a drunken junkie at that. You couldn't have missed the publicity. They roasted me alive and when I was dead they fed off the carcass. Sonia, old son, never became a film star."

"Opportunity'd be a fine thing." She picked over the cakes with exaggerated care. "You okay now? Physically, I mean, after the accident. You were all smashed up."

"Water under the bridge. Chalked up to experience. Wouldn't have missed it for the world."

"So what are you up to now?"

I gave a vague shrug. "This and that."

I never tell anyone what I do – not unless it's absolutely necessary. Let them think I'm a fallen idol. It's as good a cover as any. "I changed my name, by the way. I'm Mark Savage now, not Sutherland. It's best not to remind people."

"Then you should wear a beard and dark glasses, old mate. You still look like jolly old Mark Sutherland to me."

"People forget. They gawp at me in the street sometimes, but they're never quite sure."

12

"Why Savage?"

"Why not? Haven't you ever felt savage?" She lowered her eyes. I said, "Can I have some more tea? I see you've married again. Anyone I know?"

She gave a smug little smile as she took my cup, her eyes suddenly mischievous. "Gerald Grantley's son."

I stared at her. "I didn't even know he had a son."

"Well, he has."

I gave a low whistle. "You're practically royal, I hope you realise that." She smirked again as she passed my replenished cup. "In my book, there are three of them left: Gielgud, Guinness and Grantley. The three G's. And what's going to happen to the theatre when they go? Who's going to take over? Nowadays they're afraid to take their hands out of their pockets or raise their voices above a mumble in case someone shouts 'Ham!' "

She smiled. "How would *you* know? You just said you never go to the theatre."

"Touché, Mrs Grantley."

"Mrs Rosner." I looked blank. She smiled over the rim of her cup. "Gerald changed his name before Richard was born. Richard's my husband. Grantley's a stage-name. Richard reverted to Rosner because he didn't want to ride in on father's back, so to speak."

"He's an actor? Another actor? You must be out of your mind. Would I have seen him in anything? On the box or somewhere?"

"You'll see him tonight. He's playing Cornwall."

"You mean the one who . . .?"

". . . digs out the old man's eyes?" She nodded. "That's the one."

"I'm beginning to wish I hadn't come."

We watched each other in silence for a long time. I was remembering the happy times, the first year she and I had come together, like two heavenly bodies on collision course. And she'd certainly had a heavenly body. Still had, if it came to that, I thought, my eyes on the wander.

I also remembered the impotent rage and despair I had felt when I received her letter in the hospital informing me that

13

she'd just *had* to go off on her dreary little tour, because she could *hardly* walk out of it now, could she? – being under contract and all that crap.

"What are you thinking?"

I came back to her in a haze. "Not a lot."

She stared at her plate. "You were hating me."

A clock was striking somewhere. I looked at my watch. Five o'clock.

I shrugged. "Nothing I haven't learned to live with. We just overspent what little we had, that's all. We should have had a good roll in the hay and called it a day before the novelty wore off." I touched her hand. "I'll try not to think any more unkind thoughts."

But I did, of course. With a promise to go back-stage after the show to tell her what I thought of it all, I dropped her off at Smith's, then prowled back the way we had come and along the river bank where they were building the new Swan Theatre, and where I settled down to quite a number of unkind thoughts about her.

I didn't want to see her again, or meet her bloody husband, even if he were the son of one of my own theatrical triumvirate. I didn't much want to witness her Regan either. She wouldn't get within a mile of the part; she was too vapid, too small and hadn't got the guns.

I now began to wonder whether perhaps I shouldn't go home and forget the whole thing.

The urge to see Sir Gerald Grantley's King Lear had come upon me unexpectedly. A profile of Grantley in *The Times* had got me reaching for the telephone. Trevor Nunn, not only the artistic director of the theatre but also an old buddy of mine, had said that the place was sold out, but yes, he thought he could fix a house-seat for me. So, since Mitch, my assistant, had taken herself off on a long weekend pony-trekking in Wales – just the sort of daft thing she gets herself involved with – here I was, wallowing in the stagnant shallows of a soured and ancient love affair and indebted to the director of the theatre who might well challenge me to a duel if I paused to fling his generosity back in his face.

I decided to stay, went back to the hotel, showered, shaved

14

and dined, patted the Honda on the tank and went off to join the ambling throng converging on the theatre.

Seated smartly in the stalls, I battled my way through a long and densely written programme note by the producer of the play who thought it necessary to explain why he had bothered to direct the piece at all and why he had decided, against his better judgment, to set the play in the somewhat nebulous period for which it was originally intended by the author, "though the introduction of news-reel clips of World War II projected on the cyclorama during the final act will do much to flesh-out and clarify the usual confusion of Shakespeare's somewhat sketchy handling of battle scenes."

I took a note of the man's name to remind myself to keep my hands in my pockets should I find myself in the unhappy position of being introduced to him; my first inclination would be to punch him smartly on the nose.

"It's Mark, isn't it?" whispered a soft, lavender voice beside me. "Mark Sutherland?"

I turned my head. Gerald Grantley's wife was settling herself into the seat beside me. "Connie." I greeted her warmly, genuinely delighted. "What a lovely surprise." I took her tiny gloved hand and leaned in to kiss her cheek. "I had no idea I'd be sitting next to you."

She smiled sweetly. "So you'd better behave yourself."

She took a minute mirror from an equally minute purse and peered at herself with a critical frown. "Oh dear, oh dear . . ." She prinked at a perfect hair-do.

Her presence put paid to any thought of the hasty retreat I had been considering should the entertainment prove too much for me, but it was also a bonus; should either of us need a shoulder to cry on there would be one readily available.

She leaned in towards me. "What in the world are you doing here? We haven't seen anything of you for years. And on a first night too! You should know better."

"I wanted to see him, didn't I? It's not every day he plays Lear."

"Thank the Lord."

I grinned. "Has he been difficult?"

15

"I've almost forgotten what he used to look like. Never mind," she squeezed my hand. "Seeing you again will cheer him up. It's lovely of you to have come." She was peering nonplussed at the dimly-lit open stage, which stared back, bare and depressing, devoid of anything which might conceivably serve as scenery other than something which looked like an uprooted tree-stump dead centre. "How do you like the set?" she added in an undertone.

"I'd prefer not to talk about it."

She gave a little snort of amusement. "The theatre," she whispered as the house-lights began to fade, "ain't what it used to be."

What little light there had been on the stage also disappeared leaving us in Stygian darkness. In front of us someone chose the moment to rip a yard and a half of cellophane from a box of chocolates.

The first act was over. A desultory smattering of applause had greeted the final words of the Earl of Kent sitting alone and despondent in the stocks while night, in the guise of a lingering fading of lights, descended upon him. Most of the audience, curiously subdued, had departed for bars and cloakrooms. Neither Connie nor I had moved. A silence louder than the sporadic gunfire of tip-up seats lay between us.

Presently she laid a tentative hand on my knee. "I'm supposed to be in the manager's office imbibing gin and tonic."

I grunted. "So am I."

Another silence. "I really don't think I could. How about you?"

When eventually I shook my head it was like a gesture of betrayal. I took her frail hand in mine. "Would you like some fresh air?"

She gave a wry smile. "It could kill me."

A further brief pause, then I pulled myself together. "So . . ." The word had a petulant sound. "It wasn't a good first act. So what? He's got another two to go. He could lay the world waste in twenty minutes, let alone two acts. Come on, Connie darling, let's risk it – the fresh air, I mean, not the manager's office."

Stratford was on the verge of demonstrating the distinctive brand of magic I remembered so well from the past. The sun had almost gone; a few stars pierced the purple sky; below us, the murmuring river, now almost devoid of traffic, glinted darkly. The still air was heavy with the scent of someone's cigar. The surge of bodies about us, the conversation, low laughter and the clink of glasses, seemed to increase our sense of solitude rather than lessen it.

I glanced at my diminutive companion. Both hands, one of them clutching her tiny embroidered purse, gripped the rail of the terrace, the knuckles white with tension. She was staring out at the river, her eyes fixed implacably on a point midstream as if witnessing some enigmatic event – Excalibur, perhaps, being drawn irrevocably beneath the surface of the water. There was something about the rigidity of her stance and the glitter in her eye which gave off an appalling sense of loss and finality – the mystical sword gone? Never to be seen again until the mortally wounded king came back from the dead to reclaim it.

I placed a gentle arm about her shoulders. "Stop it, Connie. It's a first night, for God's sake; it happens all the time, even to the best."

She shook her head with sudden vigour. "Not to him, Mark, never before to him. He was just lost – as if he had never been on a stage before. He was standing up there like a small lost boy. I've never seen him like that . . . never!"

I tried to comfort her. "Most people wouldn't even have noticed it. You know him too well." She didn't seem to be listening. I tried again. "Has he been very worried about the play – unduly so, I mean? After all, it's not the fun part of the year, is it? It's got a pretty murky reputation – unplayable and all that. It would scare the pants off me, I know that, but then, I'm only human – Gerald's a colossus."

She frowned. "He's been pretty tense, of course, but that was only to be expected. He's never played Lear before – and at his age . . ." She left the sentence unfinished. "He's been going off on his own quite a bit, walking, studying, mumbling his lines over to himself rather than with me as he usually does. Mind you, he's never been really happy with the set-up

17

here. He's never hit it off with Paul What's-his-name, for instance, the producer – Twit-face, Gerald calls him. What *is* his name?''

"Braidy – Paul Braidy. Twit-face will do."

"In fact, quite early on Gerald actually walked out. He's never done that before. Never. Once a contract was signed it was holy writ. But he just couldn't be doing with any of it. Originally the setting of the play was to be the twenty-first century, after the bomb if you please! Everybody dragging about in rags with burns and blisters all over them. I ask you! What sort of kingdom would that be to divide up between your three daughters? Who would want it? Gerald said no, he wouldn't do it.'' She gave a heavy sigh. "It's a fetish with producers nowadays – to be different just for the sake of being different. It's not as if they have anything new to say. Anyway, rather than lose him, the management talked Twit-face into revising his ideas and Gerald went back, much against his will, but having made his stand, he felt it was enough, and they'd been quite magnanimous about it. Now I wish to God they'd let him go. This will destroy him."

"Connie darling!" A shrill parrot voice in my left ear almost leapt me out of my shoes. "I've been looking for you every-where. How absolutely gorgeous to see you!" A tall, frowsty-looking female with erect grey hair and an enormous painted mouth housing a portcullis of large yellow teeth, shoved me brusquely to one side and planted a resounding kiss on Connie's cheek. "Isn't that man of yours just divine? Aren't you proud of him?" Over her shoulder she narrowed pallid, myopic eyes in my direction – mascara'd eyelashes like park-railings, breath like a gin-palace. I swayed gently back on my heels. "Sorry to bust in on you like this, young sir, but I just had to say hello to Connie." She grabbed my hand and pumped it up and down. "I'm Arden," she informed me confidentially. "Lizzie Arden – no relation to the forest or the make-up lady, but a boon companion of my dear Connie here, isn't that so, Connie? Oh my dear, isn't Gerald being quite, quite shattering. No one has any right to be so mas-culine!" She was back with me again. "When are you going to introduce me, Connie?" She leaned in towards me. "I can't help feeling that we've already met somewhere. We haven't, have we?"

"My name is Hinchcliffe," I leapt in before Connie could utter. "John Thomas Hinchcliffe."

"Heathcliff?" Several people turned to look at me.

"Hinchcliffe, Miss Arden, with an 'e'."

"*Mrs*, alas, Mr Heathcliff, *Mrs* Arden. Well . . ." She squinted at a large watch pendant on her flat chest and shook her head in despair. "I really must get back to my party. Connie darling, *lovely* to see you; you and Gerald simply must look in for drinkies tomorrow a.m., you simply must, and I insist on you bringing Mr Heathcliff with you, even if you have to tie him hand and foot – oh, how lovely *that* would be! I'd just love him to meet God. And Emma, of course. You're not an artist of any sort, are you, Mr Heathcliff?"

"I'm afraid not. I'm in submarines."

"Submarines!" More people turned to look. "How romantic. A sailor! Connie sweetheart, I simply must away. Give Gerald a great big buss from me, won't you? And *au revoir* to you, John Thomas," she added archly. "It's been an oodle of pleasure." With a jangle of bangles she departed as suddenly as she had come.

At the same moment the bells went, recalling the faithful to the auditorium.

I stood for a second staring nonplussed at Connie now a helpless heap of silent laughter. "Pull yourself together, Connie," I told her severely.

"Submarines!"

I took a handkerchief from my pocket and held it to her mouth. "Spit," I said. "You have Arden's lipstick all over you."

As I scrubbed gently at her cheek she hung on to my arm. "Oh Mark, you evil boy, you've made my evening; everything's better now. John Thomas Heathcliff . . .!"

"Hinchcliffe," I said, "with an 'e'."

" 'Who put my man i' the stocks?' "

Head lowered, feet splayed, the old king, fiery-eyed and challenging, stood foursquare like an angry bull, his voice

19

low and ominous presaging an archetypal outburst of rage. A shiver of expectation ran through the theatre. Connie's hand sought, found and clutched mine, her nails biting into my palm.

The old maestro was back in the saddle. Whatever had been bugging him in the first act had gone. The strain had left him; he was breathing deeply and easily, pacing himself, carefully gathering up the reins. I had the feeling that those with him on the stage were in for a rough ride. I almost envied them.

I had once played a six-minute dialogue sequence with him in a film called *Fall-Out*. We did it in one take – a miracle in itself. If I could place a finger on the most exciting moment of my film career, it would have to be that. We raced neck and neck, he making the running, daring me to lose ground, at the same time carrying me with him to the crest of a second-to-none theatrical experience. When we'd done, the technicians applauded, something I had never before heard on the floor, and the director's triumphant 'Print it!' was as close to an accolade as I had ever been.

Sporadic lightning flared across the darkening stage. In the full flight of his fury the old king paused abruptly, frowning, peering upwards, head on one side, listening; an endless pause, then blindly groping for the support of his fool's shoulder: " 'Oh fool!' " he whispered in a voice barely audible, " 'I shall go mad . . .' "

The silence which dogged his steps into the desolation of insanity was broken only by the rumble of distant thunder. No one in the theatre seemed to be breathing.

Connie was trembling violently. I turned my head. Her eyes were tight shut; a lone tear glistened on her cheek. I knew what she meant.

From thence onward the performance took wing. Gerald Grantley seized by the throat that unplayable part and shook it until its teeth rattled. The disintegration of the arrogant and vindictive old king was played out with a sureness of touch which took my breath away. In his challenge to the elements, he himself became elemental, hurling back the thunderbolts with the unbridled fury of a demon, Jacob wrestling with the Angel, Lucifer flouting God; and when madness eventually

20

stilled his rage and drew him down into the darkness of his own sick mind, he held court with an assemblage of phantoms so vivid that the onlooker was hard pressed to swear that they were not visible.

About him, the cast rose to the occasion. Sonia, as Regan, seemed to grow in stature as she and her husband – both on stage and off – ganged up on the old Duke of Gloucester and gouged out his eyes with their thumb-nails. At this point someone behind us gave a low groan and got up and left, followed by an alert member of the St John Ambulance Brigade.

What production there was – and there was precious little of it barring sound-effects, some very wet rain, and bits and pieces of furniture carted on and off by stage-hands in black catsuits – resulted in a lack of discipline which enabled the actors to indulge in what looked suspiciously like spur-of-the-moment improvisation; somehow they seemed to release themselves from the confines of the stage and were doing it 'for real'.

It was a unique and harrowing experience, one which continued to the end of the act, throughout the interval and on until the play eventually had run its course.

The stage lights faded for the last time and after what seemed an interminable silence the applause began, sporadic at first, then rising to a roar as with a mighty thunder of tip-up seats most of the audience leapt to its feet and cheered its head off – something I had seen only in American movies and would never have thought possible in stuffy old England.

The company, a motley collection of puppets bobbing erratically on strings, took their calls. In the centre Gerald Grantley, tall and unsmiling, inclined only his head, making no attempt to take a separate call; when the gallery took up his name in a rhythmic chant he remained unmoved.

A small man bustled on from the wings, important in a tight blue suit and club tie, stride too long for his legs and loose black hair obliterating any eyes he might have had.

"Twit-face!" crowed Connie in loud derision as the applause noticeably diminished and a couple of lusty boos were added for good measure. Paul Braidy spread his hands and folded

21

himself in half a couple of times; when he turned away to join the line-up nobody seemed inclined to let him in.

Eventually Grantley was winkled out of the line by his fellow actors; two of the women led him down to the stage apron and left him there to get on with it. The house fell in about his ears. There seemed to be no doubt in anyone's mind that theatrical history had been made.

Chapter Two

Connie and I allowed a decent interval to elapse before venturing backstage to the dressing-rooms. The usual crowd of first-nighters, friends and relations was on the ebb as we shoved our way through the thinning numbers still throwing congratulatory verbal bouquets over their shoulders.

Gerald had evidently made short work of any visitors he may have had for when Connie stuck her head in his door with a loud view-halloo an answering bellow came from the shower. "Con? I'm in the shower. Come in, shan't be a second."

She picked up a towel and thrust it through the plastic curtains. "Put that round you before you come out. I have a visitor for you."

"Male or female?"

"You just wait and see." She gave me a grin as she lowered herself wearily into a leather armchair. "Don't want him prancing about in that saggy old birthday suit of his, do we?"

"I heard that!" came a shout as the shower was shut off. "Who've you got out there?"

He erupted from the shower, wet and steaming, Neptune rising from the ocean bed, huge and god-like, fastening the towel about his middle. There was no sagging flesh about him. For his age his physique was magnificent. When he saw me he drew up in his tracks; the towel flapped dangerously and almost fell.

"I don't believe it . . ."

"Isn't he a lovely surprise?" smiled Connie comfortably.

"Mark, my dear boy . . ." He lumbered over to me and took me in his arms like a great bear. "To hell with the wet," he growled kissing me on the forehead – he was three inches taller than I which made him six feet three. He held me away from him and blinked down at me with true affection, rivulets

23

of water pouring down his face from his streaming mane of hair.

"Just look what you've done to his jacket," moaned Connie.

"I'll buy him a new one. Mark Sutherland, dear boy. Well, well. If I'd known you were going to be in front I'd have shown you the mettle of my pasture. How are you, boy? What have you been up to? Where've you been all this time? And why haven't you been up to see us and what in the name of hell do you think you're doing, coming to an opening night without even a by-your-leave?"

"Shut up, Gerald," expostulated Connie with a despairing shake of the head at me. "Let him get a word in for goodness sake."

"Who are *you*?" asked Gerald turning and frowning down at her. "Well, hello old Dutch, how are you then?" He stooped and kissed her loudly. "How was it?" He looked back at me. "You haven't said a bloody word yet, do you know that?"

"Chance would be a fine thing," said Connie.

"How was it?" he asked again, no hint of anxiety in the question.

I grinned. "Will 'bloody marvellous' do?"

"For openers I guess it'll have to. You wouldn't kid me?"

"I was knocked cold."

He stared at me intently for a brief second and turned back to Connie. "Is he telling the truth?"

She stretched out a hand and took his, tears in her eyes. "You did it, dear old man, you did it."

"And how!" I added fervently.

Snatching up a towelling bath-robe he shrugged into it, and slumped into the chair at his dressing-table looking suddenly deflated. He let out a long breath. "Thank the Lord for that," he muttered half to himself. "They've all been in. 'Darling, you were *marvellous*!' – 'Congratulations, old man' – 'How do you remember all those *words*?' – 'Soopah, darling!'" He stared gloomily at his reflection. "People like me are too old to be called darling." He squinnied at me over his shoulder. "Hello, Mark darling, how are things with you? Speak up boy. What the hell are you doing up here?" He picked up a towel and began scrubbing at his wet hair.

24

"Came to see you, didn't I?"

"Good God, not a one night stand?"

I nodded. "Back to the Big Smoke in the morning."

"Where you staying?"

"The Swan's Nest."

Connie said, "Why don't you come and stay the night with us? Tell us all your news in comfort."

I hesitated.

"He just said he's booked in at the Swan's Nest," put in her husband abruptly. "He can't just walk out on 'em like that — not when he's booked." I met his eyes in the mirror; they shifted quickly away from mine. "Tell you what, though — come back and have something to eat with us, a noggin or two, open a bottle or three."

"I'd like that."

Connie interrupted. "You're not forgetting the first-night party?"

"Bugger the first-night party."

"Now Gerald, you must go."

He flung the towel into a corner. "They can stuff it."

I caught Connie's look of appeal. "You only need to show yourself for a couple of minutes," I pointed out. "A couple of drinks and away. Nobody'll expect you to stay the night."

He gave a loud theatrical sigh. "All right, all right. I'll go if you go."

"I'm not invited."

"You are now."

I looked at Connie; she frowned and gave a little nod. "Okay, if that's the way you want it. And while you're getting dressed I'll go and say hello to Sonia. I said I would."

"You know Sonia?"

"Don't be silly, dear," put in Connie. "He was married to her for two years."

"I didn't know that."

"Of course you did. You just don't listen."

He winked at me. "That should make you and Richard husbands-in-law, or something, shouldn't it?"

"If it does, you're my father-in-law once removed."

25

He chuckled. "We'll give you five minutes. Hey!" I paused at the door. "Not thinking of starting all that up again, are you?"

"All what?"

"My daughter-in-law."

"And have you on my back for the rest of my life? Never."

The party was a parochial affair and should never have happened. Apart from the cast, the stage staff and the theatre management, only a handful of invitations had been issued, and those to prominent burghers and their wives who stood about in their party frocks clearly wishing they hadn't come. Had I not made an entrance with Gerald, whose appearance merited a ragged round of applause, I would have stuck out like a sore thumb.

When I caught Trevor Nunn's enquiring eye I raised a couple of embarrassed shoulders and made a face which renounced all responsibility for my presence. He came over and forgave me, talked about old times and asked why I didn't act any more. I told him I'd grown out of it. He didn't believe me, gave me his wisest smile and drifted away to say hello to the mayor who had just arrived wearing his chain of office.

"Isn't this awful?" muttered little Connie at my elbow. "What's happened to everybody? It's like a wake. These do's are usually so jolly."

"They're all in the dog house."

"Who are?"

"The company. According to Sonia, Twit-face has been storming around the dressing-rooms tearing strips off everybody."

"Whatever for?"

"For buggering up his production."

"But there wasn't any production."

"*You* know that and *I* know that, but nobody's told *him*. That's what's bugging him." I snatched a couple of glasses of white wine from a passing tray. "He says they deliberately sabotaged it."

"And did they?"

"Well, there were certainly some very odd things going on, most of them initially perpetrated, I may say, by that wicked old husband of yours. I think he just got fed up with being strapped into a strait-jacket. That's what was worrying him all through the first act: the whole thing was going down like a lead balloon until he charged off on his own. Much, it seems, to everyone's relief. The rest of the cast fell in behind him – even when he wasn't on the stage."

"Hi, you two," said Sonia, insinuating her tiny presence between us. "You're both being far too serious. This is supposed to be a party."

"That's what we thought too," smiled Connie kissing her cheek. "How are you, darling? And congratulations on a perfectly horrid performance." A tall cavernous shadow hung over us. "Hello, Richard dear – you were pretty nasty too. I hope you don't behave like that at home. You haven't met Mark, have you? This is my son, Richard – Mark Sutherland."

"Savage," countered Sonia and, while Richard and I exchanged a flabby handshake, put Connie in the picture about my change of name.

Richard Rosner could only be described as louring, his best and worst features being his eyes: wide, dark and deep-set, they burned with some inner and inexplicable rage or frustration, vying with the hand he had offered me which was like something long dead and recently exhumed. He stood over me like the Ghost of Christmas Future, large-nosed and doom-laden, defying me to feel at ease.

"Why did you change your name?" His hot eyes homed in on mine in an accusing, all-consuming stare. His voice was his second-best feature, rich and resonant like his father's.

"Change of life, I guess," I shrugged. Why should I tell him why I'd changed my name?

"My father changed his name." His eyes left mine and quartered the room like those of a bird of prey. "He didn't like being a Jew."

It was my turn to stare and before I could find my voice he had turned on his heel and gone.I watched him forge his way without ceremony through the guests.

If he was anything like that at home Sonia had exchanged the frying-pan for the fire. As the ex-frying-pan I still had the edge on charm. I was wondering what he was like in bed when Sonia

27

threaded a confiding arm through mine. "Don't worry about him. He's just looking for someone to hate."

"I thought it was going to be me."

"Rubbish. He likes you."

"I'd just hate to be someone he loathed."

"He was always a funny boy," said Connie in a preoccupied voice; she was standing on tiptoe trying to see over the tops of nearby heads. "Can you see my husband anywhere?"

Gerald's shaggy grey head reared above the rest on the far side of the room; before I could point him out Connie went on, "Do you know what he once did when he was still at school? He smashed up the face of another boy simply because the boy said he didn't want to play conkers with him. Broke his nose, I think."

"Gerald broke a boy's nose?"

"Richard, silly. You're as bad as Gerald, you don't listen. Can you see him anywhere?"

"Richard?"

She gave me a playful slap on the arm. "Gerald."

"He's over there," I nodded. "Where the bar is, I imagine."

"I'd better go and rescue him. I don't like him cruising around on his own – especially after what he's been through tonight. He needs to unwind in peace." Turning to go she hesitated. "Sonia, is it true what Mark said about that awful person careering around backstage picking fights with everyone?"

Sonia made a hideous face. "Quite true. He certainly told Megan and me where we got off and what he thought of our performances. He burst into our dressing-room like a blue-arsed fly – didn't even knock – hissing at us and wanting to know what the hell we thought we'd been doing all evening. Megan was wonderful. She's nearly twice his size. She told him we'd all been doing our best to get what he laughingly called his production off the ground. You should have seen her! Except for her panties she was stark naked and for some reason hadn't taken that terrible wig off. She looked like Frankenstein's mother. In the end she actually manhandled him out of the door. 'On your way, you silly little man,' she said, 'before I strike you down.'"

Connie was frowning. "I wonder if he included Gerald in his ravings?"

Sonia shook her head. "They'd already had their session before the curtain went up. We could hear them through the wall. Anyway, he's called a full rehearsal for Monday so we can expect the fireworks then."

I grinned. "Gerald will have him for lunch."

Connie sighed. "Don't joke about it, Mark. He really can't stand that man. Now, I must go and winkle him out."

Again she was frustrated, this time by the advent of the mayor's wife who gave her a genteel hug and congratulated her on Gerald's acting. I made several indistinct noises at Sonia, shook myself loose from the group and shouldered my way through the guests in the general direction of Gerald. The party appeared to be hotting up a little; someone had put on a tape; above the hubbub nobody could hear what it was doing but it was a step in the right direction even though, from where I stood, it did sound a bit like the Dead March from *Saul*.

Several strangers smiled and nodded at me; somebody said, "Hi Mark, how goes it?" as if he'd known me for years. I realised then with something of a jolt that contrary to what I'd told Sonia earlier in the day about how soon people forget, Stratford-upon-Avon was one of those places where I would most likely be remembered and recognised – not because of what I'd done in this particular theatre, but because the town usually seethed with people interested in Acting with a capital 'A'.

My only brush with the Royal Shakespeare lot had been way back in the late sixties and early seventies when I had walked-on and held spears, said a couple of lines in *Henry VIII*, flirted with Sheila Burrell in *Richard III* and fallen head over heels in love with a blonde and buxom blue-eyed beauty of a stage manager who went by the name of – what the hell was her name?

A painful prod in the ribs followed by a voluptuously vocal "Hello, you old bat," sent me pivoting on a heel to face a blue-eyed blonde, no longer buxom, who went by the name of . . . "Ba!" My face fell open with astonishment. "By all that's wicked – Barbara Sterling. I was just this very second thinking about you."

"I'll bet." Colour was welling up in her cheeks, one of her most endearing traits; you had only to look at her in a certain way and she would blush all the way up to the gunwales. She had always complained that such a malady was unfair to girls.

I handed my empty glass to yet another fortuitously passing tray, took her by the shoulders and gave her an enthusiastic kiss. "This is wonderful. You're not still working here surely? Not after all these years?"

"I am too." Her voice was low and husky and purred a little. "Only now I'm company manager."

She was looking extremely toothsome. Not that she had ever looked anything else, but now that she had exchanged her erstwhile mandatory stage managerial costume of grubby jeans, shapeless sweaters and down-at-heel sandals for a short chic number in white linen with a plunging neckline and a scarlet sash, she was positively unnerving. In a roundabout way I also managed to notice that her small, smartly shod feet and slender ankles rounded off a stirring pair of legs.

I was still staring when she said, "You haven't darkened these doors for years, have you?"

"Not since you and I made a go of it."

She shook a regretful head. "A lifetime ago." She peered into her empty glass for a second. "I saw every one of your films – several times. Cried through most of them."

"They weren't those sort of films."

"They were to me."

After an awkward pause I asked how things were. "I suppose you're an old married woman now?"

She shook her head. "Footloose and fanny free."

"No one?"

"I didn't say that." Another pause. "How did you enjoy the piece tonight?"

"Apart from the first act, it was about the biggest thing I've seen in the theatre to date."

She made a wry face. "You wouldn't have thought so if you'd been backstage just now."

"Paul Thing?"

She nodded glumly. "If we hadn't got everyone's contract sewn up, we wouldn't have a cast on Monday. Adolf Hitler pales beside him. He's a lunatic. However . . ." She gave a dismissive shrug. "So how long you here for?"

"The night, that's all." I added, "Unfortunately."

Her eyes lifted, narrowing slightly as she frowned at me, the blood once again suffusing her cheeks.

"Do you mean that? – the 'unfortunately' bit?"

I nodded taking her hand in mine. "And if that isn't bad enough I've promised Connie and Gerald to go back to their place, otherwise. . . ." I hesitated, considering the possibility of easing my way out of their invitation. As I did so a sudden shattering of glass from the far end of the room was followed by the sound of a voice raised above the general babble around us. "Don't you dare mention the word professionalism to me, you young pipsqueak. I've seen and heard enough of your pig-headed pomposity and your posturing mediocrity to last a lifetime."

In the ensuing deathly silence Barbara Sterling's whispered "Oh my Christ!" sounded like a shout of panic. As she threaded her way roughly through the throng of guests another voice was raised, querulous and defensive. "I don't give a damn what you think of me. Tonight you deliberately sabotaged my production, and the rest of the cast followed you like sheep because you left them no alternative. That was *your* responsibility – as the so-called leading man, that was your frigging responsibility."

"Tonight, little man," interrupted Grantley, "you have history on your hands and will be remembered only because, God help us, your name happens to appear on the programme."

Barbara caught desperately at his arm. "Gerald, please . . ."

"Keep out of this!" With unexpected violence and without even a glance at her he threw her off; I caught at her shoulders as she stumbled back against me.

"Gerald," I said quietly over her head. "You're making an exhibition of yourself."

He turned on me like a madman, eyes blazing. I felt Barbara shrink away from him; for a moment I was sure he would attack me.

"Gerald . . ." It was Connie's voice, gentle and calm – as casual as if she were calling him to lunch.

We watched the wild flare of fury fade from his eyes, the ugly

31

lines of violence leave his face. The crowd parted as Connie stepped from among them, the tips of her fingers deliberately touching mine as she brushed past. I was aware of Paul Braidy moving stealthily back a couple of paces at her approach.

For a silent second or two she stood before her husband, smiling a little, holding him with her eyes.

The hand he reached out for the support of her shoulder trembled as if with an ague. His eyes were tight shut. "Oh Con," he whispered. "Take me home, for God's sake."

Chapter Three

The Grantleys had a cottage in a village some five or six miles north-east of Stratford. The name of the village was Grantley.

"I was born here," Gerald explained when he and I were installed in his comfortable and unpretentious sitting-room, imbibing a cool, sparkling wine from Italy. Connie had taken herself off to the kitchen to make tea and sandwiches. "When I decided to change my name Grantley seemed as appropriate as any other – I've always loved the place."

"How long ago was that?"

"When I became an actor," he said shortly.

Neither he nor Connie had mentioned his outburst at the party and it was certainly nothing to do with me. When, in the car-park, I had suggested that I should slope off and ring them in the morning to say goodbye, it was Gerald who practically begged me to go back with them. "Talk me down . . . out of this . . ." had been his words. So I'd picked up the Honda and chugged along behind them at a relentless twenty-five miles an hour, Connie, a careful driver, having managed to get to the driving seat first.

Now, heaving himself to his feet, he opened a window and leant out into the steamy night. The scent of late roses crept into the dimly lit room; the thin whine of a motor-cycle climbing the hill was the only sound.

A large portrait of Gerald as Hamlet dominated the wall opposite; even from where I sat I recognised the technique of the artist. It was a famous picture, reproduced every now and again in such prestigious journals as *Country Life* and *Connoisseur*.

The brooding, troubled eyes stared implacably at someone or something behind me – the ghost of his murdered father perhaps, the dead Polonius, the yawning abyss of melancholia . . . I found myself stirring uneasily, only by an effort of will resisting the urge to glance over my shoulder.

"I could be bounded in a nutshell, and count myself a king of infinite space," quoted Gerald softly, "were it not that I have bad dreams."

He had turned from the window and was watching me intently. "Ever played him?" I shook my head. "Every actor should have a stab at Hamlet."

"I don't think I'd have had the nerve."

"Nonsense! Nothing to him. A lot of rubbish has been spoken and written about him; he's become a sacred cow. Tell you one thing, he's a damn sight easier than Lear or Macbeth or Richard Three. Mind you, you have to be strong as an ox to do any of them justice, but that's what acting's about, isn't it? Real acting, I mean, not all that phony movie crap you and I were once engaged in. One minute's work and then hang about for an hour and a half while they rebuild the bloody set and change the lighting . . . that's not acting." He stopped. "Mark . . ." He moved in front of me, his great bulk between me and the picture. "Mark, I'm devastated about what happened tonight. What do I do? Apologise?"

I shrugged, said hesitantly, "To the theatre management perhaps – for upsetting their party. Otherwise . . ."

"And what about . . .?"

"Twit-face? Bugger him. From the little I heard you were merely putting a point of view, a criticism – somewhat forthrightly but I've read worse in the daily press. Forget it, Gerald. He shouldn't be working in the classics anyway."

"Exactly. He has no bloody background, that's his trouble, precious little education and certainly no psychology. He has no idea how to cope with *people*. Every actor is an individual, for Christ's sake, usually with an ego the size of the Albert Hall, but he treats us like school kids – herds us around like cattle. Worst of all, he has no vision. How the hell can anyone produce anything without vision? Arrogant little bastard."

He drained his glass, made a face, and strode over to the drinks table where he poured himself half a tumbler of Scotch. He waved the bottle at me. "Something stronger?"

I shook my head. "I'm off it."

34

He glanced at the clock on the mantelpiece, then at his watch. "That was one of your hang-ups, wasn't it – the hard stuff?"

"I keep a leery eye on it."

He tramped restlessly about the room. The uneven, polished wooden floor creaked and vibrated beneath his heavy tread, setting glass and china ornaments on the tinkle; each time he trod on a particular carpet the standard-lamp went out.

"You should have that lamp seen to."

"It's not the lamp, it's the wiring." He was at the table again replenishing his glass. "What are you up to now, Mark?" he asked suddenly. "You must be doing something. You're not the type to sit around all day studying your navel."

Only for a second I hesitated, then, "I'm in the P.I. business."

"What the hell's that?"

"Private investigation."

"You're a detective?"

I gave him a modest smile. "I don't do a lot of detecting. Most of it's pretty bloody boring – routine stuff. I get knocked down occasionally, of course, beaten up, which is quite fun in a painful sort of way, but I'm not your Philip Marlowe and all that mob."

"Who's Philip Marlowe?"

"Humphrey Bogart usually."

Connie reappeared carrying an outsize tray laden with tea things. She eyed her husband sternly as I relieved her of her burden. "I guessed it was you thudding about. Do sit down, there's a dear; everything in the kitchen is on the move. These old houses!" she confided, clearing a space on a coffee table for the tray, "you just can't move a muscle without setting everything on the jangle. Sandwiches coming up," and she departed once again.

Gerald had slumped obediently into the deeply cavernous armchair which was clearly his personal preserve – not all that preserved either by the look of it. Apart from the sofa on which I sat it was the largest piece of furniture in the room and was battered and disfigured beyond recall. An enormous, triffid-like pot-plant standing alongside gave the uneasy impression that it grew out of the chair itself. He frowned at me solemnly from between his knees.

"Maybe I could put some detective work in your way," he said thoughtfully. He put a finger to his lips. "Not a word to Connie though." He took a diary from his blazer pocket. "Put your address in the back of that somewhere, will you? Never know. I might want to get in touch with you. What time you leaving tomorrow?" Any time, I told him, scribbling my office address and returning the diary, I was easy. "How about in the morning then, when Con's gone to church? About elevenish? How'd that do? If you're interested, that is?"

Connie returned at that moment. He gave me a warning look. I said, "I'm always interested in old churches."

"You talking about our church?" asked Connie, making room on the table for a large plate of sandwiches. "There, help yourselves. Tongue in the white bread and smoked salmon in the brown. Has he told you about his tower?"

"I was just getting around to it," said Gerald glancing covertly at his watch once again. Did he want me to go, I wondered. "That tower's fifteenth century, you know. Sometime or other, someone installed a clock into it with a chime of bells. As I told you I was born here, lived here till I was ten years old, and in all that time that bloody clock stood at a quarter to eleven. Nobody, but nobody, ever got the thing to work. When the war came I went off with everybody else . . ."

"Milk, sugar, Mark?" whispered Connie passing me a dainty cup of tea. I shook my head. "Gerald?"

"I'll stick with the hard stuff, thanks," said Gerald huffing and puffing himself out of his chair to swill yet more Scotch into his glass. I gave Connie a sidelong glance but she was intent on pouring tea. At a rough estimate Gerald must have put away the best part of a tumblerful of Scotch in a quarter of an hour. Already I could detect a slight thickening of his speech.

"Not too much of that, dear," warned Connie voicing my thoughts. "You'll be impossible in the morning."

"Where was I?" asked Gerald, sorting through the sandwiches.

"You'd just gone off to war, dear, with everyone else," said Connie, "and please don't pick at them, they're all the same."

"What's in the white ones?"

She sighed. "You see what I mean, Mark? He never listens to a thing I say. Tongue in the white, salmon in the brown."

"I'll have one later. I'm not in the eating mood at the moment. Too excited, I expect."

When he fell into his chair the house shook.

"All right then," he went on, "now I've just come back from the war, battle-scarred, fed up, not a job in sight. I had no urge to go back to my old job – chartered accountancy, believe it or not."

"Gerald, dear," put in Connie a shade querulously, "Mark doesn't want to hear your entire life story."

"I'm not telling him my entire life story, I'm telling him about the tower."

"You're going a very long way about it."

"Be patient, dearest chuck, will you? Well, the turning point came one night when I went to the Stratford theatre – the Memorial Theatre it was in those days – and saw a production of *Love's Labour's Lost* – '47 I think it was. And that was it. My course was set. I would be an actor. Well, years passed . . ."

"Thank the Lord," muttered Connie.

"I met Connie . . ."

"Hip, hip," she munched.

". . . and married her."

"Hooray!"

"And we came here to live."

"Best thing we ever did," said Connie.

"And do you know what?" Gerald cocked an eyebrow at me. "The bloody clock still stood at a quarter to eleven."

"Well done, that, man. So what did I do?"

"You got in the experts."

"And put in a new clock with chimes, at my own expense, and gave it to the village as a gesture of thanks for letting us come and live here. The church, along with the village, God bless 'em – also as a gesture of goodwill – gave me the freedom of the tower, and a large brass key to go with it. Unofficially, it's my very own tower, what do you think of that? And there," he stabbed a finger at a dark corner, "is the key to it, see? Hanging on the wall. I go up there and tramp around to my heart's content. The view from the top is stunning. On a clear day you can see Land's End to the south and John o'Groats to the north. I do most of my learning up there. I can bawl my head off. 'Blow winds and crack your cheeks' at the top of my voice and there's not a soul to say me nay."

"The whole village says you nay when the wind's in the right quarter," said Connie. "Still," she smiled at me, "it gets him out of the house. You can imagine what his shouting does in here – the plaster comes off the ceiling. Do help yourself to sandwiches."

"And do you go up there with him?" I asked clutching at a salmon sandwich.

"Oh no, no, no." She raised a horrified hand. "I couldn't, I really couldn't, never in a month of Sundays. I have the most awful thing about heights, you see, and if that isn't enough, I'm a martyr to claustrophobia. I tried once but I couldn't get past the first half-dozen steps. It's not only pitch black in there, it smells horribly – bats, I think, mice, and all sorts of creepy crawly things you can't see. And it's so damp and cobwebby." She shuddered. "Oh no, it's not for me. I really would love to go up to the top just to see the view, shout with Gerald, be with him, but I just couldn't. More tea?"

As I passed my cup she gave me a nudge, nodding at her husband. Gerald's chin had fallen on his chest, his eyes closed. "He's tired out, poor pet."

"He's not tired out at all," muttered Gerald thickly. "He's just bloody tight." He opened bleary eyes. "What was in that Scotch, I wonder?"

I half rose to my feet. "I'd better be off, let you get some rest."

"Just finish your tea like a good boy," said Connie handing me my cup. "And please eat some sandwiches – they'll only go to waste if you don't. Gerald, how about you? Please have one. Did you eat before the show?"

"Enormously." I offered him the plate and sat patiently while he made a great song and dance about which he would have, then decided against it. "Mark, old lad," he said suddenly à propos of nothing. "I'm going to give you some good advice. Come back and do some acting. You don't want to bury a talent like yours farting about in a – what was it? Con, do you know what this idiot child does for a living now? You'll never guess. He detects." He nodded heavily. "He's a detective. Would you credit that?"

Connie's eyes widened. "You never told me that, Mark. A detective? Is that really true?"

"I'm a private investigator."

"But how exciting."

"They knock him down," nodded her husband.

"Who does?"

"And beat him up. That's what he told me."

"Why do they knock you down?" Connie sounded alarmed.

"They don't do it all the time," I told her through a mouthful of sandwich.

"But sometimes they do?"

I was utterly at sea. "I *have* been knocked down in my time, yes, battered about a bit, yes. But it comes with the territory. It's not my fault, it's the company I keep."

" '*One of the ruins that Cromwell knocked abaht a bit,*' " supplied Gerald breaking into song.

"Oh, do shut up, Gerald," sighed Connie. "I think you'd better go to bed and sleep it off. And take some Alka Seltzers."

"Good idea," said Gerald. "Will you excuse me, dear boy?" He gave a cavernous yawn. "Suddenly hit me. Too much excitement for one day, that's what it is. May I give you that?" He handed me his empty glass and made a couple of sketchy attempts to get to his feet, neither remotely successful. He held on grimly to the arms of his too low-slung chair. "I wonder if you would mind giving me a hand, kind young sir?"

Together Connie and I levered him upright and he stood between us, swaying slightly.

"I'm ashamed of you," said Connie with no censure at all in her voice. "Making a spectacle of yourself."

"I've been a spectacle all my life, too old to give in now. Just point me in the right direction and I'll manage." He stood for a second blinking up at Hamlet. "There he is, look, the man with the bad dreams. No bad dreams for me tonight, Hamlet old thing. Tonight I shall sleep the sleep of the very dead." He gave a topply bow. "I can manage now." He made his way slowly to the door where he paused and turned, a histrionic hand draped on the door jamb. "Should it interest you, Mark, I have been denied my wife's bed – no comfort, no solace these nights. She tells me I snore – arrant nonsense, of course. 'Good night, good night! parting is such sorrow, That I shall say good night till it be morrow.'"

"Go to bed," said Connie. "I'll come up and tuck you in later."

He smiled at me wanly. "Good night, sweet prince."

For a moment his eyes seemed to clear and look through me, then, waving an airy hand, he was gone.

Chapter Four

Back at the hotel I put the Honda to bed and dragged up to my room with the feeling that I had just lived out my autobiography. It had been a retrospective and unsettling day.

I sat in front of the mirror and stared moodily at Barbara Sterling's first lover who, one starlit night among the tombstones of the parish church, had relieved her of her novelty – her own colourful, if cynical designation of virginity; at Sonia Rosner's ex-husband whose two brief years of unloving coupling had climaxed in mutual indifference and desertion; at the erstwhile stuntman, actor and film star whose meteoric screen career had exploded in a conglomerate of accident, surgery, alcohol, pot and the venom of a witch-hunting press. On the credit side stood the earnest and moderately successful agency which kept the roof over an office in the vicinity of St Paul's Cathedral – *M. Savage Private Investigation*, the Honda and a gratifying group of faithful and valued friends among whom Gerald and Connie Grantley loomed high on the present count-my-blessings list for the day.

The mood predominating this introspective canter down Memory Lane, however, was one of uneasiness and apprehension, inexplicable in the light of the nostalgic mellowness of my evening with the Grantleys – Connie's gentle persuasiveness on most counts and Gerald's humorously abrasive outlook on all things, to say nothing of his soul-shaking interpretation of King Lear about which, with an ego somewhat less in magnitude than the Albert Hall, he had neither provoked nor uttered a word.

But something was wrong and as I kicked off the duvet an hour later and lay sweltering in the oppressive heat, that 'something' bedded itself down to the last few minutes of my visit to Grantley. A man with bad dreams . . . not Hamlet, but

Gerald. Was that it? Something was on his mind. "I could put some detective work in your way." Something clearly personal. "Not a word to Connie."

I had no idea what time it was when sleep eventually claimed me; I do know that when the telephone squawked its way through a shadowy sequence of breakfast with the Queen of England, it was just coming up to four thirty. It was still dark and I sent a glass of water flying in a frantic effort to silence the bloody thing.

"Mark . . .? Mark, is that you?" It took me a second or two to recognise Connie's voice. She made no attempt to identify herself but rattled on without a pause. "I'm terribly worried, Mark. It's Gerald . . . he's gone. He's not in his room. I thought at first he'd gone for a walk but then I noticed the key to the tower was missing . . . Mark, are you there?"

"Yes Connie, I'm here."

"I'm so sorry to bother you, dear, at this time of night but you were the only one I could think of who might be willing to help."

"Connie . . ." I shook the sleep out of my ears and concentrated hard. "Listen. Gerald's not in his room, okay . . . What makes you think he *hasn't* gone for a walk?"

"He never has before – not in the middle of the night and without a word. I think he must be up in the tower. The door was open and I called and called . . ."

"Connie," I interrupted her. "I'll come over. Try not to worry. Just stay put and I'll be with you in ten minutes."

"You're an angel, Mark dear . . . please forgive me."

"Nothing to forgive. By the time I get there he'll probably be back."

"Oh I hope so, I hope so."

"If he is, I'll sue. I'm on my way."

The Honda woke up half the neighbourhood as she streamed along the narrow ribbons of roads. She hadn't liked getting up in the middle of the night and coughed a couple of times to air her displeasure. "Shut up," I told her. "I don't like it any more than you do. Look on it as an errand of mercy." Having jumped into my leathers I rather fancied myself as a knight errant in gleaming black armour – which is the only safe way to feel when you've been winkled out of bed to go blasting off on a wild goose chase – because that's exactly what I thought it was: Connie over-reacting. But then Connie was Connie and I *had* been worrying about her husband, hadn't I?

When I got to a place called Butlers Marston which sounded more like a Shakespearean actor than a place, I knew I'd gone wrong somewhere but the Honda took things into her own hands, doubled back through Pillerton Hersey and there we were, Connie on the doorstep in her dressing-gown looking like a mad woman, waiting for me as if there were no tomorrow. My heart sank a little. I had half-hoped that Gerald might be back and all would be well.

She explained in a few short breathless sentences how she had awoken to feel a stillness about the house which had made her uneasy. "He's such a restless sleeper, you see, and is usually snoring fit to bring the house down." He was not in his room and his discarded pyjamas were on the bed. He had dressed and gone out. The house was empty. Then she had noticed that the key to the tower was missing. "The door to the tower is open but the key's not in the lock so he must be up there. I called several times but there was no answer."

"But you didn't go up?"

She shut her eyes tight. "I tried, Mark, I really tried, but I just couldn't. Isn't that dreadful? He could be dying up there . . . I feel so guilty. There's something – not quite right about that place. Even for Gerald I couldn't do it. And then I thought of you . . ."

"Quite right too. Now you just go on inside, make a cup of tea or something and I'll have a scout round. There's bound to be some perfectly rational explanation. He probably couldn't sleep and went off on the prowl."

With a defiant little gesture she drew the sash of her dressing-gown tighter around her. "I'm coming with you." She ran her fingers through her dishevelled hair. "I must look a terrible sight."

Pausing only to pick up a flashlight from the Honda we made our way through the sleeping village, she taking my arm and galloping along gamely beside me. I was aware that her uneasiness must have sprung from that same feeling of

43

apprehension that had rendered me restless and wakeful earlier on, otherwise she surely wouldn't have called out the cavalry simply because her husband had, to all intents and purposes, gone for a midnight stroll.

"You don't think anything could have happened to him, do you?" she panted anxiously.

"In a sleepy little village like this? What could have happened?"

"He was funny all evening." A frown was in her voice.

"How do you mean, funny?"

"I don't quite know. He just seemed so on edge the whole time."

"Well, he did have quite a day yesterday, one way and another."

"And then there was the way he kept looking at his watch."

"Did he?"

"I'm surprised you didn't notice it. I nearly told him to stop it. It's so rude to keep looking at the time when you have guests – it makes them feel unwanted. And that's not like him at all. He just loves company, having friends around him, talking and laughing."

The tower reared up foursquare before us. High above our heads the gilt hands of Gerald's clock gleamed dully in the darkness; they stood at five minutes to five. "The chimes are automatically shut off at midnight," whispered Connie in case I wanted to know, "so's everyone can get some sleep."

She led me up three crumbling steps to the door which stood wide. "There," she whispered, "it's open you see?"

"Why are we whispering?" I asked in a bantering tone.

But she wasn't having any. She lifted her face to mine and even in the darkness I could see the near panic in her eyes. "I just hate this place, Mark."

I touched her hand gently. "Please go back to the house."

She shook her head stubbornly. "I'll wait here, in case you need me."

As I switched on the powerful flashlight she drew a sharp intake of breath. "What is it?"

"The key," she whispered. I directed the light on to the massive lock from which protruded a large brass key. "That wasn't there half an hour ago." I couldn't make out whether the tremulous edge to her voice was fear or hope.

"You're sure of that?"

"Positive. I'd swear to it. He must have come down."

"Why don't you go back to the house and check up?"

She hesitated. "We didn't pass him, but he could have gone the longer way round." She gave a quick nod, turned and went back the way we had come.

I stood for a second or two in the claustrophobic porch wrinkling my nose in distaste. She was right about the smell – dampness and decay mostly, with the added stink of a predator's lair where small rodents and birds had died, leaving bones and feathers to rot. The bright beam of the flashlight was the only comfort. Stone steps spiralled upwards, the narrow treads worn smooth over the centuries.

"Gerald!" I called loudly.

The echo was awe-inspiring and produced a couple of outraged squawks and a flurry of wildly flapping wings; a small body thudded somewhere and scurried off. The only other sound was the laboured *tock-tock* of the tower clock way above my head. I didn't expect an answer from Gerald and didn't get it, but I went on yelling his name every now and again if only to keep up my own spirits.

Dust and dirt gritted beneath my feet as I climbed. I wondered idly why the place hadn't been swept out – as church property it surely should have merited even a token effort from somebody's brush-and-dustpan.

Halfway up I paused for breath at a narrow, unglazed window set deeply into the massive wall. Below in the shrouded countryside burned a single light – the Grantley cottage probably. Beyond it the sky was tinged with the first hint of approaching dawn. The light from the torch touched on an inscription scored meticulously into the stone of the sill at my elbow. *J.D.* it read. *1786*. Two hundred years ago J.D. had stood on this very spot scratching his way to posterity. My finger traced the engraved figures; an ice-cold drop of sweat trickled between my shoulder-blades. I shivered slightly, turned away and continued the climb, to pause again almost at once, aware of a new sound, barely audible, which vied with the monotonous clacking of the great clock: a stealthy whisper of movement interspersed every now and again with a sharp clicking sound – no pattern to it, intermittent, something almost sinister about it.

Switching off the flashlight, I havered for a second, listening, trying to identify the sound, then moved on, still in darkness, my hand against the rough stone wall to guide me. For some reason I was treading more quietly, no longer shouting for Gerald. I felt the draught from two further windows as I climbed. The noise from that bloody clock seemed to take over my entire being and when eventually I came abreast of it I again switched on the light – not a moment too soon: another step and I would have walked into a blank stone wall six inches in front of my nose.

To the right of it, a set of half a dozen or so steep wooden steps led up to a makeshift sort of landing from which a low door, slightly ajar, gave access, presumably, to the roof.

My head was on a level with the landing when an unexpected gust of wind filled my eyes with a fistful of grit, so violent and painful that for a moment I was convinced somebody's foot had been behind it. I all but let go my tenuous hold, clinging on to the top step like a maniac, blinking away the dust and watching the door slowly creaking outwards. A cobweb strung itself stickily across my face.

Again I plunged into darkness. Above the cacophony of the clock I could hear that soft slither of sound, louder now, until with a low grunt the door swung to again and it was gone.

Muttering angrily I lurched up on to the landing, brushing away the cobweb with my sleeve; I jabbed at the button of the flashlight, made aggressively for the door and roughly shoving it open erupted on to the roof yelling "Gerald!" in a voice which didn't sound a lot like mine.

What the hell was the matter with me? Who did I think would be up there lying in ambush for an innocent private dick concerned only with the whereabouts of a missing thespian friend? Private dicking, I concluded sourly, was bad for the heart; every shadow concealed an armed adversary, every niche a lurking assassin.

And there were plenty of them up here – niches not assassins.

The tower platform was larger than I had expected: at a conservative guess, twenty feet square, bounded by chest-high crenellations with a lofty ornamental pinnacle at each corner. Small, skirmishing breezes, contrasting with the sultry stillness below, sent eddies of dust swirling about my feet.

Again that stealthy sussuration of sound. I swung the light to my right. *Click, click, click* . . .

A flagstaff clamped to the battlements; something flapping against it sluggishly at half-mast. A flag? I moved towards it. A black flag. In the torchlight small roundels of metal winked back at me, like buttons. They *were* buttons – brass buttons, belonging to a black blazer suspended from the halyard. Gerald had been wearing a blazer with brass buttons earlier that evening.

A sudden gust of wind had me spinning on my heel, probing the dark with the torch. I was as jittery as a kitten.

Turning back to the flagpole I unfastened the ropes and slowly lowered and detached the jacket, only then realising with a sudden sinking of the heart the possible significance of its flying at half-mast.

As I bundled it up I studied the battlements. For someone slightly unsteady on his feet – or drunk perhaps – clambering about up here in the dark could be lethal. The lower level of each crenellation – the crenel, is it? – was little more than knee high. A stumble and . . .

For a second or two I stood, rigidly conscious of a responsibility I had no wish to shoulder. If Gerald himself had run that blazer up the mast what purpose had he intended it to serve? If, on the other hand, someone else had done it . . .

I put down the jacket and with a stifling feeling of dread, knelt on the nearest crenel and directed the powerful beam of the torch downwards some seventy or eighty feet. Slowly and meticulously I quartered the ground below; a clutter of tombstones huddled, higgledy-piggledy, against the foot of the tower, ancient stones now moved and stacked together for preservation like so many playing cards.

Satisfied, I moved towards what I judged to be the north wall and, repeating the exercise, found myself looking down on the gravelled path leading to the steps of the tower's entrance, and, at a right angle, the west entrance of the church itself.

The east wall of the tower rose above the actual roof of the building. With no more than a cursory glance over a jumble of grey slates and pinnacles, gulleys and gutterings I passed on to the south side.

I have no idea how long I hesitated before I made the final effort, the thought uppermost in my mind, I remember, being that this was like playing Russian roulette, with the desperate odds almost at zero. I also remember the sweat seeping saltily into my eyes, making them smart.

I cast the beam of the torch downwards.

The long drawn-out groan I heard came from my own lips.

The twisted body was splayed crudely across a grey expanse of monumental marble, the face pale as alabaster, huge gleaming eyes staring like glass alleys, the mouth gaping wide, frozen in a silent scream; the hands, like claws, flung wide in crucifixion, the white shirt black with blood.

I rested my forehead against the cold stone of the parapet and shut my eyes tight.

I have no memory of my descent, only of reaching ground level and catching sight of the forlorn figure of Connie standing silhouetted against the greying sky with her back to me, waiting.

I felt myself swaying on my feet as I stood staring at her, my mind a rag-bag of confused and barely suppressed emotions – anger, sorrow, disbelief and, most insupportable of all, the monstrous reality of the truth.

She must have felt my eyes upon her for she turned swiftly as if someone had tapped her on the shoulder. With nothing for her but heartbreak I emerged slowly from the shadows and stood in silence at the head of the crumbling steps while minutes, it seemed, ticked by on the great clock above our heads. Sparrows chittered in the trees, a blackbird whistled and far off a train clattered its way through the misty dawn.

Hesitantly she moved in a couple of paces. "What is it?"

"Connie . . ."

"What have you got there?" A tremor was in her voice.

I came slowly down the steps holding the blazer. She took it in both hands, examined it briefly as if for defects, then cradled it gently in her arms as if it were a sleeping child.

"Connie, there's no way I can . . ."

She read the truth in the helpless spread of my hands. "He's gone?" The words were barely audible. I nodded. "How?" She was now too calm.

"He fell."

Her eyes held mine unwaveringly, then raising her head she stared blankly at the summit of the tower, slowly crushing the jacket to her breast. "Oh dear God," she whispered. "Oh dear, dear God."

Gently I took her in my arms and held her. Her frail body was hard and rigid. I have no idea how long we stood there.

"Where?" she whispered at last. "Where is he?"

"I think we should go back to the house. Do some telephoning . . ."

"I want to see him."

"No."

She pushed herself from me. "Where is he?"

I caught at her. "No, Connie!"

"God damn you!" She flamed with strident anger, striking out at me with a clenched fist. "I asked you where he is."

She clapped a hand hard over her mouth and shut her eyes tightly as she fought desperately to control herself. At last, "Show me, please, Mark dear, please. I need to see him."

Unwillingly I placed an arm about her shoulders and led her silently through the graves and around the dark rearing bulk of the tower.

It was worse than I had imagined. Far worse.

He was impaled on an iron fencing which bounded the grey stone monument I had seen from above, half suspended in air, half resting grotesquely on the tomb; one cruel lance-like spike had thrust itself through his chest.

I tightened my hold on her as a sudden spasm ran through her, followed by an ague fit of trembling; with a little whimper she buried her face against my chest. I took her away, half carrying her back to the house, placing her at last on the sofa where we had sat so happily such a little time before.

Her eyes stared stonily at the ceiling.

I made her take a small shot of brandy, then went to the kitchen to make some tea. While the kettle was coming to the boil I phoned the police and ambulance, and, helping myself to a larger shot of brandy, sat beside her on the arm of the settee, holding her hand, waiting.

Chapter Five

I stood at the open bay window and watched the police ambulance bearing the earthly remains of Sir Gerald Grantley move slowly past the house and through the long dappling shadows of the little copse on the brim of the hill. The sun was up at last, the pale sky blue and blameless. I watched the darting flights of the few remaining house martins, listened to the full-throated song of a thrush, and heard the steady brazen notes of Gerald's clock booming out the hour. I glanced at my watch. Seven o'clock.

At the creaking gate at the foot of the garden path a uniformed policeman stood in lofty conversation with a couple of scruffy individuals who could only be press: one had a pencil stuck in his ear, flourished a notebook and looked as if he couldn't even write. The other, in a battered tweed hat to match an equally unfortunate tweed suit, was elderly with a white drooping moustache and a cynical, seen-it-all expression on a discontented face of puce sponge. He was ignoring the policeman and was far more interested in my Honda perched alongside the garden fence minding her own business; as I watched he took a ball-point and a folded newspaper from his pocket and made a stealthy note of her number. Even from that distance I recognised *Sporting Life*. I had a feeling I was going to have trouble with him.

The garden was what the Victorians would have called a picture, with roses of every colour and strain.

A quiet voice behind me said, "Roses were Gerald's speciality. A passion. Never showed them – just grew them and delighted in them – they both did – never allowed them to be cut and brought into the house."

It was the local GP, Dr Nathan, called in by the police at my request to minister to the stricken Connie. A spare, handsome man in his middle fifties, he wore blue Marks and Spencer pyjamas and a bright orange dressing-gown belted over them. In the early morning sunlight the grey stubble on his chin had the appearance of iron-filings.

"How is she?" I enquired.

"She'll be all right." He put the traditional doctor's bag on the table and joined me at the window. "She's a tough old bird and a dear lady. Terrible shock, of course, terrible. I've given her a sedative. We always do, don't we, we doctors? She'll sleep 'til midday. I imagine she's been up most of the night?"

"Certainly since four."

A silence fell between us, companionable and unawkward.

Another entity had arrived at the gate, a small gnarled gargoyle of a creature, a garden gnome wearing a school cap. With head on one side and a malignant snarl on his lips he was doing his best to shove past the policeman who had placed an official and repressive hand on his chest.

Dr Nathan leaned out of the window. "Officer." The policeman turned. "He's the gardener. I'm sure it will be all right to let him through." While the doctor was still speaking the gnome had removed the law's hand from his chest with a pair of fastidious fingers and now ducked beneath it and through the gate. "Life must go on," muttered Nathan. "Morning, Arch," he called as the gnome skittered up the path on depressingly bandy legs.

"Arrr," grunted the gardener touching his forelock.

"You could drive a coach and pair through those legs," muttered Nathan as the man approached. "Best gardener in the district though."

"What's 'e doin' there?" demanded Arch, aggressively coming abreast of the window.

"There's been an accident, Arch."

Arch's face twisted with alarm. "Not the missus?"

"Sir Gerald."

"Bad then?"

"Dead, I'm afraid."

The misshapen body sagged visibly. "Save 'im," he whispered hoarsely. "Saw the ambulance, never thought it was one of mine." He pulled the school cap slowly from his balding head. "Save 'im," he said again. " 'E was a fair gent." He screwed up his eyes and looked at me for the first time. "What do I do then, guv? You the law too? You ain't no local – nor 'im down at the gate. How's the missus took it? 'Ard, I 'spect. She'd like me to carry on I reckon?"

I nodded. "I'm sure she would. She's resting at the moment. You carry on as usual. And Arch . . ." I added as he drew on his cap and turned away. "I'm not the law."

"Glad to 'ear it." He wagged his head mournfully. "Poor lady, she'll be 'ard 'it, and that's a fact. 'Ow did it 'appen?"

"He fell," I told him with a glance at the doctor. "From the church tower."

The little man drew in his breath with a hiss. "There you go, then." He clicked his tongue. "Knew 'e'd do it one of these days. I seen 'im up there raving away. Like the devil 'isself . . . Beelzebub on the rampage. Knew it'd 'appen one o' these days."

We watched in silence as he ambled off and disappeared around a corner of the house.

Dr Nathan said with a smile, "He's devoted to them both; Connie as a latter day Mary, Mother of God, and Gerald as the latest thing in Beelzebubs – as you gathered. He's been with them ever since they came here – and probably before. I wouldn't know, I'm a stranger, only been here twenty years." He glanced at his watch. "Well, I'd better be getting along, I suppose, get some clothes on and have a shave."

I scratched at my own chin. "Join the club."

He hesitated. "You staying on here for a bit?"

"I was going back to town, but," I shrugged, "seeing how things are . . ."

He nodded. "It would be nice for her if you hung on a little. You don't have to do anything or worry about her, she'll sleep for quite a time, and I'll look in on her at lunchtime, see how she is."

"It's no sweat," I told him. "I'll pick up my things from the hotel. Presumably she'll be all right while I'm away? The hotel's in Stratford."

"She's dead to the world. Anyway," he nodded at the copper

53

on the gate, "he'll be around. And Sherlock Holmes will be back from the church when he's finished looking for clues. Has he talked to you yet?"

"We bandied words."

"He will."

"Doctor," I called him back as he picked up his bag and prepared to depart. He paused in the doorway. "What do you think happened?"

He came slowly back into the room, rested his bag on the table and stared down at it for a long time in silence. I leaned back against the sill and waited.

At last he gave a shrug. "Three alternatives. He fell, he jumped . . . or he was pushed. The outcome is the same." He glanced at the constable through the window. "The choice is theirs. I'm concerned only with the outcome, distressing as it is, but I would prefer . . ." He hesitated for an age. "I would prefer it to be the first."

"That he fell?"

His eyes met mine for a long moment, then he gave an abrupt nod. "Good morning to you," he said, and turning on his heel was gone.

I watched him tramp briskly down the garden path, the fact that he was in pyjamas and dressing-gown appearing to worry him not at all. The policeman opened the gate for him, doing his best to ward off the members of the press. Others had joined them, including a couple of females, one with glasses and wearing what looked like an ancient steel helmet but which turned out to be steel-coloured hair cut in the shape of a helmet. They pressed around Nathan, books, pencils and tape-recorders at the ready, the helmeted female standing four-square in front of him, the sun flashing aggressively from her glasses. Nathan sidestepped her with the adroitness of experience and outstripped the rest of them as they ambled after him half-heartedly before deciding that better pickings might be had by remaining where they were.

Turning away from the window I slumped heavily on to the settee and stared glumly at Gerald's huge empty chair with that ghastly plant growing out of it. The doctor's words thudded in my ears: he fell, he jumped or he was pushed.

Accident? He had certainly drunk too much – more than his usual quota according to Connie – and in such a condition, prowling about in the dark up there . . . Thinking back it seemed to me that there had been a moment when he had deliberately set out to hit the bottle. Why? Had he wished to curtail the evening? His inhospitable clock-watching certainly encouraged the idea. He had wanted me to go. So why invite me in the first place? I hadn't exactly thrust myself upon them.

He had said he would sleep the sleep of the dead; with the amount of liquid refreshment he had taken aboard it would have surprised no one if he had slept throughout the night and most of the following morning – yet there he was, a few hours later, dressed, up and about, and climbing to the top of that bloody tower. There was no way the effect of the alcohol he had put away could have worn off; he would still have been muzzy-headed to say the least, and one false step . . .

Suicide? Never. Not Gerald. One, he wasn't the type – if indeed there were a type; two, he had far too much to live for: Connie first and foremost, for whom, quite clearly, he had a deep and abiding love; his work – the overwhelming Lear he had thrust upon the theatrical world only a few hours before; his home, his roses, his undoubted joy of living. And if that wasn't enough he had made a date to meet me this very morning. "About elevenish? How'd that do?"

And so saying he plunges to his death from the top of a church tower?

Or was he pushed?

I roused myself. Someone had come into the house. I scrambled to my feet and hoofed it out into the hall.

A man stood silhouetted in the open front door, black against the bright colours of the garden beyond, tall, slim, bareheaded.

"Ah, Mr Savage . . . Splendid. I was hoping to have a further word with you, sir."

The voice was soft, careful and full of courtroom promise; somewhere it also contained a threat, no more than was deemed necessary from your run-of-the-mill investigating policeman, but a threat nonetheless. I had forgotten his name. I had met him only briefly before he had gone shinning up the tower on his own; he had looked me over with a good deal of naked suspicion, his eyes loitering over my leatherwear as if it contained the answer to all his problems.

He caught my blank look and stepped forward into the light. "Hunter. Sergeant Hunter. We met at the scene of the – uh – accident."

I invited him in to the sitting-room and he stood for a moment sniffing the air like a featherweight bloodhound, taking in the furnishings and the decorations with the appearance of one who would remember every detail until long after the day he died.

He was good-looking for a policeman and in a long sort of way, long face, long neck, long body – even his feet were long; fair haired and blue-eyed he slid gently into the Leslie Howard mode. He had a prominent Adam's apple which glided stealthily up and down like a genie in a bottle. He gave out intellectuality.

At the window he took in the now fair-sized crowd at the gate. "How the hell do they get on to these things?" he muttered half to himself. "There's someone there from the *Birmingham Post* – thirty miles away – and you only discovered the body . . . when?"

He swung round on me so fast that I started like a guilty thing.

"Er . . . five-ish, thereabouts . . ."

Now he had his notebook out and parked himself on the window-seat, burrowing in an inner pocket for the inevitable ballpoint.

"A few questions, Mr Savage, do you mind?"

I shrugged and humped myself down on the arm of the settee.

"You're a friend of the family, right, sir?" I nodded. "Visiting?" Another nod. "From where?"

"London."

"And you arrived when?"

"Yesterday."

"Departing?"

I hesitated. "Today."

"But?" he queried, catching the hesitation.

"I was just wondering whether I oughtn't to stay on for a bit, give Connie, Lady Constance, a hand. She may need some support."

"Right." He nodded amiably and doodled in his book. So far he hadn't written anything down. "Any particular reason for your visit?"

"I came to see the play."

"What play?"

"*King Lear*. In Stratford. You know, the Royal Shakespeare Theatre? Sir Gerald Grantley was an actor of some repute. He was playing the King. Last night was the first night." I don't know what he made of that but it sounded pretty funny to me.

Heavy suspicion was wrought all over his face. "You came all the way from London just to see a play?"

"I went all the way to Bremen once just to see a performance of *Fidelio*."

"*Fidelio*?"

"Yes, the one where the girl dresses up as a boy."

He nodded, "I did it at school. I can't say I go a lot for Shakespeare."

He wasn't an intellectual.

"No, well . . ." I said giving him a wobble of the head. "There you are then . . ."

He was frowning at me intently, his head on one side, face screwed up trying to remember something. "I've seen you before somewhere."

"Have you?"

"We haven't met?"

I shook my head. "I would have remembered."

"How well did you know Sir Gerald?"

"Not all that well. We were acquaintances of long standing."

"How long?"

"Six, seven years."

"And yet you come all this way to see him act?"

"Sergeant," I said quietly. "As an actor Sir Gerald Grantley was something of a phenomenon. He was even knighted for it. In the theatre last night were people from all over the world, there specifically to witness his interpretation of King Lear. Unlike yourself, I go a bundle on Shakespeare and have

57

admired Grantley's work since long before I was born. How's that?"

He wasn't in the least put out. In fact he positively beamed at me and shook his head almost playfully, like a slightly shocked parent indicating that such things shouldn't be said in public.

"So what can you tell me about last night?"

"He took twenty-one personal curtain calls."

"*After* all that." He swept *King Lear* under the carpet. "Did you stay the night here?"

"No. I'm staying at the Swan's Nest and would be grateful to get back there as soon as possible to collect my gear before they dun me for another night."

"The Swan's Nest," he repeated, writing in his book for the first time. "But you came back here with him after his – uh – twenty-one personal curtain calls?"

"They invited me back."

"What time would that be?"

I shrugged. "Twelve-ish, I'm not sure."

"And after your drinks you returned to the Swan's Nest?"

"Right."

"And a few hours later you were back discovering the body?"

"Right."

"How was that?"

"Lady Constance rang me. It was past four. Her husband, she said, had disappeared. She sounded desperate so I came over."

His eyes strayed over my leathers. "On your motor-bike?" I nodded. "Were you surprised she sounded so desperate? After all, he could have just gone for a walk."

"I told her the very same thing. She wasn't convinced. She thought he might have gone up into the tower. She's terrified of the place, wouldn't go near it. Claustrophobia, agoraphobia, vertigo – you name it, she's got it."

He ticked something off in his book. His Adam's apple, on an upward trend, thought better of it and sank back again. "Then what?"

I told him about my adventures in the tower and my subsequent discovery of the body. I left out the bit about the

58

blazer flying at half-mast. I don't know why except that for some reason I wanted to keep it to myself. I also didn't mention the fact that Connie had remarked on the absence of the key to the tower on her first visit and its later reappearance. I was perfectly well aware that I was withholding information but I needed to think some more before officially "remembering" them. Those two items together could argue the presence of a second person up there on the tower platform which could open up a very sinister can of worms.

"I'm sorry?" I said. Hunter had asked a question I hadn't heard.

"I wondered if you had an opinion?"

"About what?"

"The cause of Sir Gerald's death."

I gave the impression of deep thought. "I guess it was an accident. It must have been pretty dark up there. The moon had gone long before. He could have been a bit unsteady on his pins perhaps. Even I felt a bit shaky after tramping up all those bloody steps and I'm half his age. Didn't you?"

"Feel shaky?" He considered for a moment. "No, I can't say that I did. Had he been drinking?"

"He'd had a few."

"How many?"

"I didn't count. Let's say he was on the jolly side when he went to bed, that's all – no more than you and I would have been under the same heady circumstances."

"What heady circumstances?" He was being very obtuse.

"Of having given the world a stunning interpretation of one of the most difficult roles in the annals of theatrical history." I sounded a trifle prim.

"Ah, yes, I see." He thought for a moment. "Actually I don't drink."

I nodded. "Bully for you."

Now he was writing. And went on writing. The first chapter of a new novel perhaps, judging by the time he took over it. I studied his narrow features. He might not be sold on Shakespeare but there was quite a lot going on in that long narrow head of his. It would be wise not to underestimate him. I wondered briefly whether it was a mistake not to tell him about the blazer

59

halfway up the mast, but then dismissed the thought. That was my pigeon. If Gerald himself had hoisted it he would have done so either as a gesture of defiance or remorse, prior to flinging himself off the battlements – a sour if uncharacteristic attempt at black comedy. If, on the other hand, someone else was responsible then it was a cynical salute not only to the eminence of his victim but to the perpetration of murder. Whichever way I chose to look at it, one aspect of the case was becoming ominously clear: the possibility of accidental death was slimming down by the minute.

I cleared my throat.

Hunter grunted, wrote on for a couple of seconds then drew a line across his page. End of chapter one. He looked up.

"Is that it?" I asked. "Can I go now? Pick up my rubbish at the hotel?"

"Will you be coming back here?"

"I'll certainly look in."

"And should you decide not to stay on, you'll be heading back to London?"

"I guess so."

"Then perhaps you'd be good enough to give me your home address, sir. We shall need you for the coroner's inquest, I'm afraid."

I told him where I lived. At the mention of Wimbledon he brightened considerably. Tennis was clearly up his alley. I could see him in long white shorts and long white tennis shoes.

"Get to the championships this year?" he asked scarcely able to restrain his enthusiasm.

I felt mean so I told him drily that watching grown-ups batting balls to each other was not my particular bag.

He looked at me as if I had sprouted a second head, then with a small shudder pulled himself together. "What *do* you do, Mr Savage?"

"Do?"

"For a living."

"Not a lot these days," I said jovially. The other thing I wasn't going to tell him was that I was a private dick; the average cop's idea of a private dick is rarely the flavour of the month. I gave him a winsome smile. "I suppose you could say

I'm an actor, though it's such a long time since I worked I've probably forgotten how to do it."

Ten out of ten for truthfulness anyway. He didn't bother to write it down. "Anybody ever tell you that you look like Leslie Howard?" I asked gently to take his mind off it.

Somebody evidently had; his blush was almost as stimulating as Barbara Sterling's. "Can I go now?" I added before he could confess.

He stood up abruptly. "Yes, sure, why not?" He stowed away his book and pen. "I can count on you not to flee the country, I suppose? I may have a few more questions for you when things have sorted themselves out."

I left him at the window and ponced down the garden path to the accompaniment of bovine stares from the assemblage at the gate, the sudden silence among them broken only by a sultry wolf-whistle from the lady in the steel helmet. She was obviously a leather fetishist.

As the bobby on duty opened the gate and waved his arms about to clear a way for me, a storm of questions burst around me, not one of which I heard clearly.

While unearthing my crash-hat from the Honda's box I did an admirable job of ignoring them until the elderly early-riser with the white moustache and tweed hat pushed his way importantly through the throng. "Is that your bike?" he demanded with forked and bibulous tongue.

"Who wants to know?" I asked mildly.

I was about to place the helmet on my head when a camera flashed. "Thank you, Mr Sutherland," smirked the lady with the steel hair, winding on her film and backing stealthily into the crowd.

I jammed the key into the ignition and engulfed them in a noxious cloud of exhaust fumes. That, I thought sourly, was all I bloody needed.

Chapter Six

BBC Radio ran the story on the eight o'clock news. I perched on the edge of the bed and listened.

"The body of Sir Gerald Grantley was discovered early this morning in the churchyard of his native village of Grantley, Warwickshire. He is believed to have fallen to his death from the eighty-foot tower of the church sometime during the night, and although the police have refused to comment further on the manner of his death they have nevertheless indicated that foul play is not suspected.

"Sir Gerald, at the age of sixty-eight, was one of Britain's most eminent Shakespearean actors, his interpretations of Hamlet, Othello and Macbeth at the Old Vic during the sixties and seventies receiving great critical acclaim. Knighted in 1974, his subsequent appearances have been rare. His long-awaited King Lear, premiered only last night at the Royal Shakespeare Theatre, Stratford-upon-Avon, was received tumultuously by an enthusiastic audience. It was to be his last performance. BBC Radio 4 will be assessing Sir Gerald's long and distinguished career in a special edition of *Kaleidoscope* at nine forty-five tomorrow night . . ."

I collected razor and toothbrush from the bathroom, decided against breakfast and went down to pay my bill.

"I just can't believe it," said the man at the desk. "He was here in the dining-room only a couple of nights back, large as life . . . Wish now I'd seen him act – sounds like I've been missing something."

The attitude was typical, I thought sourly, stowing my gear into the Honda's box; only when someone took off unexpectedly for the next world did the majority remember how large he had loomed in this one.

I sat for a second or two straddling the bike, wondering

where I was going. I didn't particularly want to return so soon to Grantley; Connie wouldn't be surfacing yet awhile and I needed the company of Sergeant Hunter like I needed a hole in the head. I might also be tempted to put a certain press-person's camera out of action, an intemperance which could prove costly.

I felt out of sorts and in dire need of sleep. I'd get out into the country somewhere, breathe some fresh air, winkle out a quiet pub and a ploughman's lunch perhaps, then dawdle back to Grantley in my own time.

I screwed on my helmet, let fly with the engine and swung out on to the A34 where in no time at all I became obsessed with the pink shorts and the comely legs of a young lady jogging merrily along on the offside pavement. Female legs have always worried me and this particular pair was no exception. It wasn't until I was almost alongside that I realised with a gulp that not only were they familiar but they belonged to the delectable Barbara Sterling.

I slowed, allowing her a little headway, then, sliding down the tinted visor of my helmet, swung the bike on to the wrong side of the road and bubbled along a couple of yards behind her. Her smart blonde pony-tail twitched irritably as she became aware of my presence.

"Hi!" I called sexily through the Perspex, hoving up alongside her.

She glanced across at me, her face puce with exertion – or was it a blush? She shouted something rude; I couldn't hear what it was above the rumble of the Honda but I read her lips; an unladylike couple of words.

An approaching truck trumpeted at me like it was the end of the world, the driver, bearing no resemblance at all to the Angel Gabriel, bawling frenziedly from his cabin. I almost came to grief as he drove me into the gutter. I pulled up in a sweat, pushed up the visor and cut the engine.

"Serves you bloody well right!" shouted Barbara as she thudded past.

"Now that's not very friendly, is it?" I called after her.

She pounded on a few paces, broke stride, then turned her head to look at me. I removed the helmet and sat smirking at her like an idiot. Her face fell open. "Sorry," I said. "I just couldn't resist it."

"You silly sod!" she panted, pulling up. "You could have got yourself killed." She leaned forward, spread her hands on her knees and drew half a dozen deep breaths. "It was a damn fool thing to do," she gasped straightening up at last and glaring at me severely, the severity softening a little, however, as her eyes lingered over my sable armour.

"You look obscene," she whispered with a broad smile and a blush which welled up slowly from beneath her T-shirt.

"You look pretty good yourself," I countered. "How long has all this jogging been going on?"

"Don't ask." She drew a sweaty arm over her face. "Where are you off to, the Big Smoke?"

I shook my head. "Mooching."

"Harassing defenceless females. Had any breakfast?"

"No."

"How about . . .?"

Suddenly I felt like breakfast. "Jump up," I said quickly before she could change her mind, and reaching back into the box I produced the spare helmet held in readiness for just such an opportunity. "It's the law," I pointed out as she eyed it rebelliously. "You'll look divine in it." She did. "Now, where can we get breakfast at this hour?"

"My place. Bull Street, Old Town. Know it? I'll direct you."

Starting up the bike I snuggled back against her as she got up behind and slid her arms sensuously about my waist.

It was only when I swung the machine around and set sail for Clopton Bridge that I realised with a sickening jolt of the stomach that she couldn't yet have heard about Gerald; if she had, she wouldn't have been jogging mindlessly along the Shipston Road; as company manager she would be sweating on the top line at the theatre wondering what the hell was going to happen to the next performance of *King Lear*.

Bull Street was trim but undistinguished, with terraced, narrow-fronted late Victorian houses opening immediately on to the street. No 62 was almost opposite a pub called The Sportsman and right next door to a discreet betting-shop. At least her proprieties were right.

I tripped over a doormat just inside the front door and she fielded me into a small room on the right, opening off a narrow passage. "You hang about in there for a tick while I have a quick shower, then I'll get us some breakfast. Eggs, bacon, toast . . .?"

"Great. You live here on your own?"

"Uh-huh."

"Why?"

"Why not?" She sashayed down the passage into a smart kitchen with me in hot pursuit. "Why are you following me?"

"I thought I'd put the kettle on, sing a song, make the tea, coffee . . . which?"

"Tea for me."

She disappeared through another door at the end of the kitchen, peering back at me around the edge of it. "And keep out of here." She grinned her wide grin and closed the door slowly in my face, shooting a bolt on the far side. "Hard luck!" she chuckled loudly through the door.

As I filled and plugged in the kettle, banged my way through numerous cupboards looking for cups and saucers and the like, I brooded over the impact that Gerald's death would have on Barbara, let alone the theatre itself. The second performance of *Lear* scheduled for tomorrow, Monday, would necessitate either cancellation or the rehearsing-in of an understudy, each of which would involve her in a frantic reappraisal of what could have been an enormously pleasant Sunday afternoon.

A telephone rang somewhere.

"Ba!" I bawled over the running water. "Telephone."

"Answer it, will you, Mark? It's in the front room. Tell 'em I've died."

The front room was like a movie set for the latest remake of *David Copperfield*; everything was vintage Victorian except the telephone and I couldn't find that. Eventually I discovered the cord and ran it to earth lurking beneath what looked like an embroidered tea-cosy. I barked the number into the mouthpiece.

"Barbara?" demanded an imperious and querulous voice.

"She's in the shower."

"Who are you?"

"Her father. You want to leave a message?"

A laboured sigh. "Tell her I want her at the theatre at the double. My name is Paul Braidy."

"Hang on – I'll get a pencil." A groan this time. I stood for some time staring idly about the room wondering why she had furnished it like Queen Victoria's front parlour. He snarled a couple of petulant "hello's" in my ear before I said brightly, "Hello, here we are again, pencil at the ready. Sorry to have kept you waiting. Now, Saul who was it?"

"Paul! Paul with a 'P'."

"Paul with a 'P', got it. And who else were we? Grady, was it?"

"Braidy . . . B-R-A-I-D-Y. Paul Braidy, the producer."

"The what? Sorry, I'm a little hard of hearing."

"Just tell her I'm at the theatre, will you? And get her to ring me back as soon as she can. It's top priority."

"Does she know you, Mr Brody?"

"Just give her the message." He banged down the phone. Silly sod, I thought.

"Who was it?" called Barbara through the bathroom door as I returned to the kitchen.

"Wrong number. Someone wanting a psychiatrist."

I was making the tea when she edged past me in a cloud of steam and a large blue towel. "Two minutes," she called disappearing up the passage, and was as good as her word; three minutes later she was breaking eggs into a pan and thrusting bacon under the grill with the speed and dexterity of a thirty-second TV commercial.

We sat opposite each other at a circular bijou table under a window through which bright sunlight slanted in over a confused and careworn patch of back garden. The chat and laughter was of the past and what we'd said, done and meant to each other so long ago; no strangeness, no awkwardness, each content in the other's company; the long years might never have been. And squatting between us like a death's head was the knowledge that I had to break up this merry reunion and ruin the rest of her day.

We had finished eating. She said, "Let's take our tea into the other room."

I put out a hand and touched hers. "Let's stay here for a bit—in the sun." The news was lamentable enough without having to break it in Queen Victoria's murky front parlour. "I have things to tell you."

The sun behind her transformed her drying hair into a mesh of fine spun gold. The sudden sobering of her eyes she caught from mine.

"It's about Gerald . . . Gerald Grantley . . ."

I told her as gently as possible; how gentle can you be about a dear and valued friend plummeting eighty feet to his death in the middle of the night? No matter how soothing the voice, how careful the words, the imagination is remorseless. Throughout the short recital she sat quiet and frozen, shadowed against the bright rectangle of window, colourless except for the translucence of her hair which blazed like a halo.

When I had done I was unable to look at her; I fiddled with my knife, aimlessly shoving a crust of toast around my plate. "The phone call just now . . ." I mumbled, "Braidy. Wants you to ring him. I thought you should have some breakfast inside you before facing all that."

She made no move. I glanced up at her. She had turned her head and was staring blankly into space, her eyes large and bright. "I just can't take it in. Why?" She shook her head slowly. "Poor Connie . . . poor Gerald. He would never have . . ."

I took her hand. "Gerald was no suicide, you know that as well as anyone. It was an accident – it had to be. He had – drunk quite a bit. He was well away at the party, as you know, and later at home he had quite a bit more. He could have misjudged his footing up there in the dark, lost his balance. He might even have had a heart attack. All the same . . ." I trailed off, thinking about that bloody blazer.

"What in the name of God was he doing up there in the middle of the night?" she cried suddenly in a loud overwrought voice.

"That," I said quietly, "is something I intend to find out."

She glanced at me curiously. "I ought to be getting along to the theatre. There'll be a lot to cope with." Her voice was now under control but still she didn't move. "All the same what?" she asked abruptly. I frowned at her. "You said, 'All the same . . .'"

After a second's hesitation I said slowly, "Listen, Ba, I haven't made up my mind yet, but the chances are I might decide to stay on here for a bit – until I'm satisfied about one or two things. If I do stay I'd be grateful for your help. For one thing I'd like to be able to prowl around the theatre without anyone getting their knickers in a twist. As an old flame of yours they'd accept me, wouldn't they?"

She nodded vaguely. "I still don't understand."

"That's because I haven't yet told you what I do for a living." And I told her, adding that the revelation was not for public consumption.

. "A private investigator?" she repeated wonderingly. "You mean you're going to ask questions about Gerald?" I nodded. "But if he didn't commit suicide, if it was an accident, I don't see . . ." She broke off, staring at me with slowly dawning disbelief. "You don't mean . . . ?" She brushed a tear impatiently from her cheek.

"Don't jump to conclusions," I begged. "A couple of things are worrying me, that's all. I just want to set my mind at rest."

The telephone rang again. "Oh blast the thing!" she muttered, edging herself out from behind the table. She called over her shoulder as she thudded barefoot across the kitchen floor, "That'll be God Almighty again."

The ringing stopped. "Yes?"

Even from where I was I could hear the discontented clacking at the other end. I got to my feet, strolled up the passage and leaned in at the door. She shook her head at me and raised her eyes ceilingwards as the disembodied voice babbled on. Eventually a break occurred in the tirade and she jumped in. "Okay, okay, I hear you. Simmer down, for God's sake." It started again. "Paul!" she snapped suddenly. "While I'm listening to you pontificating I could be halfway there. Why does it always have to be you who suffer? You're not the only one in a jam. There's the company too. Have you been on to Trevor? Well, why the hell not? He's the one who's got the decisions to make, not you, and certainly not me."

She threw the instrument on to its rest with a clatter. She was

trembling, pale with suppressed anger. "That blasted little . . .!
He makes me want to vomit. He's like a tenth-rate prima
donna. Someone's got to tell him that the whole bloody world
does not revolve about him alone."

I went to her, took her gently by the shoulders. About to
shrug me off, she thought better of it, hung her head for a
second, then rested it quietly on my shoulder. When she spoke
again the tears were flowing freely, her voice taut with emotion.
"Do you know what that unspeakable lout said just now? He
said . . ." She drew a deep breath. "He said, 'That senile old
ham has just chucked himself off a church tower and left me
with no bloody Lear tomorrow!' Can you believe that, Mark?
That anyone could be so . . . so . . ."

"Sure I can believe it." I held her tight. "I think I'm
prepared to believe anything of him."

When, in fact, I actually came face to face with him a short
while later I found myself revising that judgment; on first
impression I would have considered him capable of almost
nothing, any ability he might have had being locked away
behind an overweening demonstration of self-importance, the
result, I would guess, of a chronic sense of insecurity. He
strutted, stuck out his chest, uttered platitudes with carefully
rounded and elongated vowel sounds as if to conceal a regional
accent he wished no one to know about. The top of his round
head was no higher than my shoulder, something I never
consciously hold against anyone, unless that "anyone" begins
to stand on tiptoe or climb the nearest steps to gain a frail
ascendancy.

I took an instant and important dislike to him.

When Barbara Sterling and I ran him to earth he was
parading around the dimly-lit stage like a prisoner-of-war
doing a circuit of the camp perimeter.

"Ah!" he shouted peremptorily, "there you are! You took
your time." He peered aggressively at me looming unostenta-
tiously behind her. "Who's that? Is that your father?" The
question floored Barbara since I had omitted to acquaint her
with the finer points of our telephone conversation.

I shuffled forward into the light. "Step-father actually, Mr

69

Brody." He didn't much care for what he saw: I was too tall for one thing and the black leather clearly made him apprehensive. "The name is Braidy, Mr Sterling, Paul Braidy," he pointed out prissily.

"And mine is Savage, Mr Braidy, not Sterling." Barbara at my elbow gave a snuffling sort of snort as he turned abruptly on his heel and took up his peripatetics once again.

He flung over his shoulder, "So, Madam Sterling, what are we going to do about this god-awful mess?"

"Well," she replied calmly with a weary glance at me as she seated herself sedately on the scenic tree which sprawled centre-stage, "I, for one, am not about to do anything at all until I receive some sort of directive from someone up top – Trevor or Terry. As I said on the phone, it's their decision, not mine. Nor yet yours."

He swung on her bawling like a maniac. "It's time we're up against, woman, time, for Christ's sake. We're wasting time. Who's the bloody understudy?"

"Mel Morris."

"Well, get him here. Let's do some work on him. Does he know the part?"

"I have no idea. I'm not responsible for understudy rehearsals. You haven't contacted Trevor yet?"

"No, I haven't. I can't get him. There's no reply. And Terry's in London."

She gave a loud sigh and got up. "You sure you were ringing the right number? I'll go and have a try. He's probably just nipped out for a paper, or gone jogging or something." She made for the wings, winking at me as she passed. "Get acquainted you two, why don't you?" adding for me alone, "Do your best not to assassinate him."

I squatted disconsolately on the tree and watched him for a couple of seconds in silence. Then, "Mr Braidy," I said with a falsely avuncular note to my voice, "why don't you come and sit down? You'll make yourself ill. If the captain is up-tight, the men will be too."

I thought for a second that he was going to tell me to shog off and mind my own business, but surprisingly he slowed down, relaxing a little, and eventually came to a standstill. He liked being called captain. He shoved his hands in his pockets and edged over in my direction. He had neither shaved nor done anything about his hair which hung, lank and black, over his eyes. He wore the regulation outfit for today's important director: faded concertina jeans and an outsize T-shirt which draped forlornly about his puny frame and bore the inscription *New York Giants* in large red letters across its chest. It was joking of course.

He came and stood over me. I stared stonily at his smelly-looking, off-white trainers. "You've heard what's happened?"

"Barbara mentioned something."

"That mindless old fart!" he suddenly exploded. "If he wanted to knock himself off why the fuck couldn't he have waited a couple of weeks until the bloody play was run in?"

"Come on . . ." I growled with only a tenuous hold on my temper. "The man's dead."

He snarled, "Okay, okay, so he's dead. So I'm sorry. But I'm not responsible, am I?"

He began moving around, throwing his arms about in gawky, angry gestures, his voice shrill and petulant with self-justification. "He should never have been cast for the part in the first bloody place. He was way out of his depth right from the beginning. He was just too old. He hadn't got the guts, the energy to carry a part that size. Nor the imagination." His voice dropped to an angry mutter. "It's always the same with these old hams. Ask 'em to do anything new, experimental, imaginative, and they're down the drain. I was dead against having him right from the start, but everyone knows better than the director of course!"

"'Tis ever so," I quoted, nodding sententiously. "It makes one wonder why you got yourself involved in the first place – that being the case, I mean. You must have known his work – known *about* him anyway."

"I'd never seen him act. I hardly ever go to the theatre – most of it's crap these days. Anyway he hadn't done anything for centuries. And are you surprised? Who'd want him buggering up their show? Only in the first act last night did he *begin* to be Lear – and that was because he was sticking to *my* directions and doing what he'd been told. After that, what the fuck did he think he was doing? I'll tell you one thing, if he hadn't chucked himself off that bloody tower last night, I'd now be clamouring to have him fired. Him or me. That would have been my ultimatum. That'd have made 'em sit up!"

"Why didn't you walk out?"

"Because he beat me to it, that's why."

He reached into his pocket and produced a battered pack of cigarettes. His fingers trembled as he set light to one with a match. "And because I wanted to do *Lear*. It's still a passable piece in its way. Flounders towards the end, of course, but most of the old bard's plays do. But the rest of it – the family group, their squabbles, feuds, politics, ambitions – they're so vital, so immediate. It's like a bloody great missile projecting itself through space into the future. I wanted to set it bang in the middle of the twenty-first century – after the bomb – everything in ruins, nothing to live for, nothing to fight for, but everyone living and fighting just the same, because all their problems are parochial – sex, jealousy, family, local government . . . It could have been so *meaningful*. But no! That doddering old idiot wouldn't see it, couldn't if he tried. So he swep' out, didn't he, just like that. I knew he was trouble the moment I clapped eyes on him."

His hands were back in his pockets and, suddenly deflated, he mooched around, jabbing his toes petulantly into the stage-cloth, like a small boy kicking a stone.

"Well, needless to say I was overruled – he was allowed back on his own terms, blocked me every way he knew how, argued about every move I gave him, every sodding word I wanted changed. I don't think he even understood what he was talking about most of the time. And now, having ruined everything, alienated the cast, undermined my authority, he goes and does himself in."

"We don't actually know that, do we?"

"Know what?"

"What you just said."

"Of course he did himself in. He realised he'd made a hash of it and wasn't prepared to face the consequences."

I gave a sad shake of the head. "I can only say I must have seen another show. I quite enjoyed it."

72

"With another Lear and my original setting you'd have been shattered by it."

I shrugged. "Twenty-one curtains . . . not bad for an old ham."

"Curtain-calls! I don't give a fuck about curtain-calls. There's always a mob element ready to shout and scream no matter how bad the thing is. You only have to see those sodding awful sit-com shows on the telly with a so-called live audience to know that. Old Grantley probably had a well-paid claque up there in the gods. I wouldn't put it past him. They all had 'em at one time – the old hams who were on the skids."

"You're protesting too much, Mr Braidy. People will think you're bitter."

"And they'd be right too, I am."

In the short silence which followed I sensed in him a lifetime of frustration and hostility . . . wormwood, wormwood . . .

Scuffing his feet he moved irresolutely downstage and stood crookedly on the edge of the apron staring out into the black maw of the auditorium, his round head sunk into hunched shoulders, hands deep in the pockets of his crumpled jeans. Blue smoke from his cigarette eddying about his head and shoulders added an air of disquieting unreality. He looked unfinished, deformed – everyone's idea of Richard III, hump-backed and lame.

I caught myself wondering about him. Who was he? Where had he come from? Like him, I was an infrequent patron of the theatre, so perhaps it wasn't surprising that until yesterday I had never heard of him; but to be invited to produce a play of the stature of *King Lear* at one of the most prestigious theatres in the world must surely argue a track record of some note.

He was muttering to himself, his voice barely audible. The yawning dark of the empty theatre swallowed the words, regurgitated them and sent them back in an echoing whisper as stealthy as a fledgling stirring in the nest. I strained my ears . . . "When churchyards yawn and hell itself breathes out Contagion to this world . . ." The musings of a would-be killer . . . "now could I drink hot blood, And do such bitter business as the day Would quake to look on . . ."

73

On the heels of violent death the quotation made my scalp crawl. I was beset by people quoting *Hamlet*.

I got to my feet and joined him on the apron. He made no move, no acknowledgment of my arrival, but after a second or two: "Look at it," he whispered in a tight manic sort of voice, "and just sense the power an actor feels when he stands here alone in the light. Out there in the darkness a thousand people hang on his every word. It's godlike." He glanced up at me briefly, muttering disparagingly, "But if you've never acted you wouldn't understand."

He trod his cigarette into the stage-cloth.

I let a moment go by. "Did *you* ever act?"

He was silent for a long time as if making up his mind whether or not to confess. At last he said, "I played Hamlet once." It was almost a whisper. "At college – ten years ago. It may not have been the greatest Hamlet in the world, but I bloody played it." A long pause, then almost inaudibly he added, "Acting's the only thing I've ever cared about."

"So what happened?"

"So I became a producer."

"Why not an actor?"

He swung on me suddenly, almost hissing the words. "Look at me, will you? I could play bloody Richard the Third without make-up!"

He turned abruptly and prowled off into a corner out of the light. The querulous voice echoed from the shadows. "Why the hell am I talking to you like this? I don't even know you."

"Perhaps that's why. Sometimes it's good to talk to a stranger.Therapeutic, I'm told, better than wasting your money on analysts."

He was silent. I couldn't see him. I could hear him breathing, short staccato intakes, as if he had been running. I moved slowly towards him.

In the dim light I almost fell over him. He was sitting cross-legged on the floor, elbows on knees, head in hands, disturbingly vulnerable. I squatted beside him, suddenly involved, my initial dislike of him receding. He had problems like other people had mice. Perhaps he really didn't want to be the producer people loved to hate; it must be pretty lonely –

being hated. We sat in companionable silence for a short space, neither feeling the need for communication. I wondered what had happened to Barbara. Perhaps she had left the country.

I watched him light another cigarette.

He said suddenly, "What did you say your name was?" I told him. After a second he said, "I had a friend at college called Mark. Tall, blond, beautiful. He was the Horatio to that Hamlet of mine." Another long silence. "I'm a failed actor. That would seem to be the trouble." He went on without a pause, the words almost tripping over themselves. "I didn't want to play bloody Richard Three, crippled and deformed. I wanted to play Henry Five, Romeo, Mercutio – all the beautiful ones." He sniggered. "Can you imagine it? Me! I'm too bloody small and too bloody ugly. It's pathetic."

"Edmund Kean was no giant," I told him. "Five foot six, if an inch."

"Who cared about height in those days? Acting was the thing that mattered then. Nowadays all the lousy leading actresses are five foot ten. I'm lucky if I come up to their armpits!"

He fell silent again. There wasn't a lot I could say to comfort him. It was true. A Romeo as tall as Juliet's armpit just wasn't scheduled to be the romantic wow of the evening.

"Well," I said at last to jolly him along, "there's nothing you can do about it other than wear high heels or lifts in your boots. But why let it spoil your fun? You seem to be doing quite well; you wouldn't be here otherwise, in this revered temple of the classics."

"Were you in last night?"

"I was."

"What did you think?"

"About what?"

"The production."

I took a deep breath. "I don't think you really want to know what I thought."

"I don't think I do either, but I'm asking just the same."

"All right then, on your head be it. I thought it was a shambles."

"Wrecked by Grantley."

"Saved by Grantley."

75

He took it in silence, sat for a minute, drawing on his cigarette, then he rose slowly to his feet as if everything hurt and wandered off into the light, chin on his chest, watching his feet. Pausing centre stage he looked back, a travesty of a smile on his lips. "Talk again sometime . . ."

And in came Barbara, dead on cue. "I've contacted Trevor," she said brightly. "He's on his way. Rather than put in an understudy he's more or less decided to reschedule, and chuck *Lear* altogether for the rest of the season – it's only six performances here, and we can re-cast for the Barbican. At the moment he wants three *Romeo*s, two *Merry Wives* and a *Troilus*."

For a couple of seconds Paul Braidy stared at her in silence, then, with a brief nod, he walked off without a word. I heard her mutter, "Well, fancy!" She then remembered me and began wondering where I'd got to.

"I'm over here," I called sexily, "lurking in the shadows."

She came over uncertainly. I reached out and caught her by the ankle. "What are you doing down there?"

"Lying in wait to seduce some poor unsuspecting female."

She sank to her knees. "Am I poor enough?"

"Oh yes, I think so – at a pinch. Come and share my small dark corner."

Chapter Seven

From the upstairs window I watched the patient group of reporters waiting around for a statement which said something more than the one about Sir Gerald Grantley falling off a tower and getting himself killed. What they wanted were the whys and the wherefores.

Didn't we all?

New faces had replaced some of the early originals. Tin-wig was still there, a cigarette wedged firmly in the corner of her mouth. I missed the elderly gent in the tweed hat but then caught sight of him trundling down the road from the village pub grasping a couple of bottles of Guinness and a large bag of crisps.

The policeman, with his back to them, leant, arms folded, against the low garden wall and dozed. There was no sign of Sergeant Hunter. The distant sound of singing was borne on the still air; morning service coming to an end. Hymn-singing always depressed me. This morning it was all I needed to fill my despondent cup of hemlock to overflowing.

I glanced over my shoulder. Connie, mercifully impervious to it all, slept, her face smooth and without expression – like a child's.

Perching on an uncomfortable upright chair in the window-bay I closed my eyes. I badly needed sleep. It may have been only twelve noon but I'd already had a long day.

When the distraught Trevor Nunn had eventually turned up at the theatre I had slunk off into the shadows leaving him to sort out his troubles with the other two; I chugged slowly back to Bull Street.

Barbara had pressed a spare key into my palm with murmured instructions to make myself at home and put down roots for as long as I needed refuge in Stratford. I exchanged my stormy leathers for the light relief of shorts, T-shirt and trainers and wandered off on a tour of inspection of the pert little property.

Barbara Sterling had obviously become a dyed-in-the-wool Victoriana nutter. The place bulged with megalomaniacal lumps of louring furniture which dared you to sit, lean or lounge on them. Tables, bookcases, chiffoniers and mantelpieces groaned beneath inlaid wooden work-boxes, epergnes, pots of aspidistras and clocks which had long since ceased to operate. In a corner of the front room an outsize harmonium looking like the inside of a church with brass candelabra and panels of red silk, eyed an unlovely wind-up gramophone with a rearing green horn lurking in the shadows of the corner opposite. Every wall was infested with ancient photographs: wedding groups and christenings, ladies in hats the size of mill-wheels and majestic Wagnerian gents with beards and waxed moustaches leaning on fortuitously placed piles of books. Biblical texts invited the pious to *Serve the Lord with Gladness*, but warned the wicked that *The Wages of Sin is Death*.

In the lavatory a pair of beady-eyed stuffed deerheads followed your every move. Over the door and most confusing of all, a notice in Gothic script read *To The Chapel – up – Left – up –* confusing because there was no "up", and "left" was a dark store cupboard stacked with bottles of preserved fruit and bread bins.

Only the kitchen and the main bedroom, which sported a bed the size of a cricket pitch, had been by-passed by the nineteenth century. Around the dressing-table mirror a photographic display of healthy masculine faces and bodies represented, I guessed, a head-count of those with whom she had dallied upon that monumental bed.

I was quite chuffed to find a bedraggled picture of myself tucked away among them – even though I had no knowledge of that particular bed; our lascivious cuddlings and couplings had been confined to the somewhat less yielding tombstones of the parish churchyard and a narrow bed over a fish-shop in Henley Street.

I came to as I was about to fall off the chair. I got up and stretched, blinked out of the window, then at Connie, sleeping soundly and snoring a little.

On a low chest at the foot of the bed lay Gerald's blazer, its brass buttons reflecting sunlight. If it weren't for that bloody blazer I might have been prepared to accept a verdict of death by accident.

With an eye on Connie I went through its pockets. Nothing but a couple of sugar lumps and a pink rose with a broken stem, withered but not yet dead. What the hell was he doing with a pink rose in his pocket? I peered at it closely. The end of the seven- or eight-inch stem was splintered as if it had been torn from the bush with some violence; it had then been bent double and stuffed into the jacket pocket.

I took it to the window and narrowed my eyes at the front garden. There, pink roses grew in abundance – and red and white and yellow – no discernible pattern to them. Dr Nathan had mentioned that roses were neither picked nor brought into the house. Someone had picked this one.

The traffic on the road outside was hotting up. Lethargic groups of homeward-bound church-goers in their Sunday best loitered curiously outside the cottage, some pausing to confer shyly with members of the press, who seized the opportunity to produce notebooks and jot down irrelevant views and sentiments supplied by incautious locals. There were many shakings of sorrowful heads, mournful eyes peering at the house.

I placed the rose on the dressing-table and turned away from the window.

Peering inquisitively into the wardrobe and a drawer or two, I was about to wonder where Gerald's things had got to when I recalled what he had said about being banished from his wife's bed because of his snoring.

It was my day for viewing houses so I decided to have a quiet look at this one.

A second door in the bedroom led directly into a spacious, well-appointed bathroom and lavatory which, in turn, opened on to a wide warmly carpeted corridor lit by three latticed windows. It ran the full width of the house and overlooked the stairwell. Through one of the windows I caught a glimpse of the

79

church tower and hills beyond. Every board of the corridor seemed to creak as my weight bore down on it. Creeping about the place at night one would have been hard pressed not to arouse the entire village.

The only other door on the corridor led into Gerald's room, a strangely makeshift affair giving the impression that occupation was of a temporary nature only – until such time, perhaps, that Connie relented or Gerald adjusted his unfortunate night noises.

The outlook was similar to that of the main bedroom. A low chest of drawers wedged into the small window-bay bore a couple of silver-backed hair brushes, a throat-spray, some loose change, a bunch of keys and a bottle of Aramis after-shave. A narrow bed in a corner was unmade and his pyjamas sprawled where he had thrown them. I lifted the crumpled pillows in the hope that he might have left a note beneath them. He hadn't.

Open and face downwards on the bedside table was a copy of Alec Guinness's *Blessings in Disguise*. Keeping up with the Jones's, I smirked to myself, making sure he hadn't missed anything. Alongside the book was a jam jar containing a selection of sweets and more sugar cubes.

A tallboy revealed a couple of suits, several jackets, trousers, shoes and a pair of green Hunter gumboots. Two side-drawers contained underclothes and socks; the chest in the window, shirts, sweaters and cardigans, while the drawer of the bedside table was chock-a-block with a variety of patent remedies for strained eyes, stuffed-up noses, sore throats and troublesome ears; embrocations for the chest, liniments for muscles and salves for feet. A cardboard box contained a hypodermic and several glass phials of colourless liquid – insulin? – and a bottle of something called Orinose. Could Gerald have been a diabetic? If he were then the lumps of sugar in his pocket and in the jar on the table were something more than the cravings of a sweet tooth.

Thoughtfully I sat on the edge of the bed. Hadn't I read somewhere that the condition of a diabetic on his way to a coma could be mistaken for drunkenness?

Putting my head between my knees I peered inquisitively

80

beneath the bed; a shoe-box tucked up tight against the wainscotting. I hauled it out.

Inside was a rumpled square of chamois leather, some loose cartridges and a lanyard which had once been attached, I guessed, to a service revolver. The leather smelled strongly of oil, and not stale oil at that, and had recently been folded about the missing weapon, its imprint still visible on the material. The calibre of the cartridges was .38 – a big weapon, capable of putting a hole through someone's head at eighty yards – there were six of them. I shook them in my hand like dice, wondering whether they represented the full supply of ammunition; if so, why would anyone bother to drag about an empty and useless gun with him?

I folded the cartridges into my handkerchief and stowed them away in the scanty pocket of my shorts where they made an unseemly bulge. Replacing the box with its lanyard and leather beneath the bed, I sat for a further couple of minutes puzzling over why a man like Gerald maintained what looked like a fully loaded gun under his bed – and where was it now?

A last idle look around the room; on the mantelpiece a framed photograph of Sonia and Richard on their wedding day, she looking very much as she had on our wedding day; the dress was different, but the smile was the same. A studio portrait of Connie, enchanting in a straw picture hat, stood alongside a colourful birthday card – *To a Wonderful Husband*.

I let myself quietly out of the room. Facing me was the head of the stairs. Connie had said no one could move around the house without setting everything on the tremble. I took myself in hand and edged across the corridor, negotiating the first of the three steps downward with an appreciable lack of sound; the fourth gave out a complaining whoop but otherwise I managed fairly well. If a stranger could do it, Gerald, conversant with every creak and groan of the place, could have got around quietly enough had he needed to.

Opposite the front sitting-room was a large and gloomy, book-lined study occupied by heavy leather club furniture and a littered desk facing lofty French windows. The room had a musty smell. I unbolted the windows, pushed them open and stood for a second looking out over a trim, walled garden, manicured lawn, more roses and a thriving oak beneath whose spreading branches huddled a set of white painted garden furniture. A few hundred yards away the uncompromising bulk of the church tower jutted menacingly into bland blue sky. The gold-fingered clock face stood at half past twelve; even as I looked, the bells chimed.

I turned back into the room. The desk looked as if a hurricane had struck it head on. Gerald had cleared a space to write and that was all, his pocket diary open, oddly enough, at my address which I had given him the night before. The rest was an accumulation of months: letters, opened and cast aside along with their envelopes, bills and dog-eared receipts under a brass paperweight, a small pile of manuscripts, one of which, open, stood propped against the telephone; photographs, garden catalogues, a book on roses . . . I shook my head in despair.

I picked up a script and riffled through it. The dust of several months made me dive for my handkerchief. I sneezed a hail of bullets all over the floor.

I was on my hands and knees recovering them when I became conscious of a pair of unfashionable boots planted firmly on the mat just inside the French windows. I looked up. The business end of a hoe was within three inches of my nose. Against the bright rectangle of the sky the dwarfish, bandy-legged gardener loomed very large indeed.

"Oh," I mumbled, "hello . . ." What the hell was his name? The hoe didn't waver. "What you doin' in 'ere?"

The last of the wayward cartridges lay six inches from his left foot. I reached for it. The unsightly boot came down upon it with a determination which almost took my hand along with it. "I asked you a question."

I felt as if I'd lost my trousers in a public place. "We met this morning, don't you remember? At the window – with Dr Nathan."

I couldn't see his expression but the hoe made no move. "You was snoopin'."

There was no available answer to that.

With a gusty sigh he got down on one knee and, scrabbling

about beneath his boot, held the cartridge between grubby fingers. "What's this then?"

We faced each other like a couple of spare book-ends. "A bullet?" I hazarded.

"Where'd it come from?"

"I dropped it."

"Where'd *you* get it?"

"It was in my handkerchief." That got him. The blade of the hoe faltered a little. I opened my hand and showed him the other five bullets. "Along with the rest of them."

He stared at them in silence for a moment, then, "What they doin' in your 'anky?"

"I had nowhere else to put them, did I?"

"You ain't got a gun?"

I raised my arms. His eyes wandered over my scanties. "You're sittin' on it."

I rose warily to my feet, the hoe rising with me.

"Turn round."

Where did he think I could pack a bloody great gun?

He grunted, momentarily satisfied. "So what you doin' 'ere, then?"

I hesitated, wondering whether to take him into my confidence. Clearly a stalwart lad, he had been with the Grantleys for some time and with careful handling might well prove to be a mine of information.

I came to a decision. "Investigating," I told him.

"Snoopin'."

I wobbled my head at him. "Okay, snooping."

"So you're a cop?"

"Arch," I said, his name coming back to me in a rush, "I told you this morning I'm not a cop. I'm a friend of the Grantleys. Look, if I let you into a secret, will you try not to pass it on to anybody?"

He looked baffled, glanced over his shoulder and blew down his nose. For the first time I noticed his eyes: ice-blue, bright and intelligent.

"Depends, don't it?"

"On what?"

"On what it is you're goin' to tell me."

"Take a chance, why don't you?"

Slowly he lowered the hoe. "Right. 'Ave a go."

I nodded towards the garden table and chairs beneath the oak. "Why don't we go and sit over there?" I recovered the cartridge from his grasp, added it to the rest in my handkerchief, and strode off across the lawn, Arch scuttling along beside me, two steps to each of mine. He carried the hoe at the rest, like a spear.

"Once upon a time," I told him when we were sitting comfortably, "I was an actor – that's how I came to know and work with your gov'nor. But now, I'm a private detective." He blinked and drew breath. I galloped on. "Not many people around here know that, and I prefer to keep it that way if possible, so I can get around and about and ask questions without people clamming up on me. Right?"

He sat swinging his legs, his feet not quite touching the ground, eyes sparkling like bright blue diamond chips. The shaft of the grounded hoe rested across one shoulder. He nodded enthusiastically. "James Bond like?"

I grinned. "I don't have a licence to kill, and he wasn't all that private either." I leaned in towards him. "Arch, I'm worried about the way your gov'nor died." The legs became still. "Would you say he was the sort of man who'd do away with himself?"

The answer came like a bullet from a gun. "Never!"

I nodded. "Yet you said this morning that you knew he'd do it one of these days. 'Raving away up there,' you said, 'I knew it would happen one day.' What did you mean by that? You did say that, didn't you?"

"I didn't mean 'e'd 'ave chucked 'imself over – not on purpose. I meant 'e'd bleedin' *fall* over one day. Accidental like . . . flingin' his arms about the way he did. 'E used to practise his actin' up there – least, that's what we all thought 'e was doin'." He paused for a second wagging his head. " 'E'd never 'ave done 'imself in – not 'im. Besides which, 'e'd 'ave been 'ighly insured, wouldn't 'e, gent like 'im? Wouldn't you say?" He went on without waiting to know what I'd say. "Well, stands to reason, then, don't it? Insurance don't pay out on suicide. 'E'd 'ave known that. 'E didn't leave a note nor nothing, I suppose?" I shook my head. "Gent like 'im would 'ave left a note; 'e always liked things just so, know what I mean?" He gave an emphatic shake of his head. "Nope, never, not 'im. Don't care what nobody says. 'E never committed no suicide. 'E'd never 'ave left his missus up the spout like that – not able to get insurance – never."

There was a silence between us. A jumbo jet rumbled overhead. I watched it disappear behind the dense foliage of the tree, then I said quietly, "Maybe he made it *look* like an accident – staged it – so an insurance claim wouldn't be affected."

Another silence. The wizened face crumpled its way through a lengthy and morose succession of thoughts. Finally, "Why would 'e go and do a thing like that? Why would 'e want to knock 'imself orf? 'E 'ad everything goin' for 'im."

"How long have you known him?"

He gave a little snort. "We go back donkey's years. I was 'is batman in the army – 'is right 'and man. Been with 'im ever since. 'E was always good to me. So was the missus. It's like I've known 'em for ever."

"Do you go back as far as the war with him?"

He nodded. "Forty-four we met up. 'E was a Major Rosner then – changed 'is name later. We went through the last year of the war together – me taggin' along be'ind. We was in Berlin at the end – and a right un'oly mess that was, an' no mistake . . . Fuckin' 'Itler!"

"Why did he change his name, do you know?"

I thought I caught the slightest flicker of caution in his eyes. He shrugged. "'E liked Grantley better than Rosner, I suppose. I don't know, do I? 'E was born 'ere and liked the place. When 'e got 'is bowler 'at and got caught up in the actin' lark, I s'pose 'e thought Grantley'd look better up in lights than Rosner. Did to, I reckon."

"He's Jewish, isn't he?"

"So?" The eyes took on a flinty look. "What's that got to do with anything?"

"His son Richard said . . ."

"Oh *'im!*" he interrupted me. "Don't want to take no notice of anything *'e* says."

I shrugged. "Seems odd to change your name when you're halfway through life and a major in the army to boot. Just looking for a reason, that's all. Maybe he didn't care for a Jewish name."

"I don't think 'e cared one way or the other. 'E never did nothing about bein' a Jew – like plaitin' 'is 'air, or growin' a beard; nor did 'e go in for wearing big black 'ats neither, nor go to no synagogues, not when I was with 'im anyway. Never even went to this church over 'ere either – if 'e did it was only to please the missus. Old Bun's always droppin' in for a cuppa and a crumpet – 'oping to convert 'im one day, I 'spect. But not 'im. He could take it or leave it, could the gov'nor. As far as 'e was concerned, God was on 'is own. Let sleepin' gods lie, was what 'e always said."

"Who's Bun?"

"'Im up at the church. 'Is reverence. Chancey Bun. E. Chancey Bun is what 'e 'as on the board outside. Ernie, Eric, Enry – nobody knows what the 'E' stands for. I told 'em up at the pub one day it stood for Ermingtrude. Met 'im, 'ave you?" I shook my head. "You'll see what I mean when you do."

"Arch," I said after a moment. "Why would Sir Gerald have a loaded gun about the house?"

His eyebrows went up. "'Ad 'e? Did 'e?"

"In a shoe-box under his bed."

"Smith & Wesson .38, is it?"

I shrugged. "A .38 certainly."

"That'll be 'is old service revolver, I reckon."

"Smith & Wessons are American."

"Right. They issued some to our lot in '41 instead of the old Webleys. Fancy 'im keeping it all these years. A lot of 'em lost their guns – accidentally on purpose like, you know? Nothing in that. Souvenirs, that's all." His eye wandered mischievously to the erotic bulge in my shorts. "Drawn its teeth now, though, 'ave you?"

"What sort of enemies did he have?"

"'E didn't 'ave no enemies."

"You haven't met his director at the theatre."

"What, old Poofy Pants? Peter what's 'is name – Grocer 'n it?"

86

"Paul Braidy."

"That's the bugger. Knew it was something like that. Twit-face was what the guv called 'im. 'E said 'e was a lolloping great poofter who didn't know 'is 'arse from 'is elbow, so I told 'im the last thing a poofter'd get mixed up with 'is elbow'd be 'is arse." And with a wild cackle of laughter he shoved my elbow off the table and all but sent me sprawling on my face.

The unseemly bout of merriment was short-lived and cut off at source. "Oh my Gawd!" he muttered staring wide-eyed in the direction of the house. I followed his gaze.

A gaunt white face hanging disembodied against the gloomy backdrop of the study gave me, too, quite a turn. When it moved slowly forward into the light I heard myself give a little whinny of relief as I recognised the formidable figure of Lizzie Arden, she of the portcullis teeth and fuse-wire hair. Framed against the proscenium arch of the white-painted French windows she looked like an elderly tragedienne taking her final curtain. Raising a hand in greeting she called, "Mr Heathcliff," in a lustreless voice.

I heard Arch's neck creak as he turned his head to look at me. "Thought you said . . ."

I nodded. "I did. It's she who's got it wrong." I rose to my feet. "Talk to you again soon. Thanks for your time."

He raised his school cap in salute.

As I tacked across the lawn towards her I became ridiculously self-conscious about the bulge in the front of my shorts. Mae West's inimitably famous line, "Is that a pistol in your pocket or are you just pleased to see me?" flashed irresponsibly through my mind.

"Mr Heathcliff," she said brokenly as I approached. "Isn't this just *the* most *dreadful* thing? I came over as soon as I dared, just in case there was anything at all I could do for poor, dear Connie."

"She's probably still asleep." I took the huge limp hand she offered me.

"John's with her now – Dr Nathan. I think he's expecting her to come round soon. He gave her a sedative earlier on, poor dear." She pressed a large damp handkerchief to her mouth, her distraught eyes welling with sudden tears. "How could he *do* such a thing? Such a shock for poor Connie."

"And for him too, I would suspect," I said with the slightest chill in my voice.

"Oh yes, indeed, indeed." I caught her eyeing my shorts curiously and, feeling a flush come on, pushed unceremoniously past her into the comforting shadows of the study. With my back to her I removed the handkerchief from my pocket and palmed the cartridges.

Roaming about the place I looked for somewhere to deposit six rounds of live ammunition; Lizzie Arden settled herself into Gerald's chair behind the desk and watched me with huge, El Greco eyes. "Whatever could he have been thinking of – climbing up that gruesome old tower in the middle of the night?" she moaned. "And how could he have got out of the house without Connie hearing him . . .?"

A small box of tooled Venetian leather sitting on a side table caught my eye. When Lizzie next hid her face in her voluminous handkerchief I slipped the bullets inside the box.

"Then there's this other man . . ." she was going on.

I turned quickly. "What other man?"

She was a little taken aback by my abruptness. "This utter stranger." She waved her handkerchief in the air. "The one who found poor Gerald. I can't remember what his name was; John talked to him but he didn't know him from Adam. The whole thing's a mystery. What was he doing up there in the first place, this stranger? – that's what I'd like to know. And now he's just disappeared. Heaven only knows what he was up to. John says he was a friend of Gerald's, but I know *all* Gerald's friends . . ." She broke off to blow her nose with a loud trumpeting sound. "I'd never even heard of him. If I were that policeman I'd send a search party out for him – indeed I would. There's more to him than meets the eye, you mark my words."

"Mrs Arden . . ."

"Oh *Lizzie*, please, Mr Heathcliff, *Lizzie*. For goodness sake let's not stand on ceremony in this dark hour."

"It was I who found Gerald."

"No, no, Mr Heathcliff – may I call you John? – it was

88

somebody else entirely. Let me see, what *was* his name? Carvick . . . Cadbury . . .? I'm sure it began with a C . . ."

"Savage."

"That's it. Savage."

"I'm Savage. Mark Savage."

She blinked her large swimming eyes, one tear slipping its moorings and coursing down her furrowed cheek. "But your name is . . ."

"Savage." I shook my head. "There must be some misunderstanding."

She stared at me in silence for a moment. "But how very extraordinary. I met a man at the theatre last night who was the image of you. His name was Heathcliff – I remembered it particularly because of *Wuthering Heights*, you see. You really must excuse me, dear Mr Savage, but he was your double I tell you! John Thomas Heathcliff – a little less hair than you perhaps, and I'm not sure now if he didn't have a little moustache – no, perhaps not. But one thing I am sure of is that he was a sailor, a submariner of all things. He told me so himself."

I was beginning to wish I had never started this when the situation was saved by the entrance of Dr Nathan, no longer in pyjamas and dressing-gown, but resplendent in a bright yellow open-neck shirt and smart white jeans – not at all what the well-dressed GP should be wearing.

"Mr Savage," he greeted me. "I was hoping you'd be here. Lady Constance is demanding a private audience with you. Go and have a word with her, will you, there's a good chap?"

"How is she?"

He shrugged and pulled a glum face. "We'll have to keep an eagle eye on her 'til she's on her feet again, but she'll manage all right. Try not to tire her, eh?"

As I left the room I overheard Lizzie Arden telling him how extraordinary it was that a man she had met at the theatre last night, a submariner called Heathcliff, "was the spitting image of that young man . . ."

I knocked gently at Connie's bedroom door and receiving no reply stuck my head into the room. She was staring blankly at the ceiling. "Connie . . .?"

She came to with a start. "Mark dear . . ." She stretched out a hand. "Do come in."

I perched on the edge of the bed at a loss for words, her hand cold between mine, wishing I could think of something comforting to say to her.

"You've been playing tennis," she smiled, eyeing my shorts.

I shook my head. "I forgot to bring my bat and ball." I gave her hand a squeeze. "How is it with you?"

"I'll be all right. You mustn't worry about me."

I nodded. "I thought I might stay on a bit up here. In case you need anything, errands run and so on."

She smiled. "You don't have to do that. I shall be all right. I have lots of friends."

"There's one downstairs," I grinned. "Lizzie Arden."

"Oh Lord . . . Lizzie. We were to go there for drinks this morning." Her lips twitched as she added, "Weren't we, Mr Heathcliff?"

"Ah, yes. We were trying to sort out that one just now. The doctor rescued me. She's convinced there are two of us."

She wasn't listening. She said with a frown, "I wanted to talk to you alone, Mark. I hope you don't mind."

"Talk away, please. That's what I'm here for."

She closed her eyes and for a second or two I wondered whether she had fallen asleep again, but then she was watching me narrowly, eyes clear and blue. "I haven't been entirely honest with you. I'm not apologising. There was no reason why I should burden you with domestic problems. But . . . in the light of what's happened . . ."

She fell silent and, turning her head, stared blankly at the bright rectangle of window. I made no attempt to prompt her, but sat holding on to the tiny, bony hand waiting for her to go on. I watched her eyes focus and narrow. "What's that? On the table over there. A flower is it?"

"A rose, yes."

"It should be in water. They die so quickly in this heat. Gerald was always against them being picked."

I hesitated. "I have a feeling he picked this one himself."

I told her where I had found it. She nodded, then shook her head. "Mark . . . do you think Gerald . . . killed himself?"

"No, I don't."

"Then it was an accident?"

"What else?"

"And yet he knew that place like the back of his hand. He could have walked up there blindfolded and never come to grief."

"He'd had quite a bit to drink," I reminded her. "He was half-seas-over when he went to bed."

Her eyes came back to me. "That was a performance," she said in a gently chiding tone. "He was no more drunk than you were." She nodded. "A performance, I promise you."

"Connie darling, he drank more than a tumblerful of neat whisky in about half an hour."

"Yes, yes, I'm sure he did. And whisky was never his drink, was it?" She was half talking to herself. She stirred restlessly. "Something has been going on in that head of his for some little time now. I really couldn't fathom it. Whenever I brought it up, the answer was always the same: *King Lear*. I couldn't argue with that. Any actor would be half demented with *Lear* hanging over his head. But," she added patiently, "I lived through his Macbeth, his Othello and that dreadful Volpone of his, and they were never like this. This time it was something more." She blinked down at our clasped hands. "You see, dear Mark, if he didn't deliberately throw himself off that tower, and if he didn't fall accidentally, then . . ." she broke off, her eyes tight shut, glutinous tears squeezing between the ashen lids, ". . . somebody must have been up there waiting for him . . ."

I said nothing, refusing to air my own shaky conclusions until I had heard her out. Mistaking my silence for scepticism she gripped my hand hard. "Call me a stupid, fanciful old woman if you like, but I haven't lived with him all these years without being able to read him like a book. Last night he was like a cat on hot bricks. You were there, you saw him, stamping about the place and looking at his watch every few minutes as if he were expecting something to happen – someone to call. Well . . . *I* think he was going to meet someone – there, now I've said it . . ."

"And the heavy drinking was a put-up job so he could break up the party?"

She nodded. "Do you remember what he said about the Swan's Nest when I suggested you come back here for the night? He didn't want you here – not for the night anyway."

"So why invite me?"

"He wanted your company, wanted to talk to you – if only for a short time. He was a great admirer of yours. He was, I promise you," she added as my jaw fell open. "He used to say what a pity it was you'd never kept in touch. Outraged, of course, that you squandered your talents on the screen instead of the stage. He even wrote you a note when you were in trouble, but didn't post it – thought you might think him presumptuous."

Presumptuous! I couldn't help thinking how much even a note from him would have helped; I would probably have framed it.

She released my hand and touched my knee with the tips of her fingers. "If there's anything at all in what I've been saying, then he must have been feeling very – lonely . . . vulnerable . . ." She gave a little shrug. "I'm sorry, Mark, I'm not making sense, am I?"

I let a moment go by, then said gently, "You're making a lot of sense. He did have something on his mind. He made a date with me for this morning. I gathered he wanted me to do some work for him – professionally."

"What sort of work?"

I shook my head. "At that moment you walked in with the tea-tray and Gerald embarked on the story of his life."

I told her about the blazer at half-mast on the church tower and my subsequent ponderings over it. "Is it likely he would have hoisted the thing himself?" I asked her.

"Why would he do that?"

"Why indeed?"

She thought for a long moment. "Mark, if somebody killed him, that somebody must believe he had a very good reason . . . you don't go out and kill someone just for the sake of it – not unless you're a lunatic. Supposing it was something – bad, something derogatory to Gerald, something that would – harm him, his memory – I don't think I could bear that. I trusted him implicitly. He never stepped out of line, never did anything dishonourable, even remotely reprehensible." Her voice dropped to a whisper. "But somebody – if what we're thinking is true – somebody must have had a reason, a motive." She raised her head and stared at me levelly. "I want to know that motive, Mark. If it's something bad, I wouldn't like to see it spread over every newspaper in the country. I want him to be remembered as he really was – a good, kind, gentle man, someone who deserves what little recognition he earned. Do it for me, Mark. It's your line of country, isn't it? I'd like to retain your professional services. If he was killed I want you to find out why."

A sudden babble of voices from outside drew my attention to the window. I laid her hand quietly on the counterpane and went over to see what it was all about. Two people were pushing their way through the throng doing their best to ignore the flurry of questions hurled at them.

Sonia and Richard Rosner.

"It's your son and daughter-in-law."

"I don't want to see him." Her voice was suddenly petulant. I turned, surprised. "Go down and tell him I'm sleeping, anything, but I really don't want to be bothered with him just now – not just now."

I went back to the bed and stood over her. "I'll tell him. The doctor will field him for you if I can't." I gave her the rose I had collected from the dressing-table. She held it to her nose.

"Poor thing. The scent is still there." She trimmed off the broken stem and placed it in a glass of water by her bed. "There, that's better." She frowned, adding softly, "Why, I wonder, did he have that in his pocket?"

"Connie," I said quietly, hesitating at the door, "I'll do as you ask – if that's what you really want. But, prowling around and poking one's nose into other people's affairs can sometimes bring to light things better left in the dark, so to speak – things you might prefer not to know."

The pale eyes met mine in a long cool stare. When she spoke there was an unexpected chill in her voice. "I married him for better or for worse. I've known the best. If the worst is to come then it's right that I should know that too. That was part of the bargain we old-fashioned folk made at the altar." The hint of reproof in the remark receded as her eyes gentled a little. "No offence meant, Mark dear."

I shook my head with a smile. "None taken. But you were wise as well as fortunate – you married a friend."

Blinking a little she turned her face to the window. Fresh tears glistened on her cheek.

Chapter Eight

I encountered Richard Rosner halfway up the stairs, climbing, bull-like, head down, unaware of me until he all but butted me in the stomach.

"She's sleeping," I informed him quietly, doing my best to keep the edge out of my voice. I didn't go a lot for him.

"So what have *you* been doing up there?" The feeling was mutual. "Singing her a lullaby?" His hot black eyes held an uncalled-for menace. He did his best to shove past me but a nimble piece of footwork on my part placed me squarely in front of him.

"Please don't go up now, there's a good lad. She doesn't want to see anyone."

"She'll see me."

I placed a firm finger on his shoulder. "She said anyone."

"I'm her son, damn you!"

"I'm aware of that. But just let her sleep, will you?"

"Mr Savage is right, Richard." John Nathan stood at the foot of the stairs. "She needs all the rest she can get. She has readjustments to make. You must give her time."

Unconvinced, Richard continued to stare at me angrily, swaying a little on his feet, until I removed my restraining finger, when he turned and plunged down the stairs as if intent on doing himself an injury. Dr Nathan avoided bodily harm only by an adroitly executed side-step as the flying figure blundered past him.

The house shook as the front door slammed.

The doctor exchanged a wry glance with me as I drew alongside him. "She particularly didn't want to see him," I said in a low voice.

He gave a resigned nod. "He has quite a way with him, our Richard, don't you think?"

He turned on his heel and I followed him into the study where Lizzie Arden had broached the sherry decanter and was in the act of handing Sonia a glass.

"Ah," she said, eyeing me with a quizzical archness which put me in mind of a more than usually eccentric Mrs Malaprop, "our wayward submarine commander. Will you have a sherry, you wicked boy?"

"I never said I was a commander."

Sonia put in, "That sounded like my Richard making an exit."

"It was," nodded the doctor.

"Pursued by bear," I added sourly.

Sonia clucked irritably and passed her glass to me. "Here, you take that, it'll settle your nerves. I'd better go and smooth his feathers. He'll be shouting at the press if we're not careful, and that would never do."

She was looking devastating in a short pale green and white number which barely reached her knees, putting me in mind of those sorely lamented mini-skirts she had worn on our first dates and which were largely responsible for my subsequent capture and downfall.

"I was just telling Lizzie we would have been here earlier, but last night's excesses caught up with us and we overslept. We knew nothing about all this until a neighbour rang up and told us. Poor Connie, she's the one I feel sorry for." She hesitated a moment longer. "Well, cheers everybody, see you again, Mark, I expect."

When she had gone I passed the glass of sherry back to Lizzie Arden, whose long face had lengthened into the traditional lines of professional mourning. "How is she now?" she asked heavily.

"Sleeping."

She nodded, pulling on a white glove. "Well, she certainly won't want to be bothered with me, so I'll skedaddle. If she wants me she knows where to find me." She picked up an ethnic-looking wrap of purple and green weave and draped it over her shoulders. She hesitated, fiddling for a moment with the second glove. "Mr Savage," she smiled wanly, arch again. "Should you have nothing better to do, perhaps you'd care to join us for a little late lunch? Nothing elaborate, just salady things, cold chicken and the like. My husband would just love to meet you, I'm sure – and Emma, of course, the sculptress I was telling you about. Or *did* I tell you?" She reached for her sherry and drained the glass at a gulp. "She's been doing a portrait bust of poor Gerald – it'll be a bronze." Replacing the glass on the desk she retrieved the one lately bestowed on me by Sonia, silently toasted me and knocked that one back too. "Pity to waste it, don't you think? How say you then, Mr Savage, will you come?"

Little as I relished a luncheon session with the Arden menage, the prospect of valuable information gleaned from the lips of those close to Connie and Gerald tempted me greatly.

I glanced down at my bare knees. "I'm not exactly dressed for a lunch party."

"Nonsense. Absolute rubbish. You look divine, quite divine. Most men have knees like door knobs. Don't you think he looks divine, John?"

"Er . . ." mumbled John Nathan uncomfortably.

I unhooked him. "Well if you're sure the others won't mind . . ."

"Mind!" The room echoed with her raucous derision. "My dear boy, Emma will want to cast you in bronze on the spot – on the spot, my dear." She stared at my shorts. "Life size and in the nude, I shouldn't wonder." She cleared her throat and bared her outsize teeth. "We'll eat on the lawn if it'll make you feel better. It's such a lovely day, isn't it?" She flung one end of the wrap about her throat and tucked a tapestried handbag the size of a briefcase beneath her arm. "Off we go then, best foot forward. We can go the back way, then we don't have to argue with all those dreadful newspaper people."

As we crossed the lawn I glanced up at the gilded face of Gerald's clock and came to an abrupt standstill. Lizzie cannoned into me. "What is it?"

A flare of colour above the crenellations of the tower had caught my eye. "Someone's up there."

As we stook blinking in the hot sunlight an unidentifiable flag was hauled up the mast, slowly and painstakingly, in short

97

bursts of movement, as if whoever was on the halliard was out of breath.

"He's putting up the flag," whispered Lizzie.

"Who is?"

"The reverend, I expect. Yes," she shaded her eyes, "I can just see the top of his head, I think. Mr Bun, our minister."

The flag came to rest halfway up the mast, where it hung drooping and lifeless until a sudden breeze stirred it into a couple of coquettish flaps revealing for a second or two the red cross of St George. It curled sluggishly around the mast and was still again.

"There," murmured Lizzie in a pious whisper. "Isn't that nice? Half-mast. Dear Mr Bun, how *very* thoughtful!"

Through narrowed, jaundiced eyes I stared sullenly at the drooping flag.

Emma Hardcastle was a surprise. Never having met a real live lady sculptor I was thrown back on half-remembered television interviews where open-faced women with penetrating eyes and powerful hands bashed away with hammer and chisel at unlikely looking lumps of stone, surrounded by the sort of messy neglect which any self-respecting town council would earmark for early slum clearance.

Emma Hardcastle's face was closed and the eyes cool rather than penetrating. I searched in vain for the powerful hands. "Frail" was the word that sprang to mind as she laid a regal hand in mine when Lizzie hustled me on to the garden terrace of the Arden residence. Wondering whether I was expected to kiss it I settled instead for a slight pressure of the thumb on the back of it. There was no answering pressure. Dark, calculating eyes, shaded by the brim of the type of sun-hat associated with Christopher Robin, measured me from head to foot, removing what few garments I was wearing as they went, until I felt sure that the life-size nude intimated by Lizzie was no more than a whisper away.

Lizzie, a trifle boisterous, I thought, followed up the introduction with a rambling and totally fictitious run-down of my life and character, drew up a cane chair for me, patted peremptorily at its cushioned seat and disappeared into the house with the message that she was off to find her husband and supervise food and drink.

The ensuing silence was broken only by the sound of somebody's lawnmower and the cane chair she'd parked me in, which creaked at my every breath like an elderly lady in corsets. In time I became quite giggly and said, "I'm sorry about my chair."

She made no comment. Her eyes were closed as if to shut me out.

With nothing else to do I fell to studying her.

Small and painfully thin, she would be, I guessed, somewhere in her middle forties. She was dressed in the sort of loose garment you can buy in purples and sludge and at great expense in underground cellars on the King's Road – crumples and creases at no extra charge. Hers was purple and sludge but with a bold fleck of orange in it and it reached all the way down to her ankles. Her skin, even in the warm glow of sunlight, was sallow and anaemic-looking, while the ringless hands, placid on her lap, were long and blue-veined with no hint of strength in them. I wondered whether she could be recovering from a serious illness for there was a spent gauntness about the narrow face which would have worried me to death had I been closely related to her.

The deep-set eyes were open now, watching me.

"I must have nodded off," she murmured. "Did you say something?"

"Not a word."

A moment passed. "Have you been playing tennis?" she enquired without curiosity.

I shook my head. "Just giving my knees an airing." Silence. "Do *you* play?"

The corners of her mouth twitched. "I have no eye for tennis."

"But good enough for sculpture, I understand."

This time the silence went on for so long that I decided she'd nodded off again; eventually she said, "That's a different sort of eye."

The conversation had exhausted me. I lay back in my complaining chair and closed my eyes. The sun was hot. An insect whined about my head; I waved it away. My mind's eye was busy doing a re-play of Barbara Sterling's pink shorts and leggy legs pounding along the A34. I creaked irritably in my chair. What the hell was I doing here? I didn't want to have lunch with Lizzie Arden and this highly resistible lady stone-cutter.

"Did you know Gerald Grantley?" The question was barely audible. I opened my eyes. She was studying her clasped hands. Again there had been no sense of curiosity in her voice.

"I worked with him a couple of times."

"Amicably?"

"Very."

She cleared her throat. "Odd thing to have happened, don't you think?"

"Odd?"

"Killing himself like that – after such a success last night."

I watched a lone magpie strutting importantly across the lawn like a head waiter. "One for sorrow, two for joy" my mother used to say. I searched in vain for its companion. No joy for me.

I said, "Lizzie tells me you were doing a bronze of him." She said nothing. I persisted. "Does his death put paid to that?"

"I'd finished with sittings. There are sketches and photo-graphs enough should I feel the urge to finish it."

"You surely will?"

"I haven't made up my mind."

"Wasn't it commissioned?"

"No." She too was watching the magpie; I was faintly amused to see her eyes shift to the surrounding trees seeking out the invisible mate. "It was my idea," she said at last. "I saw his Macbeth at the Vic years ago. I've wanted to model him ever since. He should be hacked out in white marble, but I'm not up to that. So I settled for a bronze. He had a good head, excellent bones, strong nose . . . Epstein would have doted on him." She was silent for a second. When she spoke again there was a shrug in her voice. "It was a challenge while it lasted."

"You *must* finish it." I sounded almost petulant.

Slowly she turned her head and looked at me squarely for

100

the first time. "Why?" Her quiet aggression almost floored me.

I spread my hands. "He was one of a dying breed, a great actor; they don't make them like that any more. There surely should be something to remind people who he was and what he really looked like, other than a handful of touched-up theatrical photographs."

"Twice he's had portraits hung in the Royal Academy," she reminded me.

"Yes, and pretty dreary they were too, if I may say so. Anyway, a painting could never do him justice. He was three dimensional if anyone was; he needed to be sculpted. Don't waste the work you've done, for heaven's sake. Give it away if you don't want it – the theatre here would take it like a shot. They'd stick it up in the foyer where everyone will see it." I pulled myself up. "Oh, what the hell! For all I know you may be one of those ham-fisted blockbusters who don't know the difference between a head and half a pound of suet – a lump of metal with a couple of finger-holes for eyes. What do I know what you get up to when I'm not around?"

She laughed for the first time, a loud, braying, donkey-like sound, as contagious as it was unexpected. All at once I felt better about her.

As our amusement faded the dark eyes remained on my face for a further second or two, shrewd and suddenly serious, the eyes of the sculptor recording and assessing planes and bones and highlights – warts and all.

"Want to come and see?" she asked abruptly.

"See?"

"What I've been getting up to when you weren't around."

"You bet." I bounded to my feet and then stood dumb-founded as she reached awkwardly behind her chair for a couple of sticks. "Jesus . . ." I whispered.

She gave a twisted smile. "Something else you didn't know about, Mr Savage." I surged forward to help but she signed me away with an irritable twitch of the head.

She was barely on her feet, propped up by those ghastly sticks, when Lizzie breezed on to the terrace. "Oh goodie," she chortled, "I was just coming to call you to lunch. Everything's ready. Hope you don't mind, Mark – I may call you Mark, mayn't I? I thought we'd be more comfortable around a table than on the lawn." She gave my knees a simpering look. "We've all become accustomed to your legs anyway." She turned back into the house.

I glanced enquiringly at Emma Hardcastle. She gave an ungainly shrug. "It'll still be there after lunch. We can't keep them waiting – the salad will get cold."

Lunch was a somewhat ambivalent affair with Lizzie Arden, way out front, conducting herself with a rumbustious lack of reserve which stunned the rest of us into a coma.

Godfrey Arden, a dapper parchment-skinned man, bald as an egg and sporting a neat white military moustache, though brightening noticeably at the prospect of another male at the lunch table, cast an apprehensive eye over my informal attire, then sank back into gloomy obscurity as his wife took charge of the proceedings, comforting himself in a forthright attack on his own personal bottle of red Châteauneuf du Pape.

The rest of us imbibed the white variety.

Any hope of gleaning classified information about Gerald Grantley and his doings was a dead duck long before the avocados were demolished. True it was that at the commencement of the meal Lizzie had raised her glass and, fixing each one of us in turn with lugubrious and reproachful eyes, had intoned solemnly, "To absent friends," – a strangely insensate valediction, I thought wryly, for one who had plunged eighty feet to a messy death. However, she clearly meant well and, duty done, cheered up considerably and attacked her food as if she hadn't eaten for a fortnight.

Emma Hardcastle, facing me across the table, picked fastidiously at her food and, bludgeoned into silence by Lizzie's stream of fatuous chit-chat, barely uttered a word throughout the meal. Only once did she betray her feelings: reaching for our glasses at the same moment we raised them together, silently toasting each other; as we drank, her down-stage eyelid lowered itself into a stealthy and meaningful wink.

I fared little better. An occasional nod in Lizzie's direction to keep her happy, a question answered, an unheeded opinion ventured – these were the sum total of my attempt at politeness.

Poor Godfrey Arden, however, was drawn reluctantly into the limelight by repeated demands from his wife for "screamingly funny" anecdotes of his experiences in India where he had seen unwilling service in the Diplomatic Corps under the British Raj. With monotonous regularity each of his stories was vandalised by Lizzie who snatched away the tag-line and delivered it herself, thus depriving him of what little triumph he might have enjoyed in the telling of it.

While he was speaking she would interject such coy observations as "Dear God, what a card you were!" or "Oh God, what a trial you must have been!" It was not until she said, "Tell them, God, about the time you set your foot on fire," that I realised that God was Godfrey and not the Deity.

Fortunately for the rest of us, her considerable intake of Châteauneuf du Pape had been such that by the time the cheeseboard was going the rounds she became more or less incoherent and eventually appeared to fall asleep with her eyes open, a hiccup and an occasional vacuous smile being her only contribution to the remainder of the festivities.

"She'll sleep for the rest of the afternoon," confided Godfrey as if she were no longer in the room. "She's a funny old thing." He raised his voice and addressed her directly. "I say you're a funny old girl, aren't you?" She blinked and nodded and closed her eyes. Godfrey frowned. "She's one o' the best though, let me tell you, Mr Savage, one o' the very best. Mustn't take any notice of her. Upset. Grantley's suicide's turned her upside down. Never as bad as this – likes her tipple, but never as bad. They were very close, you know, she and Grantley . . ."

Lizzie was upright in her chair as if bolted to it, face drawn, eyes tight shut. Two huge tears were coursing down her raddled cheeks. Her lips moved, muttering an unintelligible word. As a gentle snore bubbled across the table her head fell forward on to her chest.

"There," said Godfrey. "There she goes, poor old duck. Better move her to the couch, she'll be better orf there . . ."

She weighed a ton and giggled a little as we manhandled her over to a chaise-longue affair beneath the window. I folded her arms on her chest like an Egyptian mummy and frowned down at her.

The more I thought about it the more convinced I became that the word she had muttered as she passed out was "Murder".

Invisible from the house and tucked away in a corner of the spacious garden stood a prime example of somebody's architectural folly – a cross between a diminutive Brighton Pavilion and an Indian restaurant. Here Emma Hardcastle had set up a makeshift studio, assiduously littering it with the messy paraphernalia essential to the sculptor at work. I would have thrown away most of it without a second thought: none of it looked worth salvaging.

On the way over from the house Emma had fairly skipped along, merrily adroit on her sticks and clearly relieved, as I was, to be away from the oppression of the dining-room and the gentle bubbling of our prostrate hostess. Godfrey had hastily excused himself and disappeared upstairs with the *News of the World* clamped beneath an arm.

The afternoon was heavy with heat; the temperature inside the octagonal gazebo, four of whose walls were of plate glass, was like the engine-room of a tramp steamer ploughing through the tropics; even my knees began to sweat. I stood panting just inside the door while Emma humped herself over to a large electric fan, set it in motion with a sharp slap of her hand, and came to rest beside a grubby tripod upon which stood the results of her recent labours mummified by shroudings of damp cloth.

"I really don't know why I'm showing you this," she muttered in a slightly cross voice as she hooked one of her sticks on to a high stool positioned alongside the tripod. "There's still quite a bit to be done to it – *if* I decide to finish it, that is . . ."

With infinite care she unwound the wrappings and lifted them clear. Gently she rotated the base a couple of inches until the light fell upon the work to her satisfaction.

I moved a few paces forward, my feet crunching debris into the polished wooden floor.

Earlier she had said that Gerald Grantley should have been hacked out in white marble and I had known exactly what she meant. Now I saw it, violent, stark, powerfully and unashamedly theatrical; no white marble, only dull grey clay, but transformed miraculously into taut flesh drawn over hard bone, a vigorous physical force stilled by the sculptor's hand, bereft only of breath. A vibrant and uncanny sense of brutality seemed to brood over the portrait, but when, after a moment of slight shock, I took a step to the right, it was gone, a sly secrecy replacing it. I moved back again; the brutality reappeared.

I shook my head in a kind of wonder.

I glanced at Emma. She had turned her back on me and was staring fixedly out of the window – hooked on her sticks like a scarecrow. A sudden surge of sympathy for her swept over me. Poor bloody woman, no wonder her face was permanently closed; in her shoes I would have wandered the earth spitting in the eye of everyone within range. But then, talent often begets misfortune; it seems to come with the territory. Milton was blind, Beethoven deaf; Caruso grew nodes on his vocal chords and Van Gogh went potty and cut off an ear.

"What do you think?" Emma's whispered question echoed about the place like the scurry of dry leaves.

My eye returned to the model.

The head was tilted slightly to one side as if listening, the mouth half open, quizzical eyes turned upwards. With a finger I pivoted the base a little as she had done; the moulded face seemed to smile, turn in upon itself, satyr-like, full of secret malice. Again I shook my head.

"It's all there," I said hesitantly. "Brute force, power, sensuality, even malevolence . . . it changes with the light. You seem to have captured it all . . ."

"Except?" There was a hint of challenge in the word.

"What?"

She turned to face me, the rubber ferrules of her sticks squealing and clumping loudly in the silence. "You wanted to say 'except', didn't you?"

I shrugged noncommittally. "I can only comment on what I see. I think it's great."

"Except for what?"

I held her eyes for a moment, still hesitating. "I'll answer that with another question, if I may. When I said earlier on that I had worked with Gerald, you asked if it had been an amicable experience – almost as if it could only have been otherwise. Why was that, I wonder?"

She stared steadfastly at the portrait, considering her answer, then with a little sigh, "He was well known to have been a difficult man."

"Was he? That's the first I ever heard of it. Though, if what one gathers about his behaviour in *Lear* be true, he was certainly thrown off balance by the set-up in general and his director in particular; he disliked them both intensely. But that doesn't mean he was a difficult man. In the film studios he was a cooing dove. No trouble. No tantrums. Temperament, yes, but what good artist is without temperament? Yourself included, I shouldn't wonder."

"So what are you saying?"

I took a deep breath and spelt it out for her. "In my own small way I believe Gerald was a good, kind and understanding man, as well as a great actor . . ."

"And?" The word was almost inaudible.

I nodded towards the head. "I can see none of those qualities there. I can see only what I've already mentioned: brutality, arrogance, malevolence. Now, don't be upset," I added quickly as she twisted impatiently on her sticks. "You asked me and I'm telling you. I do think it's a magnificent piece of work. I do believe you are marvellously talented. And because of that talent I also believe that if you could have seen any of the goodness and understanding in the man you would have put it there along with the rest of it. But you didn't see it, did you?"

She was a long time answering. Her eyes shifted to the head, staring at it intently through half-closed lids. A minute or more passed in utter silence, then she began moving around the stand, slowly and deliberately, her eyes never leaving the work, the creak and thud of her sticks on the polished floor the only sound.

She came up at last on my other side. "I didn't see it because it wasn't there," she said at length and with finality.

She hooked one of the sticks on to the stand and using my

106

arm as a support clambered awkwardly on to the high stool. Frowning, she swung her head around to face me. "I was disappointed in him." She gave a thin smile. "Perhaps I expected too much. One should never . . ." She broke off, shaking her head. "As an actor, I idolised him. As a human being, I found him arrogant, self-opinionated and not a little . . ." she hesitated, ". . . sly, I suppose, is the word. In fact, I didn't much care for him. It's as easy as that. And that's probably why I can't make up my mind whether or not to finish it." She raised a hand as I was about to interrupt. "I accept your criticism. Everything you said is probably true, even though I may not agree with it. As things have fallen out I wouldn't wish to harm his memory – which is why I hesitate to give it to the world. Because what you see there is *my* opinion – and my opinion only. A fallen idol . . ."

She fell silent, staring bleakly at her work, her head sunk deep into hunched shoulders.

I was at a loss. There was no denying her sincerity. For her, there was no compromise, no whitewashing, no romanticising. I could only respect her for that. Integrity is a built-in requisite of a true and sincere artist; without it, talent is a dead duck grubbing for gold and playing to the gallery; only the shallow and the ignorant will shout for more.

"It's worrying, isn't it?" I mumbled. She looked at me enquiringly. "A trained observer like you seeing him so differently. One of us has to be wrong."

She shook her head. "Not necessarily. Most people only see what they're looking for."

"But not you!" I turned away feeling hot and irritable. I crunched over to the fan to cool off. The air it disturbed was damp and warm and did nothing at all to relieve my mental congestion.

"No one is wholly black," I growled half to myself, "nor yet wholly white. Even a saint has to be flawed somewhere and the deepest dyed villain can love his old mother or his bloody cat just as well as the next man. Otherwise we'd all be nothing – caricatures, cardboard cut-outs. Of course Gerald Grantley was arrogant; every actor is arrogant – it's part of the make-up – otherwise he'd never be able to get up on a stage at all. But he

107

also has to have guts because he's scared rigid most of the time – and that gives him a kind of humility. One thing compensates for the other."

I turned back to her. She had neither moved nor reacted to my fuzzy reasoning; I might never have spoken. Behind me the whirring draught of damp air played on my sweaty T-shirt and the back of my neck; it felt cold and clammy. I shivered slightly. "How well did you know Gerald?" I asked abruptly.

She turned her head, eyes, dark and bitter. "Not well enough, it seems."

"How long?"

"Six weeks, thereabouts."

"And before that you'd never met him?" She shrugged. "So in six weeks he managed to destroy his own image and knock himself off the pedestal you'd built for him."

I took off again, mooching about with my hands in my pockets, kicking out at the muck on the floor and coming at last alongside the only other piece of furniture in the place – a frail-looking gilt armchair borrowed from the house, elegant and out of keeping with the rest of the rubbish – the one in which Gerald had sat for his portrait. Gingerly I lowered myself into it, stretched my legs, clasped my hands behind my head and glared at her with calculated aggression.

Only then did I sense her vulnerability and felt suddenly ashamed. What in hell had I been lecturing her about? What business was it of mine *how* she saw Gerald Grantley? If she saw him as arrogant and malicious, that was her affair, not mine. People would judge her work according to their own beliefs and understandings. As she had pointed out they see only what they're looking for. I happened to see Gerald as a lovely great talented bear of a man, but I could be just as wrong as she was, beauty, as they say, is in the eye of the beholder; so maybe we were both barking up the wrong tree; maybe he was just an ordinary mortal like the rest of us.

I jerked forward on the chair, slapping my hands loudly on my knees. "I'm sorry . . . if anyone's arrogant, it has to be me."

She made no reply. I looked up. She had eyes only for the head. For a long helpless moment I stared at her with a compassion I couldn't bring myself to put into words, then I lumbered to my feet and made for the door. I mumbled some sheepish inanity of an apology and left her.

The blazing heat of the afternoon sun beat down on my bare head like an angry counterblast from the heavens. I felt guilty and incredibly disturbed.

Chapter Nine

Passing through the house on my way out, I peered timorously into the dining-room. Lizzie Arden lay safely slumbering, whale-like, on her chaise-longue, making noises like a bandsaw felling trees.

My feeling of guilt persisted, deepened, as I carefully closed the front door behind me and slunk quietly away down the garden path.

The village of Grantley, what little there was of it, was peacefully adrift on a raft of post-prandial torpor. An elderly and ragged sheepdog emerged from the shelter of a shady doorway and plodded over to see if I was anybody; when I paused to pass the time of day, he sniffed delicately at my trainers, waved a feathery tail and appeared to fall dead at my feet in the middle of the road, lying supine on his back, mouth open and a-drool – not unlike Lizzie Arden.

I shambled on, heavy depression burgeoning about my overheated head like a storm cloud.

Why hadn't I just told her that I liked her bloody head? It would have been so much simpler all round and no skin off my nose – not much anyway. What did I know about sculpture? And what, moreover, did I care about her hang-ups regarding Gerald Grantley? Everyone had hang-ups about someone.

Nevertheless, I couldn't help grinding away at what had made her so vehement about him. She had laid into that clay like a bricklayer building a wall. What had been bugging her? What had they talked about during those lengthy sessions? What had relieved the sultry hours during which she had beaten and moulded her dislike and disillusion into clay?

At the gate of the Grantley house the police constable, now in shirt sleeves, still loitered, armpits on the sweat, eyes round and blank as marbles. The press gang had departed.

"Everybody gone home?" I asked drawing alongside.

He gave a scornful toss of the head. "Gone to put their papers to bed, I reckon, sir."

I grinned. "But what would we do without them?"

He frowned at me. "I wouldn't mind the chance of finding out." He mopped at his perspiring face with his sleeve. "You can go in if you want to, sir," he added shoving the gate open for me.

I was eyeing the limp flag drooping from the mast of the church tower. I shook my head. "I'll mosey around a bit." I ambled off in the direction of the church.

The door to the tower was locked, not a key in sight.

Sauntering across to the west entrance to the church I brooded for a second or two over the heavy oak doorway recessed into a crumbling Norman arch; laying hold of one of the great iron rings set in the doors, I gave it a turn and a hard shove. Everything clanked and creaked appallingly.

I stepped gingerly over the threshold into the coldness of a tomb. After the bright sunlight the darkness was utter. The sweat on my T-shirt froze; my bare legs seemed suddenly to be encased with ice.

Before me, a second pair of doors, murky chips of stained glass empanelled into them. I pushed through into the church.

The silence was a living thing, even the hassocks were breathing. The interior of the building was chill, lofty and smelled of dust. Steep rays of iced sunlight slanted through tall slender windows latticed with plain glass; serried ranks of uninviting wooden pews marched alongside the narrow aisles where smooth, worn slabs of stone commemorated the dead long since trodden into obscurity; then there was the golden eagle bearing the Scriptures, the carved wooden pulpit, the secretive organ console, and the altar with its mandatory gilt cross and candles backed by the east window, a kaleidoscopic concoction of red and blue glass framing a mundane and halo'd dove of peace scarily on the wing.

I shuddered – not only from the cold.

As I drew near the chancel steps the heavy scent of the altar flowers overlaid the innate mustiness of the building. To my right a low arch led off into the remainder of the church complex and passing beneath it I came to a green baize-covered door standing ajar. I pushed it open.

At the foot of a long table with his back towards me sat a man, hunched and intent, oblivious of my intrusion. A wayward ray of sunlight glinted on the crown of an almost completely bald head.

Gently I cleared my throat. With a startled whinny of sound he swung around, half rising to his feet, one hand splayed protectively over the pages of the book he had been reading. Sunlight flashed like a heliograph from gold-rimmed spectacles.

"I'm sorry," I apologised, edging into the vestry. "I should have knocked. I startled you."

"My word you did," he muttered shortly, and not, I thought, a little guiltily. "My word . . ."

He was a short, rounded man who should have been wearing the clerical collar which lay discarded on the table before him alongside a Thermos flask and a plate of cream slices. As I approached, I watched his offside hand discreetly closing the book.

"Mr Bun?" I asked gently, not wishing to set him more on edge than he was.

He looked more like a Pickwick than an Ermintrude, though as our acquaintanceship matured and ripened, I began to appreciate the aptness of Arch's uncharitable soubriquet.

His round brown eyes, enlarged by the lenses of his spectacles, blinked furtively at the discarded symbol of his priesthood, a pudgy hand, meantime, fluttering about the open collar of a fairly unsuitable shirt in pink and blue stripes which peered incongruously above the plunging V neckline of a severe black waistcoat.

"Ah . . . yes, indeed . . ." he flustered. "E. Chancey Bun, at your service. You have me at a disadvantage, Mr . . .?"

"Savage, Mark Savage."

"Ah yes, indeed." He nodded as if he'd been expecting me.

With one hand he lifted the plate of goodies and placed it with care on the book – fearing, presumably, lest my eagle

112

eye should light upon its title – while with the other he caught up his clerical collar with its black silk dickie, or whatever they call it, and did his best to fasten it about his outrageous shirt.

I raised a hand. "Please . . . please don't bother about me. You're much more comfortable without it, I'm sure – and I'm not here on official business, I promise you . . . church business I mean."

I gave him one of my most winning smiles which seemed to set his mind at rest, for he relinquished his hold on the collar and fell to studying my shorts with a certain amount of appreciation. "You've been tennising, I see, you lucky boy."

"Alas, no," I told him, beginning to be bored by the assumption that shorts and tennis were synonymous. "Like you I prefer to be comfortable."

"Is there something I can do for you, Mr Savage?" He indicated a chair. "Perhaps you would care for a cream slice – a little weakness of mine." He glanced furtively over his shoulder at the open door and edged cautiously around me to close it. I twisted my neck to read the title on the spine of his book. *Strong Poison* it was called and was by Dorothy L. Sayers. A man after my own heart.

"I have a little rest period at this time on a Sunday, you understand," he confided returning to me and reseating himself with a comfortable sigh, "before the kiddy-winkies come crowding in for their afternoon Sunday School. Well, 'crowding' is something of an exaggeration – there are seven of them to be exact, eight sometimes, even ten on a good day when visitors' children come to stay. We are not a large community." He glanced at a gold wristwatch. "I have almost ten minutes to offer you."

I said simply, "I was a colleague of Gerald Grantley."

The round face puckered with sudden distress. "Oh dear, yes. A terrible shock was that, quite terrible. What could he have been thinking of?"

"Was he a parishioner of yours?"

He gave a wry little smile. "He lived in the village, that's as near as I can say. He was never religious in the accepted, orthodox sense of the word, but he was a good man. Somewhat more so than many of those who regularly attend divine service here."

"But you knew him quite well?"

"Oh dear me, yes, quite well, quite well. One way and another he did quite a bit for this community. As you are doubtless aware he was responsible for subsidising a new clock in the tower and has many times footed the bill for various small building costs; he was also most generous in the way of gifts and donations. I hoped and prayed over the years that he might eventually have become a regular member of our congregation – in vain, alas! Please have a cream slice."

"Thank you, no. I've just fought my way through a large lunch." I cringed at the memory.

"Perhaps, then, a little something to drink?" With a mischievous twinkle behind his lenses he collected a couple of glasses from a sideboard, uncorked his Thermos flask and poured a measure of amber liquid into each, sliding one across the table in my direction. I thought he winked. "Croft's Original," he murmured. I warmed to him.

We smiled slyly at each other above our glasses. "To illicit sherry," I toasted, "to say nothing of Lord Peter Wimsey."

His eyebrows went up. "You peeked!" He removed the plate of cakes from the book. "I have an almost unhealthy passion for detective stories in general and Miss Sayers in particular; and if that's not enough I also enjoy sherry and good Italian wine. I rarely admit to any of it. You would hardly credit the narrow confines in which we of the clergy are still expected to exist – even in this so-called enlightened age." He eyed the cream slices with a faraway look in his eyes. "My little peccadilloes are harmless enough, heaven knows, but there are those of my congregation who would frown upon them; I'd be up before the bishop if they got wind of them. So I keep them to myself and a very chosen few – of whom," he added pedantically, "Sir Gerald Grantley was one, God rest his soul." He fell silent for a space, his pudgy fingers restlessly twisting at the stem of his glass. "I need earnestly to believe that he did not take his own life," he said at last almost in a whisper. "I pray he didn't."

"Would you have thought him capable of it?"

His lips compressed into a thoughtful line. "Under normal circumstances of course not, certainly not, but . . ." I waited tensely. After an indecisive moment or two he shook his head, raising his eyes to meet mine, deep distress magnified by the lenses of his spectacles. Abruptly he rose to his feet and glanced again at his watch. "For all I know you may be a bishop's man. You must excuse me, Mr Savage, I have to go; the children will be waiting."

He took Dorothy Sayers and locked her away in a drawer of the sideboard. He was replacing the cork in his Thermos flask when I said, "Would it help, I wonder, if I told you that besides being a friend of the Grantleys, I am also a private investigator retained by Lady Constance to look into the death of her husband?"

He stopped what he was doing and stared at me wide-eyed, continuing to do so until I too rose to my feet to stand over his meagre five foot four. "Neither she nor I believe that he took his own life, and you have just prayed that he didn't. Is there anything you would like to tell me *à propos* the – er – *ab*normal circumstances you hinted at?"

He was shaking his head a little wildly. "No, no, there's nothing – nothing at all. At least . . ." Again he hesitated, again I waited. He took up the flask and hugged it close to his chest like a wounded bird. "I must think . . . I must have time to think." Turning back to the sideboard he stowed away the flask and stood for a moment, swaying a little, in deep preoccupation, chewing at his lower lip. Darting suddenly to the table, he snatched up his collar and moved quickly to a mirror where with exaggerated care he fastened it about his throat, undoing his waistcoat to tuck and smooth the black bib neatly across his chest. Rebuttoning the waistcoat he said in a low voice, "Gerald Grantley was, on occasion, apt to – confide in me." He picked up a Bible and turned to face me. A new and innate sense of dignity in his bearing momentarily stilled the question on my lips. He stared blankly at my chest. "Sometimes his confidences were in the nature of confession." He lifted a hand as if I were again on the point of interruption. "A confidence of any sort, however freely given should, in my book, be regarded as inviolable until such time as one is released from the

115

obligation of silence. In this present case the responsibility must rest entirely upon my shoulders and I would be grateful to be allowed a little time to consider my position. Now I really must be off."

"Before you go . . ." I stopped him at the door. "The key to the tower. Do you keep it in a safe place?" For answer he pointed to the wall above the sideboard where a large brass key hung from a nail. "That's it?" He nodded. "There are two keys only, I understand. Gerald had one and you the other, is that right?" Again he nodded. "And do you keep this vestry locked when you're not around?"

"Rarely."

"So anyone at all could come in here and help himself?"

He smiled mildly. "There's nothing of value up there in the tower, you know."

"There *was* last night," I retorted grimly. "However . . . May I borrow the key?"

"Do, please," he said shortly and turned to go.

"And Mr Bun . . ." He stopped. "I should be grateful if you would regard the knowledge that I am a private detective also in the nature of a confession. I wouldn't care for all and sundry to know of it."

He stood with his back to me for a moment, then took off without sign or word that he had heard.

I listened to his footsteps echoing in the narrow confines of the corridor; a sudden confused chatter of children's voices as a door opened; then, just as suddenly, silence and the stealthy breathing of the building took over once more.

Again I stood panting on the platform of the tower, again looking out over the parapet, this time at a landscape flooded with September sunlight. Heat haze shimmered over the still lush countryside; afar off the splintered reflection of the Avon glittered, mirage-like, through thick clumps of trees, above which, pale as a ghost, climbed the slender spire of Stratford's parish church.

Behind me, stirred by an occasional hot breath of weary air, the flag of St George flapped soggily at its post – a grim reminder of an event to which, as yet, no cogent explanation had offered itself.

It was probably no more than a morbid curiosity which drew me once again to this place; I had little hope of discovering what had actually happened here in the dark during the early hours of the morning; any wayward clue that might have been lying around would almost certainly have been snatched up by the narrow and astute Sergeant Hunter who seemed to have spent half a lifetime grovelling about up here – with the added advantage of bright daylight to assist him.

Nevertheless, I set myself the task of combing every inch of the platform in the hope of turning up some small, seemingly insignificant item overlooked by him – a spent match, ash from a cigarette (had Gerald smoked?), signs of a struggle . . .

I must have spent nearly an hour meticulously grubbing about in the grit and the dust on hands and knees, squatting uncomfortably on haunches and bent double in the orthodox beachcomber crouch. In the remote possibility that Gerald Grantley might have scribbled a hasty farewell note or even a last will and testament and crammed it into a handy crevice, I also poked into cavities and niches caused by crumbling mortar and broken masonry. I quartered every inch of the place and came up with a large sweet nothing.

Eventually I called it a day and cautiously straightened up, every nerve, tendon and muscle on the ache. I rolled my head around on complaining shoulders, exercised my biceps and shimmied my hips like an elderly belly dancer, finally giving loud vent to my favourite and most satisfying four letter word.

At that moment, for no reason that I could remember, I stumbled backwards and struck my heel hard against the low parapet. For a second I was thrown off balance and during that second all but came face to face with my Maker. My body twisted in an arc and doubled over the crenellations, presenting me with an uninterrupted and quite sickening view of the ground eighty feet below. I can't remember if I yelled out – I thought I heard something of an outcry from somebody who could have been me – then my flaying left arm wrapped itself around something hard and smooth and I found myself clinging to whatever it was for dear life, thinking as I did so how

117

really dear the whole thing had suddenly become. I hung there between heaven and earth for what seemed a pretty tenuous lifetime, panting and sweating and staring down at the muddle of graves below.

It was the flagstaff that had come to my assistance – not a moment too soon. My arm was coiled about it like a boa constrictor. I could have hung there quite happily for the rest of the afternoon, but eventually righting the rest of me, I carefully disengaged myself from the pole and sank into a melancholy heap at its base.

If I hadn't been sweating before, I was now.

Splayed against the wall I sat staring soberly at my feet stretched out before me, looking longer and further away than usual. That's one life gone, I thought peevishly, shutting my eyes tight and feeling the sweat that had gathered in my eyebrows oozing greasily down over my eyelids.

To make matters worse, the great clock in the tower below me chose that moment to heave itself into life, clearing its throat in a sinister series of whirrings and clankings to loose off a brazen clamour of sound which shook the tower to its foundations and raised the hairs on the back of my neck. I jammed my hands over my ears and shut my eyes waiting for it all to go away. When it did, the echoes, rolling and prowling plangently over the countryside, seemed to go on for ever.

It was the last straw.

"Give it up, Mark old lad," I heard myself mumbling. "Give it all up and go back to the acting – it's safer." But then, recalling the accident that had brought my brief movie career to a painful close, I edited that opinion, opened my eyes and clambered unwillingly to my feet, backing away respectfully from the battlements.

I was trembling like that boring old aspen leaf.

I blinked up at the flagstaff. Without that . . . My eye wandered around the platform. Had I stumbled at any other spot I would have been a dead duck splattered among the gravestones for others to mourn over and mutter "Why did he do it? . . . He wasn't the type . . ."

I pulled myself together and did a couple of slow circuits of

118

the platform keeping more than a safe distance from the battlements. It had been so easy – even in full daylight with the bright sun shining . . . but in the dark and somewhat the worse for drink . . .

I stopped and once more peered up at that life-preserving flagstaff. But why that bloody blazer . . .?

It wasn't until I reached ground level again that I realised how filthy and dishevelled I was. I looked as if I had been working in a coal bunker.

I was also dead on my feet and needed sleep; I had been beavering away ever since Connie had called me from my slumbers at four thirty that morning.

Sliding back into the church I returned the tower key to its nail on the wall. From down the corridor came the echoes of a hideous cacophony of children's voices raised in some gloomy hymn or other, aided and abetted by a faltering accompaniment on a wheezy harmonium. E. Chancey Bun leading his diminutive flock in song. I wondered idly what dire confession of Gerald's lay tucked away behind that little black bib of his, and whether it would shed any light on the present problem – if and when he decided to release it to the world.

The bobby at the Grantley gate gave my grimy clothing an old-fashioned look as I hove into his sight. "I fell down the stairs, didn't I?" I told him as I tramped past, up the garden path and round to the garage where I had parked the Honda alongside the Grantleys' ancient Jaguar.

I had just clambered into my crash hat and hooked the machine off its rest when somebody tapped me peremptorily on the helmet.

It was Sergeant Hunter looking taller and narrower than ever standing on the top step of the doorway leading into the house. "Hoping I would catch you," he shouted as if I were stone deaf. "Have you got a minute?"

Whoever tried telling a cop he hadn't got a minute? I gave an inward sigh, heaved the Honda back on to her rest, removed my helmet and fell in behind him as he turned and led the way into the house.

"Just a couple more questions, Mr Savage, if you wouldn't

119

mind," he said over his shoulder as we thumped through the house and into the front sitting-room. "Shan't keep you a moment. Do sit down, won't you?"

"I haven't a lot of time," I pointed out, slumping unthinkingly into Gerald's massive chair and immediately regretting my choice. Actually there wasn't any choice: the sergeant was standing foursquare in front of the sofa where Connie and I had sat the previous night and I had no intention of sharing it with him. Share a sofa with a sergeant and there's no knowing where you might end up.

I folded up in the huge chair like an unoccupied glove-puppet and peered up at him over my knees. "I haven't got long," I grumbled again.

"Driving back to London?" he asked heartily.

"No, back to bed to get some sleep. I've been up ever since I can remember."

There was a sudden strong whiff of malt whisky in the air. I looked at him in a new light. A whisky cop? He'd said he didn't drink. I sniffed again and turned my attention to Gerald's great triffid thing which grew out of his chair. A whisky plant? I inclined my nose a trifle towards it. "You smell it, do you?" There was a modicum of triumph in the sergeant's voice.

"Pardon?"

"The plant. Strong drink."

I leaned in and sniffed at it. "Well, what do you know? Whisky grows on trees now."

Hunter sat himself down on the sofa opposite and for the first time seemed to notice the parlous state of my clothing. "You look as if you've been run over by a bus," he remarked jovially.

"I fell into a ditch." I crossed my eyes and frowned at the triffid whose root-bound pot, I now discovered, stood a few inches to the left of the chair.

"Can you account for that, I wonder?" asked Hunter.

"What, falling into a ditch?"

"The whisky in the plant pot."

"Ah . . ." I shook my head, nodded, then shook it again. I knew now exactly what had happened. Gerald hadn't drunk a

120

couple of tumblers of whisky at all; he'd poured most of it away into his plant-pot; far from being drunk he had been as bright as a button the entire time. Connie was right; it had been a performance.

But I was not about to impart that information to the law. If they suspected he had poured his drink away then it was only a step to the supposition that he was stone cold sober when he had climbed the tower, and another short one to arrive at the conclusion that he had deliberately taken wing from the top of it. Suicide. And no insurance claim forthcoming for Connie. They could, of course, bring in a verdict of murder by person or persons unknown, but somehow I still wasn't convinced that murder had, as yet, found its way into their books.

Sergeant Hunter was watching me intently from beneath lowered lids, his head on one side looking for all the world like Leslie Howard doing his Scarlet Pimpernel in an eye to eye encounter with Raymond Massey's Citizen Chauvelin.

I gave him the famous twisted Massey grin. "All right, I confess." He frowned and his head drew upright with a jerk. "I don't really drink whisky as a rule, you see – in fact, I don't really drink anything at all much. Well, last night Sir Gerald evidently decided to get me plastered out of my mind. So I lapped up a drop of each refill and poured the rest of it away into his pot when he wasn't looking. I must admit I didn't think about the pong, but even if I had I'd have been back in London by the time he discovered it." I made a vain attempt to get out of the chair. "Is that all you want me for?"

"You actually sat there last night, did you – in that chair?" he asked thoughtfully. "I would have thought that chair belonged exclusively to Sir Gerald."

"So it does," I agreed easily. "So it did. But last night he was playing the perfect host, I suppose – sacrificed his own personal domain to his honoured guest. *Toujours la politesse* and all that, what? Anyway he was much too excited last night to sit down."

"Excited?" he jumped in. "What was he excited about?"

I gave an eloquent sigh. "*King Lear*. You remember? At the theatre last night? First night? Twenty-one curtain calls? If I'd had twenty-one curtain calls I wouldn't have sat down for a week." He eyed me gloomily, obviously not understanding. "Can I go now?" I finally extracted myself from the chair.

"I suppose so, yes." He was being a bit broody. "For the time being." He too got up and moved to the window, clearly regretting that he couldn't think of anything else to detain me. Perhaps he was lonely.

At the door I hesitated. "Is Lady Constance awake, do you know?"

He shook a preoccupied head. "I've no idea."

"Mind if I go up and give her a cheery word?"

I scuttled upstairs, scratched on her bedroom door and stuck my head into the room. She was propped up on her pillows, eyes closed but not asleep. "Connie? It's Mark."

She turned her head. "Mark dear, come in."

I glanced over my shoulder at the empty corridor, closed the door carefully and sped over to the bed. "Only for a second, Connie. Listen, if that sergeant asks you where I sat last night downstairs, tell him I sat in Gerald's chair, will you?"

She looked bewildered. "Where you sat?"

"Yes, Gerald offered me his chair."

"He wouldn't do that."

"I know he wouldn't. But last night he did – let's pretend he did. I sat in his chair the whole evening, right?"

"All right," she nodded. "But why?"

"Explanation later." I laid a finger on my lips as a stealthy creak came from the stairs outside. "Now, pretend to be asleep, otherwise he'll be in here harassing you all over again. You all right?"

She nodded and patted my hand. "Off you go," she murmured.

I tiptoed to the door, opened it quietly and backed out. A loud creak behind me. I shot into the air. Sergeant Hunter stood at my elbow. "Don't *do* that!" I whinnied. "Creeping about like Boris Karloff." He was watching me through narrowed eyes. "She's asleep," I told him in a whisper. "Come on now, if we hang about here mumbling to each other we'll wake her up."

Once downstairs I took off with the mendacious promise that

I would keep in touch. He stood at the garage door and gave a theatrical wince when the doughty Honda burst into flame. I gave him a merry wave.

His reflection in the wing-mirror looked, I thought, mighty suspicious.

Chapter Ten

When I got back to Bull Street no one was in. The house was shut up and airless and smelled like the inside of a bell-tent full of Scouts. I tramped around opening all the doors and windows in the hope that even the slightest wind of change might help to lighten the omnipresent oppressiveness of Victorian history emanating from that amazing front room.

A well-deserved and highly necessary bath was the next item on the agenda.

I turned on the taps, squirted an expensive quantity of Badedas into the running water, stripped down to my Y-fronts, searched unsuccessfully for a bath towel, came face to face at the open front door with a surprised lady in a blue hat and glasses who appeared to be collecting money for a good cause but didn't stay long enough to say what cause it was, and finally, having closed the front door on that lady's fast retreating heels, climbed gratefully into the bath, only then realising, too late, that I had omitted to remove my Y-fronts.

With the fixed determination to sort out and assess the various alarms and excursions of the day, I sank blissfully beneath the bubbles and promptly went to sleep.

A door banged; a voice calling, "Anyone at home?", an incoherent barking from me in the bath surfacing from an equally incoherent dream, and Barbara Sterling shot into the bathroom like a bullet from a gun.

"Hello, Boy!" she greeted breathlessly.

"Girl . . ." I waved at her, adding unnecessarily, "I'm having a bath."

"Wow!" she growled, blue eyes wide and watchful.

"I was in need of comfort," I told her, "but fell asleep before I could enjoy it."

"You might have drowned."

"No such luck." I drew my sopping underpants from the bath. "Only my Y-fronts drowned; I forgot to take them off. And I met a lady at the front door who was collecting for somebody; she took to her heels when she saw me. There could well be future repercussions from that quarter."

"What repercussions? Why?"

"I wasn't wearing a lot – only these. I was looking for a bath towel at the time."

"In the airing cupboard." She stooped and kissed me on the top of the head.

"Of course. How stupid of me. So where's the airing cupboard?"

"Under the stairs."

"Where else?"

She disappeared calling over her shoulder, "Sorry I've been so long. All hell's going on over at the jam factory. Half the *Romeo* cast is in London and scattered about the countryside; I've been hours and hours on the blower gathering them all in. We want them for a word run-through in the morning."

She returned with a huge pink bath towel and draped it becomingly over the heated towel rail. "There," she said, and drawing up a stool, sat down, crossed her luscious legs and stared at me expectantly as if I were a performing seal.

She looked fresh and lithe and good enough to eat.

"I didn't think I'd ever see you in a bath again," she said at last, throatily reminiscent. "Remember that terrible bathroom in Henley Street over the fish-shop?"

I grinned. "Where the geyser hated me? Every time I went near it the bloody thing tried to set light to me."

"It got your hair and eyebrows once, remember that?"

"Hairless in Henley Street!"

The little room echoed to our laughter. And suddenly I was sober again. "I was up on that tower again this afternoon. That nearly got me too. It was a matter of pure luck that I didn't follow poor old Gerald all the way down to the grave-yard."

The light died from her eyes. "What are you talking about?"

I told her what had happened. She knelt beside me, her face suddenly ravished with a concern that surprised me. She fished my bubble-bespattered hand out of the bath and held it to her lips and face.

I drew it gently away. "Hey, come on, stop it . . . There's enough going on without you going broody on me." I swirled industriously at the water. "I'd better get out of here, everything's beginning to freeze over." I gave her what I hoped was a winning grin. "Come on now, missus, bung me over that towel and I'll tell you who's queer."

"Come and get it."

"Not on your nelly!"

"You dear old-fashioned thing!" She handed it to me. "I've seen it all before." She turned at the door. "How would tea and bun-cakes grab you?"

Later, sitting primly alongside each other on a shiny black horsehair sofa in that gloomy front-parlour of hers, eating buttered scones and drinking lifeless Russian tea with lemon to give it body, I told her most of what had been going on since I last saw her. There seemed to be quite a lot of it and I finished up exhausted, staring glumly into my empty cup.

"That's about it," I shrugged. "A long day and nothing much to show for it."

She replenished my cup. "So what's next?"

"Questions and answers, I suppose. No one seems to be coming clean. Old Chancey Bun, for one. He's tight as a clam at the moment, but with a bit of gentle persuasion he may think better of it. Then there's Arch, the gardener. He's keeping something locked away. Maybe it's nothing important, but he was pretty cagey about Grantley changing his name; there was a shifty squint in his eye which worried me a bit."

She looked puzzled. "I thought it was Richard who changed his name – so's not to take advantage of dad's success."

"He did change it, but from Grantley to Rosner. Dad was a Rosner long before he was a Grantley; all Richard did was to revert to the family name. Gerald apparently became a Grantley soon after the war, probably before he met Connie – but *why* he did, we shall probably never know. Perhaps he'd had a bad time in the army, it could happen. Life can still be tricky for Jews in some quarters – even in this country. You know the sort of thing: 'I've nothing against the Jews but . . .'

126

Even so, I wouldn't have thought the name Rosner stuck out like a sore thumb, like Levi or Samuels for instance. And it's not even as if he were a practising Jew. He seems to have been more buddy-buddy with E. Chancey Bun than with the local rabbi – if there is a local rabbi. According to Arch old Bun just couldn't wait to get him on the conversion table."

"And this Emma person, the lady sculptor, what about her?"

"Hardcastle – Emma Hardcastle." I gave a ponderous frown. "She's the pick of the bunch – an odd-ball if ever there was one. She's like a damped down bonfire; on the surface she's dry and brittle, cool; underneath she's really stoked up. At least, she is at the moment, but it may not be chronic. Gerald managed to get under her skin in record time and in a big way, God alone knows how. It surely can't have been that she was just disappointed in him as a man, as opposed to an actor. Damn it all, we're all disappointed in somebody at some time, but that doesn't mean we go out and do away with that somebody." I pulled myself up abruptly. "What the hell am I saying?"

"You think *she* killed him?"

"No, no, of course I don't – don't even know what made me say it. Except that she's the sort who might lash out and do something she'd be sorry for later. Not that she's sorry. Far from it. Gerald's death doesn't seem to have affected her one little bit." I thought for a moment. "If she were able to get about a bit more, she'd be top of my list of possibles. But she could never, ever, have made it up to the top of that tower *and* down again – not with those sticks she couldn't."

I got up and weaved a restless and serpentine path through the lumpish furniture.

"You really do believe he was shoved off that tower, don't you?" she asked carefully.

"I don't believe he shoved *himself* off."

"Okay. But if he was drunk . . ."

"Ah, but he wasn't. I forgot to tell you that bit." As I filled her in about the whisky-logged triffid, I busied myself with her antique gramophone, peering down the horn, lifting the heavy lid and nosing inquisitively inside. It smelled of machine oil. A ropey looking 78 disc was on the green baize turntable; I held it up to the light. "Teddy Bears' Picnic" performed by someone called Henry Hall and the BBC Dance Orchestra. I replaced it and released the stop. Nothing happened. I gave the turntable a shove.

"You have to wind it up," she pointed out.

I gave the handle a couple of turns. The turntable revolved with the speed of light; the soundbox weighed a ton and a half. I set the whole thing going. It was like lighting a fuse: surface noise reminiscent of "frying tonight" at the fish-shop in Henley Street, through which we were informed by a light but frightened baritone that if we went down to the woods today we'd be sure of a big surprise . . . "Today's the day the Teddy Bears have their picnic . . ."

"By golly." I grinned at her over my shoulder. "That was really living in those days, wasn't it? You weren't like this when we were rolling about among the tombstones."

She laughed. "I'm younger now than I was then. I must have been pretty important and fairly piggy in those days."

"You were fairly beddable, I know that." I turned off the machine. "I have scarey memories of those mini-skirts you almost used to wear. And I wasn't all that averse to the fumbling and tumbling in the churchyard either – dangerous though it was."

She gave a suppressed snort. "Hey, what about that night when the law raided the cemetery and the entire Shakespeare company rose up from the dead behind the tombstones, all in various stages of undress, and fled for cover? I've never moved so fast in my life."

I stood over her and touched her hair. "Those really were the days."

The room seemed to close in around us. I watched the familiar surge of blood to her cheeks. I could even feel my heart beating. She said huskily, "Now you're all grown up and serious and hunting murderers."

I moved over to the window. "I try not to do it all the time."

I peered almost peevishly through the heavy lace curtains at Bull Street and the pub opposite; a boy in shorts straddled a stationary bicycle, reading a comic; a woman with a pram talked to a man shouldering a garden-fork; from somewhere came the soporific pulse of pop music doing battle with a strident female voice . . .

I felt confused and saddened. What the hell was the matter with me? That she disturbed me after all these years didn't surprise me one bit; that I had all but rebuffed her, did.

The pealing of the telephone bell shattered the tension in the room. Behind me she gave an impatient yowl as she reached for it. "Yes? . . . Hi, Roger? . . . Oh God, yes, I'd forgotten . . . no, no, leave it to me . . . First thing in the morning . . . Yes, isn't it? I still can't believe it . . . Okay, see you, thanks for ringing." She hung up. "Roger Howells at the theatre worrying about Gerald's things in the dressing-room. I said I'd collect them in the morning. Perhaps you ought to come too – you never know, there might be something."

I nodded. "I'll do that."

As I moved towards her she said almost briskly, "Now, about food tonight. There's bacon and eggs and fish fingers in the fridge, not much else. Or we could eat out."

"What do you usually do?"

"Eat out, pick up some of the gang. There's not a lot of places open on Sundays."

"Somewhere quiet . . . without the gang."

"Great. Do you eat Indian, Chinese?"

"I eat anybody."

"Chinese then. The Mayflower in the High Street."

"It's a date." I hesitated. "Not yet though . . ."

"No . . ."

I knelt in front of her, took her hand gently in mine. "How would it be," I enquired slowly, "if we took ourselves upstairs to that enormous great empty bed of yours . . .?"

In the silence which followed I wasn't sure whether it was the pop music down the road thumping away in my ears or something nearer home. I was still worrying about it when she murmured, "That would be just like the good old days," adding in the smallest whisper, "without the smell of fish."

She placed her forehead against mine and we stared mutely

129

into each other's eyes for a rapt second or two, like a couple of owls . . .

The same owl-eyes were there when I unglued my lids the following morning; warm lips on mine, gossamer hair trailing seductively over my face – a golden web of trapped sunlight, tickling a lot. The *tender* trap, they call it in the trade; not at all unpleasant. So I gave her an encouraging growl, made a pair of long lips and prepared to surrender my all, which, as it turned out, was not what was required of me.

"Time to show a leg," she said, removing her lips and tugging at my ear. "Tea or coffee?"

"Coffee."

"I've made tea."

"Tea, then."

"Coffee coming up."

I hadn't the energy to argue with her; when I looked again she had gone. I blinked blearily around me.

Propped up against a pillow a few inches from my nose was a folded newspaper displaying a large photograph of some idiot in leather crowning himself with a crash helmet. Recognising the idiot almost at once, I crossed my eyes at the caption: "Screen star of the seventies, Mark Sutherland, photographed yesterday at the home of Sir Gerald Grantley."

I groaned and elbowed myself into an upright position.

A by-line said: *Savage Sutherland*. I read on:

Mark Sutherland, meteoric screen-star of a handful of box-office action movies during the seventies, who dropped abruptly out of sight after a near-fatal accident on the set of what proved to be his last film, *Dark Side of the Moon*, yesterday made a dramatic reappearance when he was first on the scene at the tragic death of his friend and colleague, Gerald Grantley.

To those of our readers who have pondered over the recent whereabouts of Sutherland, let me say that he is alive and well and bearing a remarkable resemblance to a character straight out of one of his own movies: black leathered from head to foot and straddling a powerful Honda Super Sport motorbike.

The boyish charm, alas, appears to have worn somewhat

thin and the intervening years have dealt none too kindly with those once well-known clear-cut features of his, the result perhaps of a new name coupled with a new profession. For Mark Sutherland, one-time star of stage and screen, is now Mark Savage, private investigator. Sounds like a good title for a new TV mini-series, don't you think, ladies?

The column came from someone who called herself Annabel, and I knew exactly who she was and what she looked like: steel hair cut like a helmet and glasses which flashed malice.

"Cow!" I muttered.

Barbara stood in the doorway bearing a coffee-pot.

"Thought you'd better see it while you were still lying down."

"If she wanted to write about me why the hell didn't she say so?"

She gave a wry smirk, calmly stirring at the coffee-pot. "Judging by the photo, I'd say you never gave her much of a chance."

I squinted again at the picture. The snarl below the helmet was almost in 3D. "What does she mean – the boyish charm's worn somewhat thin?" I hurled the paper across the room.

She offered me a cup of coffee. "She means you're older. Cream, sugar?"

"Black."

She squatted on the edge of the bed and poured herself some pissy-looking tea. "It's blown whatever cover you might have had, hasn't it?"

"That's for sure." I scalded my mouth on the coffee. "What is she, this Annabel, a gossip columnist or what?"

Barbara nodded. "Show-biz mainly. She hangs around the theatre a lot picking up this and that. She's Birmingham based, as is her rag, and her name actually is Laurie Marsh." She screwed up her face in thought. "Annabel used to be a man by the name of Church Washington; he was struck by lightning one summer night while sheltering under a tree. We've been half hoping that the same might happen to Laurie Marsh one day, but apparently it's true what they say about lightning."

I leaned over and kissed her on the ear. "How utterly

fascinating. Now, if you've finished your reminiscences, I'd like to show my leg."

She had clearly been up betimes, for not only had she gathered in the newspapers, she had also washed my shorts and T-shirt, now humping around in the tumble-drier.

Over bacon and eggs we studied, on the one hand, the unanimously euphoric notices of Gerald's Lear and on the other, his lengthy and detailed obituaries.

It was a melancholy experience, unprecedented to my mind, and made me think of people who had died on their birthdays, like Shakespeare and Caius Cassius . . . "This day I breathed first: time is come round, And where I did begin, there shall I end; My life is run his compass . . ."

One way and another the press had done him proud, most of them carrying photographs, *The Times* coming up with a hair-raising picture of his Lear haranguing the elements. I stared at it soberly, knowing as I did so that his performance would go with me down to the grave. In my mind's eye I was comparing its grandeur and stature with the flawed diminishment now swathed in damp cloths on Emma Hardcastle's work-stand . . . One of us just had to be wrong.

Barbara passed me the *Daily Telegraph*. "Another picture of you – almost." It was a still from one of the movies I had made with Gerald. I was unrecognisable, togged up in an army major's uniform with little more than nose and chin visible beneath the shadow cast by the peak of the cap. Gerald appeared to be doing his Lear all over again, towering above me like Mephistopheles in a white wig. The caption read: "The late Sir Gerald Grantley with Mark Sutherland in a scene from the film *Fifth Column.*" No mention of the fact that it was I who had found the body, so presumably they hadn't latched on to it – that had been left solely for Annabel's jaundiced eye.

The why's, how's and wherefore's of Gerald's demise were handled by the majority of the press with an incurious complacency.

No one asked what he was doing up there in the middle of the night; no one suggested a sudden stroke, illness or drunkenness; if there was one glancing shot at suicide it was only in repudiation: ". . . no grounds to suspect that the tragedy was brought about by any cause other than accident." The only mention of foul play was a bland assurance that it was not suspected.

Briefly and idly, I found myself wondering what conclusion Annabel had arrived at . . .

"Well," mourned Barbara, folding the last of the papers with an air of desolation, "at least his passing hasn't gone unnoticed. And the echoes will go on for a long time yet." She added thoughtfully, "Hell of a shame no one was there to video that performance."

"They'd have had to remove the first act." She frowned at me. "He was faffing about like a fifteen-year-old on amateur night. Even Connie was shaken. But no one else seems to have noticed. *The Guardian* mentioned he was a little slow off the mark. A *little* slow! It did cross my mind that he'd taken something to quieten himself down or give himself a boost – benzedrine or something, I don't know, anything. You were there, you saw it all . . ."

"After those dress rehearsals I was relieved to see him there at all; they were the worst rehearsals I've ever sat through." A thought struck her. "Mind you, he did have a steaming great row with You-Know-Who just before the curtain went up; that could have thrown him for six."

"Sonia mentioned that. Do we know what it was about?"

She spread her hands. "What else? His flaming God-awful production, I suppose, and how not one member of his cast could even begin to act, and was therefore incapable of passing on his stupendous vision to the world at large. Sonia and Megan will probably be able to fill you in on the details. I think they were both hoping Gerald would slaughter him on the spot."

"Instead of which . . ." I murmured.

"Gerald was slaughtered."

Silence fell between us.

I said, "You don't kill someone simply because he doesn't like your bloody production."

She wobbled her head. "Well, *I* wouldn't, *you* wouldn't . . ."

"But?"

She nodded. "Paul's a loony, you know. A nutcase. You

should see him in a rage. What those kids went through! I wouldn't have stood it. I'd have torn up my contract and swep' out. Let 'em sue. In the end, of course, it all became a great joke and they coped, like most actors do if it's a question of getting the curtain up at all. They did everything he asked without question, like zombies, because there was no point in doing anything else." After a pause, she added, "Interesting, isn't it, how few of the critics mentioned the production – even to carp over it."

I shrugged. "When Sir surfaced and took over, the production didn't seem to matter any more; he did his own thing and the rest of the cast followed suit – even when he wasn't on stage. He just seemed to light them up, like Prometheus bringing fire to mankind."

There was a sudden silence as the tumble-dryer clicked itself off. I finished a piece of toast and emptied my cup. "As for Twit-face . . ." I gave a theatrical sigh. "His greatest ambition is to act, did you know that? He wants to play Hamlet and Henry Five – all the good guys with the pretty faces. He doesn't really want to direct at all. And that's what's gnawing his guts away. He sees them all poncing about up there on the stage and loathes every mother's son of them."

"Like I said, he's a nutter."

I nodded. "But I still wouldn't cast him as First Murderer. In a rage he could kill, okay, but then, couldn't we all? But would he have the nerve to lie in wait for someone in the middle of the night and calmly shove him over the edge? You'd need a lot of guts to do that."

"Or a lot of hate," she murmured, staring sombrely out of the window at the tiny backyard, shadows and morning sunlight creeping stealthily over it. She shuddered suddenly.

"What is it?"

"Somebody walking over my grave." She got to her feet slowly and painfully, like an old woman, and began collecting up the breakfast things. "We ought to be moving. Do you want to wear your shorts today? I can run the iron over them, it won't take a minute."

I shook my head. "It's jeans day today."

She grinned. "It's the leathers I go for."

I smiled back at her. "I'll wear them tonight – in bed."

She came into my arms. "Oh Mark, it's so good to have you back." Her voice was muffled against my shoulder.

I held her tight. With the scent of her hair in my nostrils, my thoughts wandered crazily back over the various amorous entanglements I had engaged in over recent years. With the exception of a diminutive veterinary surgeon somewhere in Wales, Barbara Sterling was the nearest I'd been to committing myself.

Chapter Eleven

I remember my old buddy and fellow conspirator, Sam Birkett, late of the CID, telling me once that one of the more ghoulish chores he had sometimes been obliged to perform was the picking over of the effects of the recently deceased: clothes, contents of pockets, removal of wristwatches, bracelets and necklaces – sometimes even dentures.

As I stood in Gerald Grantley's dressing-room once again, eyeing the unsightly litter of his make-up table and the display board above it to which was pinned an awesome array of greetings cards and good luck messages, something of Sam Birkett's reluctance grabbed at me and made me wish I hadn't come.

Everything was just as he had left it on Saturday night, even to the soiled towel he had chucked into a corner. The cleaners apparently had been instructed not to touch the room until further notice.

Collecting the key at the stage-door, Barbara had let me in, parked a kiss on my chin and then gone off to sort out some of the chaos initiated by the unforeseen change of programme.

I sat in Gerald's chair and to cheer myself up stared critically at my image in the mirror. It didn't help much. What did that blasted woman mean by the boyish charm wearing somewhat thin? There was nothing thin about that charm. And the clean-cut features bit too? I struck a couple of Napoleonic poses, looked up my nose and down my nose, bared my teeth and then gave up. So I wasn't quite as clean cut as I used to be; the edges had fuzzed over a bit, the lines deepened, but they were lines of wisdom and understanding – experience. Anyway, I had lived a lot, for God's sake. "I've been ill," as the mouse said to the elephant. I half closed my eyes. "Distinguished" was the word I'd have used – a young Herbert von Karajan with a dash of the Leonard Bernstein's.

I was still sitting there frittering away the time when the door opened and Roger Howells looked in.

"Hi."

"And hi to you."

"Ba told me you were doing the dirty work. Very good of you."

"As a matter of fact I haven't even started yet. I've been sitting here admiring myself and thinking what a loss it was to the acting world when I decided to give it all up. Perhaps I should make a comeback."

"Ah . . ." said Roger vaguely, looking cagey.

"Can I ask you something?" Roger's face closed up like a deck-chair, panic flickered in his eye, excuses and apologies formulating in his agile brain. I said, "Richard Rosner." His face opened up again. I grinned. "There, that wasn't too bad, was it? You went all funny on me there for a minute, didn't you? You thought I was going to ask for a job."

He was as near to a blush as he could get. "It crossed my mind."

"Didn't Ba tell you about me?"

"What about you?"

"That I'm what we laughingly call a P.I."

"I read about it in the paper."

"There you are, then. That's why I'm here. I'm on the snoop, doing a job for Connie Grantley who's asked me to look into Gerald's death."

I thought he paled a little. "You mean . . .?"

"I don't mean anything at the moment, just that I'm looking into it. Connie's not satisfied, and neither am I. So tell me about Richard Rosner."

"What do you want to know?" He came into the room, closed the door and set his back to it.

"His attitude towards father, for a start."

The pause that followed seemed endless then he said succinctly, "Sullen?" It sounded like a question.

"Do we know why?"

He shrugged. "They just didn't get on."

"Did they fight?"

"Not to my knowledge. But I'm not the best person to ask.

137

Mine's a backroom job. I'm rarely at rehearsals. I like to keep in touch with the company, of course, but I don't see a lot of them. I get to hear of situations, naturally, relationships and so on." He paused, frowning. "I've heard nothing about them fighting – not in public anyway. They just didn't – associate. In fact, it wouldn't surprise me if half the company's unaware that they were related. He's a strange lad, Richard, always looks as if he's on the verge of launching into some ghastly political homily he's cooked up."

"Is he into politics?"

"You could say that, yes. A non-conformist of the first order."

"What does he not conform to?"

"Most things, as far as I can gather. Politically, I guess, he's left-wing plus – far left."

I made a face. "I bet that makes him flavour of the month with the rest of them."

He shrugged. "You know actors; they're either running up the hammer and sickle or don't know the difference between Tony Benn and Margaret Thatcher, bar the fact that one of them's female. God alone knows how Sonia manages him. Sonia's his wife."

"Yes, I know. But she's always been bolshie, so she probably manages him quite well."

"You know her?"

"Slightly, yes. I was once married to her."

This time his face fell wide open. "I didn't know that." He grinned like a Cheshire cat. "You and Sonia, well I never. Who would have thought it?"

"You don't have to make a production number out of it." I brought the meeting back to order. "Apart from being a non-conformist Jewish Marxist, what else do we know about him?"

"*Half* Jewish, actually," he corrected me gently. "Connie's one of us. And he's not a Marxist – he just leans heavily in that direction."

"And unpopular?"

"You said that, I didn't. But he's not exactly one of the boys; that's as far as I'll go."

138

I murmured quietly half to myself, "He's certainly not popular with Arch the gardener, even Connie doesn't much care for him." I squinnied up at him in the mirror. "But then, she's only his mother. He sounds a bit unfortunate to me. How about Sonia, does she like him?"

"She's married to him."

"She was married to me too, but she didn't like me much."

"That doesn't surprise you, I hope?" He twinkled at me.

"If you have nothing more pertinent than that to say," I told him, "you may go about your business and leave me to get on with mine – snooping though it might be." I stared blankly at the mess of make-up on the table in front of me. "God, this really is a sodding awful business. Poor old Gerald. I half worshipped that man, you know."

"How's Connie taking it?"

"At the moment, remarkably well, though when the shock's worn off she's going to be pretty rough – the loneliness, his things lying about, his clothes in the wardrobe, his empty bed . . . all that jazz. It must be terrible to be suddenly cut off like that." I stirred myself irritably. "Oh, yuk! Let's get on." I gave him a glassy grin. "What about you? You've inherited a fair sized headache too. How's it all going?"

"At least the cast's intact." He glanced at his watch. "They'll be running lines right now. That's the least of our problems. Rescheduling is a second-to-none bastard. We couldn't have put on an understudy tonight, not possibly. Who wants to see an understudy anyway?"

"You should have asked me," I told him blandly. "I'd have done it. You've never seen my Lear, have you?"

"King or Edward?" he asked rudely. Opening the door he added quirkily over his shoulder, "*The Night the Bed fell on Father* would be greatly up your street."

"Thank you, Mr Howells, and good night."

"And good night to you, Mr Sutherland." He departed to return a second later. "Mr *Savage*, sir. Sorry."

He closed the door delicately as if it were made of egg-shell. I listened to him trundling down the corridor humming some tuneless ditty without an opus number.

I frowned at a wig-block wearing Lear's crown and beard; a

face sketched crudely on the block with yellow greasepaint was one I felt I ought to know. A faded photograph of Connie in a small gilt frame perched on a box of Kleenex alongside a half-eaten ham sandwich, edges depressingly curled, an unopened bottle of lager and a packet of potato-crisps; stuck on the lager bottle was Lear's moustache. I transferred it to the block, let out a heart-felt groan and began to turn the place over.

From beneath the table I rooted out an elderly cardboard attaché-case fastened, in lieu of a lock long since inoperable, by a knotted neck-tie in mauve and green stripes. The case contained nothing but a couple of clean hand-towels and a chunk of nose-paste hard as a rock. I couldn't imagine what he had ever wanted with nose-paste – to add to a nose like his would have been like carrying coals to Newcastle. False noses were out now, anyway; L. Olivier's comprehensive exploitation of the nose scene had seen to that.

Gerald's make-up consisted of a couple of ancient sticks of greasepaint, a tin of Johnson's Baby Powder, a tacky bottle of spirit-gum, a greasy bottle of liquid paraffin and two obscene-looking powder-puffs. So much for the irresistible call of the greasepaint! I packed the paints and puffs into a battered blue tin which had once contained a hundred Player's cigarettes and put the lot in the case along with two small china pigs, a Paddington Bear who had clearly been around the world twice, a brass cross, a ribboned Military Medal, a tiny silver owl, a rubber mouse, a paper-knife, and a pack of grubby playing-cards – Patience during the waits perhaps – a small bottle of boiled sweets and a paperback edition of *David Copperfield*. And that was the lot.

Below the table-top, a drawer. Locked.

I eyed it enthusiastically. I'd left my piano-wires in London but locks rarely bother me. With the aid of the paper-knife I had the drawer open in three seconds flat, its sole contents, an audio-cassette with no indication of what was on it. Nothing perhaps. In a locked drawer? I slid it into my hip-pocket.

Next, I cleared the display-board of its cards and messages, reading each one and stacking them into a neat pile. I wasn't expecting any earth-shaking revelations, didn't get any, so wasn't disappointed. What they did reveal was an astonishing affection and respect for an artist of whom somewhat more than a great deal was expected. The number of distinguished signatures footing the various messages made up the sort of fan-mail that makes the rest of us want to give up. These too went into the cardboard case, which I then tied together with its neck-tie.

Someone had switched on the intercom relaying the stage goings-on to the dressing-rooms and, judging by the banging and grunting and heavy breathing, the stage-staff was busy building the *Romeo* set, brick by solitary brick. "To you, Jack." – "Got it." – "Back a bit, Jack . . . back . . . to me, go on . . . 'old it! That was my fucking foot, Jack."

I upended the waste-paper bin and sorted through its contents like a rag-picker; used envelopes, a pair of socks, a *Stratford Herald* and an empty lager bottle.

This was a waste of time. I took time off, stretched and went to have a peer through the window.

There aren't many theatres in the country where you can stand at your dressing-room window and watch the world go by in boats – it just seemed a pity that they were all doing it at the same time. A traffic-jam was in full swing. Fascinated, I watched a nimble-toe'd damsel in a bright yellow bikini crossing the river on foot, nipping pertly from one yawing craft to the next, egged on by a boisterous crowd of supporters on the far bank.

I turned back into the room.

In the hanging space was Gerald's towelling bathrobe, a tweed jacket, a plastic raincoat and a comic yellow sou'wester; below them, a pair of carpet-slippers and a sturdy blue canvas bag with a zipper. I went through the pockets of the jacket: handkerchief, a five-pound note, a pencil and an empty blue envelope with "Sir Gerald Grantley – Personal and Urgent" scrawled across it in a bold and untidy hand. The pocket of the bathrobe gave up the rest of it: a folded page of matching blue paper. As I read the contents, the drum-beats in my ears started up.

Someone over the intercom growled, "Can't believe old

141

Gerald's gone, can you? Poor old bugger. What a way to go, eh? I feel sorry for his missus."

Gerald dear, must talk to you. Most urgent. Concerning E.H. Couldn't raise you on the phone. Please ring me soonest. Love and greatest good luck for tonight.

A scrawled signature which looked like a nose, an eye and somebody's upper lip completed the message. I puzzled over it for a moment or two. "Liz!" I whispered aloud. "Lizzie Arden . . ."

With silent satisfaction I stared at it for a further couple of seconds. Lizzie Arden in a panic? Well, disturbed enough to pen a note, probably indiscreet, and deliver it by hand to the stage-door on Saturday some time before the show. *Personal and Urgent. Concerning E.H.* E.H. . . . Emma Hardcastle? Who else?

I stared again out of the window, blindly this time.

Had he called? *Had* a meeting been arranged? At the church perhaps? In the early hours of the morning? Was that why Gerald had been so jumpy, keeping an eye on his watch and doing his drinking act to get rid of his unexpected guest? "How about up on the tower, Liz? No one will disturb us there? I'll leave the key in the lock."

I folded the note carefully, placed it in its envelope and stashed it away in my back pocket with the cassette. The hairs on the back of my neck were beginning to stir. Lizzie Arden . . . the capable looking, incapable Lizzie . . .

Meticulously, I folded the bathrobe, packed it into the blue canvas bag, followed it with the slippers, raincoat and sou'wester, the soiled towel on the floor where he had thrown it, a bottle of gargle on the wash-basin, and from the shower-cubicle some soap in a plastic container.

Scouring the room thoroughly, I stole the bottle of lager and the bag of crisps and left the sandwich for the cleaners.

Chapter Twelve

I ran Barbara Sterling to earth rehearsing the theatre band. Or if she wasn't she was not minding her own business. They were perched on a raised wooden platform backstage and she was looming over them peering short-sightedly at a score and stabbing at it with a didactic finger. "That," she was saying, "is an A sharp."

"Natural," said the owner of the score wagging a good-natured head.

"Sharp," she insisted. "Look at it. You can see the ends of the little cross-pieces."

"That's just the way he does his notation."

"Well, it doesn't sound right."

"What does in this score? We play everything we see *as* we see it – fly-dirts and all. That's the way we've always played it."

"Doesn't mean to say it's right though, does it?"

I found a dark corner, squatted on a rostrum and settled down to a long wait, opening my free bottle of lager and bag of potato crisps. Listening with half an ear to the ensuing scratchings and groanings from the band, I couldn't honestly believe that the difference between an A sharp and an A natural was worth bothering about. Either way it would be misery to listen to.

Far more interesting was the garbled conversation of a couple of stage-hands taking time off for an illicit cigarette on the far side of a nearby flat.

"Doomed it was, I tell you," one was saying. "Doomed right from the start – before it even opened." It was the voice I had heard over the intercom. "What's the good of getting in a guy like Grantley an' then lumbering 'im with a pig-'eaded Peruvian ponce like that Lucy O'Grady bugger, that's what I

143

want to know? They weren't never going to see eye to eye about anything were they? Stands to reason."

A short silence was followed by a groan of complaint from his companion. "Gawd, just 'ark at that bleedin' band, will you? Makes you want to pee. Tell you one thing, George, Sat'day night I thought the two of them was going to kill each other, straight up I did."

"What, 'im and Lucy?"

"I told you, didn't I? Nearly knocked me for six, old Grantley did; came through that door like a bat out of 'ell with Fart-face yapping at his 'eels. There wasn't no love lost between them two, I'm telling you. First night too. I wonder the old man went on at all. Could 'ave put 'im right off his stroke."

"I bet that's why 'e done it," said George.

"Done what?"

"Bunged 'imself off that church. 'Im of all people. Still, we don't know the 'alf of it, do we? Might 'ave 'ad a spot of the domestics for all we know, know what I mean? And 'aving an argy-bargy like that just before 'e goes on might 'ave triggered things off like, know what I mean?" There was a long pause then George growled, "Shame it was 'im though and not Lucy. They always get away with it, don't they, the farts of this world?"

I decided to have a look at them; maybe they knew more than they thought they did. I got up and wandered casually into the light.

One of them, a middle-aged man with a crop of red hair, was in the act of pinching out his cigarette. When he caught sight of me he froze. "I don't believe it." A shower of sparks came from between his finger and thumb. "Mark, isn't it? Mark Sutherland?" I frowned at him. "Don't you remember me? George the Red? On the flying harness? You was here some years back. I used to help fly you in something or other – you was a bat or something funny like that – before you went off and became a bloody great film-star."

It all came back to me – especially the flying bit, though I was sure I had never been a bat. "George the Red," I smiled taking his outstretched hand. "Of course I remember. How are you?"

Introducing me to his friend, Jack somebody, a lean ferret of a man, we spent a couple of minutes gossiping merrily about old times and I was about to raise the subject of Gerald's death when a belligerent stage-manager waded in from a distance calling them back to work.

"Here for long?" asked George the Red, moving off backwards. I waggled an uncertain hand. "Why don't you and me 'ave a noggin' over at the Duck some time like we used to in the old days?"

I raised a thumb, "Fine." He might remember something if I jolted his memory with a couple of pints.

He waved his acknowledgment. "Sixish then?"

"George, for Christ's sake," bawled the SM.

"Okay, mate, keep your wig on," grinned George. "See you," he called back over his shoulder with a wink.

"Can I help you?" asked the stage-manager primly, bearing down on me.

"I shouldn't think so," I told him blandly. "I'm only here for the beer." I showed him my empty bottle.

"He's my property," said Barbara coming up behind and removing the bottle from my grasp. "I'm showing him the ropes. He thinks he might want to take up acting."

The disarmed stage-manager grinned, "He looks quite sane too." He went off about his business.

"Have you finished re-writing the music?" I asked her.

"Somebody should." The band was still scraping away up on its platform. "Come on, let's get out of here." She laid hold of my arm and steered me towards the pass-door.

"What is it, anyway, that terrible row?"

"Music for *Romeo*."

"Ye gods! Whatever happened to the period stuff?"

"That *is* the period stuff. Pre-war – 1936 vintage, when Mussolini was on the throne."

I groaned. "Oh God, not another enlightened production!"

"Complete with Fascist uniforms and jack-boots."

"And Mercutio and Tybalt mow each other down with Sten guns, right?"

"Wrong. They still do it with swords – though exactly why they *have* swords in the first place no one seems to care. Still, it keeps us on our toes."

145

I shook my head miserably. "I'm glad I got out when I did. Can we talk about something else?"

"Have you finished upstairs?" she asked.

I gave her the dressing-room key. "Everything's packed in two cases. I'll ferry them back to the house if you like."

"Not to worry, we'll do that." I held open the door for her. "Find anything interesting?"

I crossed a couple of fingers. "Do you have a cassette-deck at home?"

"Sure, but there's one here if you want it in a hurry – up in the sound box."

"It'll wait. You free now?"

"I've got to see Ursula at the box office."

"I'll hang about then."

She shook her head. "Could be some time. Meet you for lunch, okay?"

"Where?"

"The Garrick in the High Street? Twelve thirty?"

I walked her round to the front of house and handed her over to Ursula Selbiger of the box office who also remembered me and gave me a large kiss. It was like coming home.

So was the Garrick. It had always been a favourite haunt of mine – real Shakespeariana stuff, dark corners and oak beams and mind your head, but modernised at the back for salads and hot meat pies. The lunch-rush hadn't yet arrived. As I stood at the bar ordering a keg bitter, a deep baritone voice at my elbow said, "What's *your* name?" It was Bill, the mina bird, peering at me inquisitively through the bars of his cage, his head on one side. "Fred," I told him, to which he replied, "Eeow!" in a rich upper-class accent and turned his back.

I took my drink into a corner by the door so that I wouldn't miss Barbara when she eventually turned up. Right opposite was a slot-machine called *Special Reserve* breathing busily to itself and flashing orange and red lights. I bore it for a couple of sips then got Nick the landlord to change a pound for a handful of coins.

"Big spender," grinned Nick.

Bill the bird asked, "Want to go downstairs?"

"Not just at the moment, thank you," I told him.

"Eeow!" he said, coughed loudly and again turned his back.

The machine gobbled up the coins, regurgitated a couple, then repossessed them. When I turned back to my drink she was sitting alongside it, hugging a whisky, her steel helmet aglow, the red and orange lights of the machine flashing from her glasses.

"That's a mug's game," she said by way of introduction.

I stood over her for a silent couple of seconds until she moved her rump an inch or two to allow me room to sit, a grudging invitation I ignored, standing instead and staring pointedly at the empty seats in the vicinity.

I took up my drink. "Is this an official visitation?"

"Nothing I do is official."

"That I can well believe."

In the charged silence which followed she took a newspaper from the bench beside her and laid it on the table open at my photograph – the one crowning myself with the crash-helmet.

"I've seen it."

"And it's made you mad."

"It hasn't endeared you to me. I suppose it doesn't occur to you that people change their names for a purpose."

"If *you* did it to remain incognito then you should have included a plastic surgery job too," she said tartly. "Your face was plastered all over the world for the best part of six years. What would you expect me to do?"

"Ask, for Christ's sake," I snarled at her loudly. "You might at least have had the courtesy to ask before you burst into print."

"My dear man, if I asked permission every time I turned up a story I'd never burst into print at all."

"And a damn good thing too."

"What's *your* name?" asked Bill the mina.

"There, you see," she smiled dryly. "I'm not the only one."

I realised I was being unreasonable and not a little rude; the humorous glint behind the spectacles drew me back to some semblance of civility. "At least he asked," I growled with a shrug.

She was eyeing me shrewdly, her head on one side, like Bill the bird, but rather more predatory. "Sit down, why don't you?

Enjoy your drink. Perhaps we can repair the breach." She shoved herself to the far end of the settle taking her drink, newspaper and weighty shoulder bag with her.

I looked at my watch. "I'm expecting someone."

"Barbara Sterling?" When I made no reply she gave a magnanimous smile and raised her hand in a three-fingered Boy Scout salute. "Discretion personified, I assure you. Have no fear." She burrowed around in her bag for about twenty minutes. "Cigarette?"

"I don't."

"Silly me." I watched in silence as she chose a cigarette, set light to it and laid down a smoke-screen.

"Have you been following me?" I asked, irritably waving aside the smoke.

"Not with any real premeditation. Saw you leave the theatre, had an idea, decided to renew our acquaintance." I looked blank. "Oh, you wouldn't remember. Too long ago. You gave me your autograph at that very same stage-door. I asked you to write your favourite Shakespearean quotation. Know what you wrote? 'A poor player that struts and frets his hour upon the stage . . .' When the season finished you dropped out of sight for months and because I was a beastly cow I added the rest of the quotation in round schoolgirl hand: '. . . and then is heard no more.' One year later you were the hottest property in the movie world. I did feel ashamed."

I said nothing, but, fed up with standing around, planted a tentative buttock on the edge of the settle.

"How about a story?" she asked, watching me over the rim of her glass.

"About what?"

"*My Life as a Private Eye*? That'd do for a start."

"*Private* being the operative word." I gave a loud sigh and went on before she could interrupt. "Listen, if you were interested enough to hang around stage-doors as a schoolgirl, you couldn't fail to remember the witch-hunt specially laid on by the press for my benefit when I was in no fit state to answer back. As far as I'm concerned you can all go jump in the lake."

"Oh come on, Mr Savage! That's water under the bridge. People like you don't hold grudges, or shouldn't at your age –

148

not against institutions anyway, it's a waste of time. You know the way we work; we have a job to do, if we don't do it we're out on our ears. You also know the public taste: if it isn't sensational, if it isn't dirt, it's not news." She paused for a moment. "Now, if I were to tell you that you're investigating the death of Gerald Grantley because someone's not satisfied it was an accident, I suppose you'd throw up your hands and deny it?"

"I would do no such thing. I'd remind you that it's a cops' and coroner's job. Marital indiscretions are my line, missing persons and the like; and I do my very best to keep my nose clean."

The smirk on her lips did nothing to disperse the suspicion that she knew more than was good for me. I couldn't see what her eyes were doing; the coloured lights flashing in her glasses saw to that.

"I'll strike a bargain with you, Mr Savage."

"I wouldn't count on it."

The smirk became a smile. "I've come up with the bizarre idea that, regardless of what you've just said, you are, in fact, a one-man homicide squad." She held up her cigarette. "Please allow me to finish. If it's of any interest, I go along with you. I don't believe Grantley's death was accidental, nor do I believe it was suicide." She finished her drink, put down the glass and blew the ash off the end of her cigarette. "You knew him better than I did, so I don't have to press the point, do I?"

"It's a hunch," I said, "not a point."

"Right. And hunches are my bread and butter. Have to be followed up. That's what they're there for. And that's what *you're* here for too. That's why you've been going the rounds, nose to the ground. Lady Constance, Archie the gardener, the Ardens for lunch, Emma Hardcastle, the sculptor lady, to say nothing of his Reverence." She counted them off on her fingers. "They weren't exactly courtesy calls, were they?"

I couldn't resist a smile. "You have been busy."

"Comes with the territory."

As a gesture of truce I reached for her glass. "Anything special in that?"

"Vat 69."

149

I got her a refill and watched her light another cigarette from the first. "So what's the bargain?" I asked when the place was again seething with smoke.

She ground the discarded cigarette into small pieces in an ashtray. "If I were to give you a pointer which led you in the right direction, could I, I wonder, count on an exclusive story from you?"

"The police will be there before us."

"I doubt it. Sergeant Hunter sees no complications – he doesn't have hunches. He's still on the accident jag."

"Sergeant Hunter's not the only iron in the fire."

"At the moment he is. You could romp home with half a dozen lengths to spare." Sliding her glasses down her nose she eyed me quizzically. "Is it a bargain?"

"Is crime-reporting your bag?" I countered. The eyes were warm and brown, not in keeping with the rest of her.

"I don't see myself as Annabel for the rest of my life. Onwards and upwards is my motto. And talking of Annabel, there's a second part to the bargain: an in-depth Annabel interview with Mark Savage né Sutherland – then I shan't lose out if the other thing goes up in smoke."

"What's the pointer?"

"Your solemn oath first. An exclusive story."

I nodded. "If such a thing is possible."

"And the interview?"

"I'll want to see it before it goes to print."

She raised her glass. "Done." She drained her whisky at a gulp and, fishing a notebook and pencil from her bag, she scribbled a few lines, tore off the page and slid it across the table. "He knows something he shouldn't."

"Like what?"

"Like that's for you to find out, but it's something to do with Gerald Grantley, I'm sure."

I squinted at the paper. "David who?"

"Ravel – as in the composer."

"And who is he?"

"Paul Braidy's little piece. *Ex*-little piece. He's out on his ear now, holed up in a single room, all on his own." She smiled at me crookedly. "You're still a likely looking lad; after Paul

Braidy you'd be something of a boost to his ego. Wear those sexy leathers of yours, get him up behind you on that throbbing great Honda and you could ride off into the sunset together. There's nothing he wouldn't tell you – or show you. What's the quote? 'Misery acquaints a man with strange bedfellows.' "

I grinned. "You're an evil woman."

"That's been said before." She began collecting up her things. "Tread carefully though," she warned. "Don't frighten him off." She frowned down at her bag. "He's worried about something, and doesn't know quite what to do with it." She looked up at me, her face clearing. "You could show him perhaps." Her eyes flickered over my shoulder. "Here comes your girl." Rising, she laid a card on the table. "You can get me at that number. I'm rarely there, but keep trying. Thanks for the drink."

"Hi," greeted Barbara, edging between us, a cool eye on Laurie Marsh.

The columnist hooked her bulging bag on to her shoulder. "Good snooping," she said, slapped me smartly on the chest and went off without a word or a glance at Barbara.

"Stupid cow!" said Barbara spreading her worldly goods on the table. "So we're fraternising with the enemy, are we?"

"She jumped out of the woodwork at me."

Bill on the counter laughed raucously and squawked loudly, "Another thing I'll tell you . . ."

"Even he doesn't believe that," smiled Barbara.

We picked up some drinks from the bar and departed foodwards to the rear of the premises, with Bill calling after us, "Want a grape?" and whistling rudely.

Over shepherd's pie and salad I weighed in with the morning's happenings, beginning with the findings in the dressing-room and ending with Laurie Marsh's proposal.

Barbara stared long and hard at Lizzie Arden's note. "You going to face her with this?"

"Obviously."

"You're not getting out of line, are you?" She frowned at me. "With the law, I mean?"

I shrugged. "I'm already out of line there. I haven't come clean about that bloody blazer on the flagpole, have I? And it's

151

a bit late suddenly to remember it now. Anyway, Connie's my main concern, not the law; I shan't be taking it into my own hands, if that's what you mean. If Gerald was knocked off and I get there first I'll just have to concoct some fiendish way of leaking information to the fuzz without showing the whites of my eyes. The last thing I want is for Connie to get hurt – more hurt. Nobody wants a happy married life pilloried and picked over by a lot of muck-rakers."

"They'll do that anyway if they get half a chance."

"They will if Gerald didn't keep his nose clean," I added ominously.

A silence fell between us.

She toyed with the cassette on the table. "Then there's this," she said soberly.

"And this." I tapped Annabel's scrap of paper. "I'm going to have to force my attentions on young David Ravel."

"Poor unfortunate young David Ravel."

"Do you know him?"

"I've seen him around."

"*Is* he young?"

She nodded. "And very pretty. So watch your step. I'm sure you won't have much trouble in that direction."

I gave her a twitchy grin and told her what Laurie Marsh had said about getting him up behind me on the Honda.

She nodded wisely. "If he's as susceptible to black leather as I am, I don't give a dead duck for his chances. Can we go home now and listen to that tape?"

"You free now?"

"Free enough."

"Want to go downstairs?" asked Bill as we passed his cage.

"Piss off," I told him quietly.

"Eeow!" He coughed loudly and whistled a lot. "Have a nice day," he squawked at our backs as the door closed behind us.

Neither she nor I spoke. We sat watching the tape spooling itself on to the end, the slight hiss of its progress the only sound.

I got up, wandered over to the window and stared bleakly through the heavy lace curtains at the pub opposite. Next door in the betting-shop a telephone took up a persistent ringing.

Behind me the machine "clopped" off and the mosquito whine of the fast rewind took over. Somebody answered the telephone with an impatient shout.

I jammed my hands into the pockets of my jeans and turned back into the room. She was watching me. I raised my shoulders in a despairing hunch. The whining came to an end and I gave a nod in answer to her raised eyebrow.

She pressed *Play*.

The voice again, drearily sinister in its sneering insolence and careful articulation, speaking through a wodge of extraneous sounds, like bad surface noise on a well-worn gramophone record: "Sir Gerald Grantley?" A seemingly endless pause. "You thought you'd got away with it, didn't you? You thought there was no one to see – no witnesses. You were wrong, weren't you? I was there. I saw you kill him. Broke his back. And left him in the gutter. And now they're looking for you. I could tell them where to look. I could tell them who you are and where you live. What's your skin worth? A thousand? Five thousand? Let's say ten thousand pounds. In three days. You'll hear from me again."

She pressed *Stop*.

I slumped down in a heap beside her. Next door the phone was ringing again. She said at last, "I don't believe a word of it."

"I do," I said quietly.

"That he killed somebody? Broke his back? Gerald?"

"Gerald was a violent man. Perfectly capable of breaking somebody's back." She shook her head vehemently. "You saw his Lear. It was the most violent performance I've ever seen."

"That was acting, for God's sake."

"You can't act what you don't feel – and that was violence with the lid off."

She was staring at me wide-eyed. "You actually believe Gerald could murder someone in cold blood?"

"Nobody's said anything about cold blood."

"I thought you were his friend."

"Oh come on, Ba," I growled irritably. "The man was a soldier, trained to kill. He was six foot three in his stockinged feet and built like a bull. Of course he could kill. *I* could kill,

153

you could kill, we all could. It's the way we're made." I laid a hand on hers. "If Gerald did kill somebody I hope to God it was either an accident or in self-defence. One thing we can be certain of: whoever is responsible for that tape, knows what he's talking about. What we've got to find out is when Gerald received that tape and whether he paid up. It was in the drawer of his dressing-room, which suggests it was sent to the theatre rather than to his home – probably quite recently – *since* he occupied that dressing-room, in fact. Three, four days? A week?"

She shook her head. "Six weeks. Since rehearsals began. We stretched a point with Gerald. Usually dressing-rooms are shared, but with him living out in the sticks we thought he would appreciate somewhere to put his feet up during rehearsals. The tape could have been sent to his home, of course, and he took it to the theatre where Connie was less likely to find it – unless she already knew about it . . ."

"If she did, she'd have said so, I'm sure. What about the voice, does that do anything for you?"

She shook her head. "Could be anyone. Sounds a bit like you actually, talking through a pan-full of frying chips."

"What makes you say that?"

She grinned. "I was being unnecessary. Though it could be an actor's voice. Know what I mean? Like a radio-actor, everything concentrated in the voice because there's no visual back-up. That's the reason I don't like radio acting; it always sounds so ham. And that's what this is – ham."

"Well," I said, "there's a theatre full of it over the way."

She said slowly, "But then, anyone who disguises his voice is in the acting business. It's too easy to blame an actor. It could just as well be a bus-driver or a sailor on leave."

"But a sailor or bus-driver who knew Gerald by sight."

"Most people around here knew what he looked like. He had a heck of a lot of pre-publicity: photos, magazine articles, TV chat-shows. He was very nearly the bore of the year. When he walked around the town it was like a royal progress – even here where actors are ten-a-penny. He loved playing the old actor-laddie bit too, funny hats, walking-sticks to lean on, umbrellas to flourish. Mind you, when rehearsals began to bite he sobered up quite a bit. He became pretty difficult, sometimes at the cost of his sense of humour."

I got up and began tiptoeing among the furniture again. "Connie thinks his unrest was due to something more than just rehearsal pains, and she lived through enough of them to know what she was talking about." I leaned over and slid the cassette out of the machine. "*This* was the 'something more', I'll bet. So he had manslaughter, blackmail and *Lear* all on his plate at the same time. I'm surprised he was civil to anybody. The question is, who died of a broken back during the past weeks? When and where? And what happened to the *corpus delicti*? Somebody must have found it if he left it lying around in a gutter. Anything in the local papers?"

She shook her head. "Never touch 'em."

I gloomed on for a bit; I was at the window again staring out into the road. "The gutter . . ." I muttered half to myself. "*And left him in the gutter.*" I turned on her. "That's it. He knocked someone down in his car and left him there – in the gutter with his back broken."

We exchanged blank looks. "Hit and run . . ." we said almost in unison.

An endless silence followed, then she was shaking her head again, slowly this time and with determined emphasis. "No, never. Never . . ."

"Why not?"

"Gerald?"

I shrugged. "Must be very tempting just to drive on if you were certain there were no witnesses."

"He could have been attacked, mugged perhaps, killed the man accidentally in a fight."

"In which case he would have informed the police – justifiable homicide."

"But to knock somebody down and just leave him to die . . ."

I shrugged. "Number One first. Self-preservation and all that – I know it well. If someone shouts 'Fire in the paint locker' you make for the nearest exit. Panic's a right bugger – 'specially in a fast car. No time for mitigating circumstances; when there is, it's too bloody late, you're six blocks away. Oh Christ, what a turn-up this is! I'm sure I'm right. And some passer-by," I waggled the cassette, "this bastard, saw it happen, got the number of the car and traced it." I frowned. "How did he do that, I wonder? You can't just ring up Registration and ask, because they won't tell you without some sort of authorisation – official channels and all that."

"He could have recognised Gerald's car."

"If it was daylight. We don't even know that. We're guessing anyway. It could have happened way up in Scotland for all we know."

She was shaking her head. "You said Connie thinks his depressions began during rehearsals, so it has to be during the last six weeks. He couldn't have taken off anywhere during that time – not far anyway – because he was rehearsing every day. It's got to be fairly local."

I nodded. "Then the local papers will have covered it, and it'll be on their files. I'll have a peer at his car. If it hit someone hard enough to kill, it must have bent something – a wing, or a fender, something."

"Like some tea?"

"What?"

"Tea." She got up and trailed off into the kitchen, then came back again. "Listen, why don't I nip into the *Herald*'s offices and have a look through their back numbers. Would that help?"

"So long as you don't tell 'em what you're looking for."

She nodded. "You're on," and went out again, this time with me at her heels.

"What about the ten grand then?" I mumbled. "If he paid up, where did he get it and how was the drop made? And where?"

She was filling a kettle at the sink. "Would a bank let him have that sort of money without notice?"

"I don't see why not if the money was there. Or maybe he cashed in a life insurance, or securities of some sort. A building society, how about that? He could have got it from a building society without any trouble. God, what a mess to have got himself into. What bloody bad luck. Poor old Gerald . . ."

With sudden violence she thumped the kettle on to the stove and turned on me angrily. "What do you mean, 'poor old

156

Gerald'? If he was a hit-and-run driver he brought it on himself, didn't he? What's the matter with you?" I stared at her dumbfounded, my jaw on the sag. "What I'm trying to say is, don't let's condone what he did just because he's dead."

I took a deep breath. "Ba, we don't *know* what he did. We're just standing about here speculating. All we've got to go on is a recorded message from a grubby little blackmailer. So let's get it together and be sure of our facts before we fly off the handle."

She stood her ground for a second or two, glaring at me, fists clenched, face flushed, eyes wide and bright with angry tears, then, as suddenly as it had come, the fit passed. She closed her eyes, moved slowly into my arms and buried her face in my chest. I held on to her tightly. She was trembling. "God, how awful of me." Her voice was muffled by my shirt, her fists busily bruising the small of my back.

She desisted eventually and blinked a couple of tear-stained eyes at me. "I've made your shirt all damp." She turned away snuffling and switched on the kettle. "I do see what you mean." She wiped her face with the back of her hand. "If I knocked somebody down and killed him, I'd probably leave the country." She sniffed loudly. "Perhaps it's just as well I don't drive."

"Listen, you." I took her gently by the shoulders and sat her down at the table. "I don't want to get you any deeper into this. It's comforting to think aloud and be listened to, but you've got quite enough on your plate over at the factory. Besides," I added with a grin, "it's none of your business."

"You can't fire me now just because I shouted at you and made your shirt wet." She blinked up at me with reddened eyes. "Do you like coconut cake?"

"What?"

"Coconut cake."

"Yes, I think so."

She was on her feet and had her head in the fridge in two seconds flat. "So, who's next on your dance-card?"

I sorted through the list of possibles. "Madam Arden I think. And while I'm over there I'll look in on Connie, see how she is, and have a fumble through Gerald's desk, see if there's any sign that he's missing ten thousand quid."

157

"And what about pretty boy?"

"Who, David Ravel? What about him?"

"Can I be there when you force your attentions on him?"

"No, you can't," I grinned. "You'd turn it into a gang-bang."

Chapter Thirteen

I hammered on the front door of *chez* Arden to no avail, so fell back on a knob in the wall which said *Pull*; when I did, it came away in my hand of course. I was guiltily doing my best to thread it back into the wall when a growly voice behind me said, "That don't work."

Arch, in depressing school cap and worse wellingtons, stood grubbily on the lower step, squinnying up at me.

"And you're quite right," I nodded. "I've just pulled it out of the wall."

"'Ere, let me." He elbowed me aside. "There's a knack to it." Two blows of his fist and a "hup!" and a "there you are" and everything was back to normal.

"You work for the Ardens too, do you?" I asked.

"I work for 'em all. Without me, Mr Bond, Grantley would grind to an 'alt. Can I 'elp? 'Cept for Madam they're all out."

"Madam's the one I'm after."

He jerked his head, "Round the back with 'er feet up," and pointed the way through an overgrowth of rhododendrons.

"I'd like further words with you, Arch, when you've got a moment."

"You only 'ave to whistle, Mr Bond, an' I'll come a runnin'."

I found Lizzie Arden on the terrace, resplendent in a psychedelic tent-like garment and sprawled untidily over a wicker chaise-longue, eyes shut, mouth open and two lumps of cotton-wool sticking out of her ears. She snored gently. Except for the change of clothes and locale she might still have been wallowing in yesterday's post-prandial stupor.

On the table beside her were several newspapers, an empty wine-glass, a copy of *Gone with the Wind* – people were still reading that? – and an aerosol of fly-killer.

159

I cleared my throat and coughed loudly. The snoring ceased; one cautious hand groped for the aerosol; I moved it beyond her reach and coughed again – this time less politely. Her eyes blinked open and widened when they encountered mine.

"Great heavens!" she spluttered, "I've just been dreaming about you." She removed the cotton wool from her ears. "Ear-plugs," she explained, heaving herself into an upright posture. "Self-defence against bird-song and that bloody church clock bonging away every quarter of an hour – no disrespect to poor Gerald of course. But everything's so hideously noisy in the country. Pull up a chair, dear boy."

"You should live in London," I smiled, creaking down into a wicker chair.

She raised a wristful of clanging bangles. "Heaven forbid! Now if you're sitting comfortably, I have to do penance for my outrageous behaviour yesterday at lunch. I hope you have forgiven me and would you like some tea?"

I resisted the tea and told her there was nothing to forgive.

She wasn't listening. "I could become an alcoholic quite happily, you know. The slightest upset and I'm reaching for the nearest bottle: such a comfort!" She was staring idly at my crotch. "You're not wearing your shorts today," she murmured almost wistfully, then straightening up, she gave herself a brisk shake. "You made quite an impression on God, you know; he actually told me how much he took to you and that's most unusual. He's gone to Birmingham for the day, poor dear, so we're all alone. Isn't *that* a hair-raising thought?" She gave me a smile like a fan-vault. "It's so nice of you to drop in like this." She hesitated for a second. "Is it a social visit, or have you something special in mind?"

As I reached into my hip pocket her eyes rounded with alarm and she recoiled a little. "That was my dream," she whispered hoarsely. "You were sitting on a bus opposite me and reached into your back pocket just like that . . ." She stared confusedly at the blue envelope in my hand, then up into my face. "In the dream it was a gun. I woke up and there you were – coughing at me."

I removed the letter from its envelope, unfolded it and held it at arm's length for her to see. "That is your handwriting, isn't it?"

She took it from me gingerly and made a great show of sorting out a pair of half-lenses which she wore about her neck suspended from a chain.

Apart from the artificial colouring on her cheeks her skin had taken on a dirty mauve colour; a nerve in her jaw twitched. Half amused I watched her lips spelling out the words of the note. When she had finished, she removed her glasses, folded the paper carefully in half, then into quarters and finally into eighths until it was no larger than a match-folder. She cleared her throat. "This was a private note," she said in a subdued voice.

"That's why I thought you might like it back."

Her eyes met mine. "I've just been reading about you in the papers. You're a policeman, aren't you? You've been playing games with me ever since we met."

I shook my head. "I'm a private investigator. I was also a friend of Gerald's, as indeed you were, and, quite unofficially and for my own peace of mind, I need to know more about the manner in which he met his death." I nodded at the wodge of paper. "I found that in his dressing-room." I paused, registering the sudden stubborn set of her mouth. "Will you tell me about it?"

She folded the paper yet again, trying to smooth it between strong, spatulate fingers. "No."

"Can't or won't?"

"Both."

"Why not?"

"Because, young man, I consider it none of your business."

"Would you rather it became police business?"

For answer, she swiftly unfolded the note and tore it into small pieces which she scattered like confetti. "There, what do you think of that?"

"I have a photo-copy," I lied.

The knuckles of the strong hands clenched whitely. "This is no concern of yours, nor of the police. It was a purely private matter."

"And extremely urgent."

161

She hesitated. "It seemed so at the time."

"And a few hours after receiving it, he was dead. I think the police would find that very interesting, don't you?"

She was shaking her head like an automaton. "The poor man fell . . . it was an accident."

"Lizzie," I persisted, "almost the first thing you said to me yesterday morning was, 'How could he have done such a dreadful thing?' You were convinced he had committed suicide. Why? You knew him better than I did. Why should he have wanted to kill himself? For what reason?" I pointed to the scattered scraps of paper. "Could that, perhaps, have had something to do with it?"

"No, of course not . . . you don't understand."

"Then make me understand, Lizzie. Believe it or not I'm on your side. You'll find it a lot easier to talk to me than to the police."

"But it's nothing to do with the police, I tell you," she wailed. "Or with you. Or . . ." she hesitated and added in a lower voice, "or with me, if it comes to that."

I sat in silence for a moment then said gently, "And yet you felt it necessary to write that note and deliver it to the theatre on a first night, when you knew perfectly well he was sweating on the top line to give what was probably the most important performance of his career. Wasn't that a little thoughtless?"

She was sniffing loudly, burrowing around among her cushions. "Did he contact you?" She made no answer; instead, unearthing a large handkerchief, she blew her nose loudly and with vigour. "Did he acknowledge the note?"

"No, he didn't."

I sat back with a sigh. I had pressed her enough. If she was going to break, now was the time. I watched her expressions gallop through a gamut of emotions, from self-pitying despair, through a mixture of tight-lipped anger, pique and sullen obstinacy, to resignation and self-reproach.

At last she tried to put it into words, slowly and with a great deal of confusion. "I just – I just wanted to . . . I didn't want Gerald to be . . ." She broke off, waving the handkerchief aimlessly like a flag of surrender. "It doesn't concern any of us, you see, Mr Savage. It was between Gerald and . . ." Again she hesitated.

"Emma Hardcastle?"

She gave a reluctant nod. "Yes, Emma. It's Emma's affair, not mine. It would be wrong of me to tell you. If you want to know about it you must ask her. If I interfered it was only to put Gerald on his guard." She stopped and snuffled again into the handkerchief.

From the end of the terrace I became aware of a stealthy thud followed by a faint creaking sound. "All right," I said, getting to my feet and raising my voice a little, "I'll just have to ask Emma, won't I?"

"So why don't you do that?" came Emma's cool voice behind me.

Lizzie's head went up, her eyes widening. I turned slowly.

She was balanced precariously on her sticks, swaying slightly, an enigmatic smile twisting her mouth. "Ask me." She creaked her way slowly on to the terrace.

I glanced back at Lizzie who was staring at Emma like a rabbit facing a stoat. Her mouth opened and shut a couple of times. "He was asking about you and Gerald, Emma dear," she said with difficulty, adding hastily, "I didn't tell him anything, of course."

"Why not?" Emma came to a halt, staring up at me with mocking eyes. "Why shouldn't he know? I'm only surprised he hasn't already guessed."

"Guessed what?" My voice was steady enough but my mind rocked with apprehension.

"That Gerald Grantley was my father."

In a TV soap-opera they would have cut to a close-up, brought up the music, and cued in the commercials. As it was, Gerald's clock chose that moment to strike the three-quarters. I needed all of that time and more, for even when the reverberations had finally died away I still hadn't got used to the idea.

"Ah," I said in a knowing voice and then shook my head. "No, oddly enough, that had never crossed my mind."

"And does it surprise you?"

"You could say that." I swung my chair around and offered

163

to take her sticks. For a long tense moment we stood eyeball to eyeball then she nodded curtly. "I'll sit with Lizzie."

While Lizzie patted cushions and made room for her, I collected her sticks and helped her on to the chaise-longue.

A stained and discoloured artist's smock covered the sludge dress she had worn the previous day, otherwise she looked much the same. She was rubbing her hands together like Lady Macbeth worried about blood. "I'm filthy," she told Lizzie. "I was messing around in the studio, heard you arguing and thought you might need some help."

I said with a smile, "You haven't done anything rash to your father's head, I hope."

She frowned up at me a little distantly as if she couldn't quite remember who I was.

Lizzie intervened. "Emma tells me you weren't all that taken with it – the head, I mean."

I shrugged. "If I'd known then what I know now, I might have been less prepared to criticise. I didn't much care for my father either."

"And mine," Lizzie chimed in stoutly, "was immortalised in *The Barretts of Wimpole Street.*" She reached for the aerosol and shot down a passing fly.

"There we are then," I nodded, "welcome to Father's Day," which brought an amused squawk from Lizzie and the suspicion of a smile even to Emma's lips.

Having established a bridge-head, I set about securing it. I turned to Emma. "Since you have broached the subject, would it be in order for me to ask a question or two?"

"You can ask."

I gathered my thoughts. "I take it that this father and daughter relationship is not common knowledge."

"Not yet."

"But you've always known he was your father?"

"No. My mother told me only a few months back – on her death bed," she added primly as if it were a quotation from somewhere.

"Were they married, your mother and Gerald?" She shook her head. "But he knew about you?"

"Apparently not."

164

"Until *you* told him?" Her silence was eloquent. "And when was that?"

"Three weeks ago."

More silence. "One day, he was over there in the summer-house sitting for his portrait and you said, 'Hello, Daddy, I'm your daughter'?"

She gave a frigid smile. "Something like that."

I smiled back. "I bet he was surprised."

"He found it difficult."

"I can understand that. A man in his late sixties wakes up one bright morning to find he has a grown daughter he's never been introduced to. Very difficult. And incredible, wouldn't you say?"

"I wouldn't, no. He probably fathered half a dozen brats he didn't want to know about."

I stared at her with dislike but let it pass. "And you see no reason to doubt the truth of it?" I raised a hand before she could take breath. "Deathbed confession . . . I do see your point."

I glanced at Lizzie. With mouth agape she could have been an overlarge fledgling vulture hungering after a morsel of warm human flesh.

I turned back to Emma Hardcastle. "Your mother didn't happen to mention why she hadn't told you all this before?"

"It was not something she was proud of – 'a roll in the hay' she called it. Also . . ." she hesitated, "she was a married woman at the time."

"To Mr Hardcastle?"

"No, to a Colonel Brooks. She was twice married and twice widowed. Colonel Brooks was killed in the war and she married my father soon afterwards – Charles Hardcastle. To all intents and purposes he was my father; he gave me his name and his affection even though he knew I didn't belong."

"And you never met Gerald Grantley until a few weeks ago?"

"Never once. But I saw him act." For the first time a splinter of goodwill flickered in her eyes. "That's where I first saw you – on the screen with him." Life seemed to stir in her. "He was the only Macbeth who made sense of the play all the way through. As I said yesterday, it was then that I made up my mind to do a

165

head of him." She gave a rueful shake of her head. "I wish now I had never followed it up."

Lizzie and I exchanged glances.

She went on. "In the last stages of the war he was a major in the army – an adjutant. He was wounded and shipped home on sick-leave. His CO, Colonel Brooks, asked him to say hello to his wife – my mother. Well, he did a lot more than say hello; he fathered me." She began scrubbing at her hands again. "What little affection there had been between my mother and Brooks had died long before the war. She said he was a typical army man in the worst sense of the word – a 'man's man' she called him."

She picked nervously at her fingernails. "The war came to an end and Gerald Grantley – Major Rosner as he was then – went back to Germany to occupied Berlin. Then it was the Colonel's turn for leave. He came home to find his wife seven months pregnant." Her eyes filled with tears. "She had refused to get rid of me. She looked upon me, she said, as a love-child." There was a long silence. "I was almost the death of her. He literally beat the truth out of her. I was born prematurely – like this . . ." her hands touched her knees tenderly as if they hurt ". . . half made. She never saw him again. He went back to Berlin thirsting for Gerald's blood. And was promptly killed. Thank God."

"Was there a confrontation?"

"If there had been Gerald would never have survived."

"How was he killed? You said the war was over."

"Not in Berlin it wasn't. The occupying forces were still being sniped at by Nazis in hiding or civilians resenting the enemy tramping through their streets. He was picked off by one of them."

"And Gerald came back?"

Her smile was full of wry amusement. "Oh yes, he came back all right, but not to my mother. She thought he'd been killed. She'd had no word from him. She made enquiries but nobody knew anything, until one day, years later, she saw a picture of him in a newspaper – or somebody who looked like him. The paper said his name was Grantley and that he was an actor."

She delved suddenly into the pocket of her smock, took out a

166

man's leather wallet, leafed through it and produced a newspaper cutting. "She kept it all those years. I found it among her things."

The paper was yellowed and falling apart at the folds, the photograph faded and bearing little resemblance to the Gerald Grantley I had known: the face less distinguished and lived-in, hair slicked back, dark and sleek, but the bones were there and the wide dazzling eyes. It was a review of something he had done at the Birmingham Playhouse. I didn't read it.

"Did your mother follow this up?"

"She saw the play."

"And?"

"There was no 'and' – she didn't go round to see him, if that's what you mean. She'd just wanted to make sure it was he."

I returned the cutting. "But if they'd been so close . . ."

She snapped back, "It was she who had been close, not he. Anyway," she added relenting a little, "it was all past history. She had married again and was happy. In those days we all lived in Evesham, right next door to Lizzie and Godfrey." She took Lizzie's hand. "I grew up under your eye, didn't I Lizzie?"

Lizzie patted the hand affectionately and looked modest. "Until we moved up here, yes."

"And I went down to London to the Polytechnic. When my father died, mother came to live with me." She was silent for a second or two. "It's strange, you know, when I saw Gerald's Macbeth at the Vic, mother was sitting right next to me and never turned a hair or said a word. I don't know why she told me at all. I'd have been quite happy to live and die as Emma Hardcastle. Conscience, I suppose. Maybe she thought I'd be thrilled to know who my real father was." She gave a wry smile. "She did me no service."

We all sat looking at our hands for a time in silence, then she took a deep breath. "When I heard he was coming up here to do *Lear* I shanghai'd God and Lizzie into letting me come and stay with them and they gave me the summer-house to work in."

"You knew Gerald lived here in Grantley too?"

"By that time, I knew everything there was to know about him. I had done my homework. I asked him if I could do a head of him and he positively preened. He co-operated too, came

167

whenever he could get away from rehearsals and costume fittings and all that. But the more I got to know him, the less I liked him. I found him . . . well, I've said all that . . ." She caught my eye. "All right, so I was prejudiced, but how could I help it? I couldn't forget how he had – used my mother and then just dropped her as if she were a . . ." She left the sentence unfinished and continued more calmly. "As the sittings went on he seemed to – disintegrate: that's the only word to describe it. He was impossible, short-tempered, moody, and kept going off into a sort of daze; his face almost seemed to sag. I naturally put it down to his work. He hated everything that was going on at the theatre. Then, quite suddenly, I'd had enough of it. I was stupid enough to ask him if anything was wrong. Do you know what he said? 'What effing business is it of yours, woman?' So far as I was concerned, it was the last straw. I just erupted and told him exactly what business it was of mine – who I was and what I was. I was so mad I could have killed him, right there, on the spot. Maybe if I could have stood upright on my own two rotten legs, I would have done. Then I turned him out – told him I never wanted to see him again."

"And did you?"

"I never even went to his damned first night."

"When did all this happen?"

"Last week some time, I don't remember. I know I came and wept all over poor Lizzie."

Lizzie engulfed her in a protective and possessive arm. "What are friends for if you can't turn to them in need?" Clamping Emma's narrow shoulders to her she turned to me. "And having got it off her chest she was prepared to tell the world. The newspapers, Connie, Richard Rosner. Can you imagine what Richard would have done with it, the vicious little brute? So we talked it over, didn't we dear, and decided, in the end, that only Connie should know." She frowned at me and shook her head meaningly. "But not until the first night was over – that would really have upset the apple-cart." With her eyes still on mine she spoke to Emma. "But you won't do that now, will you, dear? Not now that he's gone. Connie's been hurt enough. Everyone's been hurt enough – you included. And it's not really Connie's fault, is it? And Gerald's

168

dead . . . You can only hurt his memory and what good would that do?"

When she attempted to kiss her cheek Emma turned away and extricated herself awkwardly from the suffocating embrace, her helplessly flaying arms and legs making me think, incongruously, of a duckling emerging from its shell. "I'd like to be on my own for a bit, Lizzie, if you wouldn't mind."

I was at her side, sticks at the ready, helping her to her feet. I could feel her trembling. Our eyes met. "Thank you, Mr Savage," she whispered. As I offered to take her arm she muttered irritably, "I can manage."

With a certain amount of regret that I had made an enemy of her I watched her thump and creak her way into the darkness of the house. When I turned back, it was to find Lizzie on her knees reaching for the littered fragments of her note to Gerald. An unexpected flurry of a breeze snatched them from her and lifted them like blue butterflies across the lawn. Resigned, she sat back on her heels. "I wanted to warn Gerald, that was all," she said in a low voice. "So he could talk to Connie before Emma got to her. After all, Gerald was a friend too."

Refusing an invitation to tea, I left her with a promise to call again, and as I retraced my steps through the rhododendrons, the church clock struck three with ponderous gravity.

I thought about Gerald, heard his loud and ready laughter, saw, in my mind's eye, his wide, frank and open face . . .

Chapter Fourteen

I wheeled the Honda up to the Grantley house – less than a quarter of a mile didn't interest her – and overtook Arch in the driveway pushing a wheelbarrow.

I drew alongside him. *"Hic et ubique,"* I greeted him.

He dropped the barrow and doffed his school cap. "I shouldn't wonder if you're not right there, guv."

"Never know where you're going to pop up next."

"I get around, Mr Bond, I get around."

"Like Hamlet's dad."

"That good or bad?"

"Depends how you look at it. He was dead at the time. You going to be around for a bit longer?"

"'Til four, thereabouts."

I pushed the Honda into the garage. "I'll look you up."

Heaving the bike on to the rest I wandered inquisitively around Gerald's elderly Jaguar. An old eiderdown had been draped over her bonnet – hardly to keep the engine from freezing up. With a fair amount of reluctance I stripped it away and felt my shoulders sag as I stared despondently at the nearside wing. There wasn't a great deal of damage but it was enough: an impacted dent about three inches across, a couple of hefty scratches, and some abrasions scored deeply into the paintwork as far back as the centre of the passenger door. There was also something odd about the wing mirror. A closer look suggested that it had been badly bent outwards and had undergone an unsuccessful attempt to straighten it. Evidence enough to drag the driver into a police court.

Why in hell hadn't he stopped? A phone call to the nearest cop-shop and it would have been a different ball-game altogether, guilty or not, and never a blackmailer in sight.

As I carefully replaced the eiderdown, I became aware of the two half-moons scoured into the grime of the windscreen by the wipers. I climbed into the driving seat. At the time of the accident it must have been raining; if so, the car hadn't been out on the road since.

Foraging through the glovebox, various pockets and compartments, I poked fastidiously into an ashtray crammed with cigarette stubs. Camels. Who smoked Camels any more? Had Gerald smoked? And hadn't I asked that question before somewhere?

I came across a flashlight and directed its beam on to the floor; dried mud on both rubber foot-mats. I brooded over the passenger mat. Had he picked someone up that night? A hitch-hiker perhaps? I eyed the prints blankly. Sherlock Holmes would have known the type, make and size of the passenger's shoes, where they were made, where bought, where they had been for the last twenty-four hours, and who the mud belonged to. Well, bully for him! He could go jump in the Avon.

It wasn't until I was in the act of closing the garage doors that it occurred to me that I was being more than usually thick.

For a lengthy moment I stood watching a number plate, painfully rejigging my thoughts.

The car I had followed on Saturday night after the show, and driven by Connie Grantley with her husband beside her, was not the car now standing in Gerald's garage. In the darkness it may have looked the same but the number prefix, highlighted by my headlamp, had been BOL – I know because I had made up a couple of acronyms with it: Best Of Luck, and Bugger Old Lear, neither of them prize winners but sufficient unto the day. The prefix of the car now squatting before me was XUC.

I back-tracked mentally to Saturday night.

Gerald had been out of the car ready and waiting for me as I had parked the Honda and unscrewed my skid-lid; Connie had already driven off "to put the car away" he'd said, taking me by the arm and leading me joyously up the garden path as is the wont of attentive hosts.

Carefully I shoved the garage doors shut.

"Something wrong, guv?"

It was Arch, sitting in his wheelbarrow, licking a home-made cigarette into shape.

171

I jerked my head at the garage. "Car laid up is she?"

He nodded. "Up the spout."

"How up the spout?"

"Old age, I reckon. They've 'ad 'er nigh on twenty years. Said 'er wouldn't start. They been renting one."

"How long?"

He struck a match. "'Ow long what?"

"Have they been renting?"

The loosely packed cigarette burst into flame like a bushfire until I feared for the well-being of his nose. Through the dense curtain of blue smoke he eyed me warily as he thumbed out the match and said nothing.

"Oh come on, Arch, you promised to co-operate. Days? Weeks? How long?"

He palmed the blazing cigarette and picked an irksome-looking strand of black tobacco from his upper lip. "Weeks, I reckon. Owbridge'll know, if you're that interested. 'E's the 'ire firm – crummy business, only a couple of cars – five minutes up the road, on the corner. They garridge it up there too. It's 'andy for them." The cigarette was back in his mouth, his eyes narrowed against the smoke. "Still, soon as the missus gets 'erself sorted out she'll let old 'Arry 'Obson 'ave a look at it, I shouldn't wonder, get 'er going again."

"No." I interrupted him. "Listen Arch . . ." I closed in on him and lowered my voice. "You mustn't let her do that, understand? Tell her anything at all, but don't let her put that car on the road again – not yet anyway."

The shrewd blue eyes widened slightly and flickered towards the house. "I can't tell 'er that. I'm only the dogsbody 'ere, not the bleeding chauffeur."

"All right, understood. But listen, if your guv'nor ever meant anything at all to you and you care about Lady Constance's peace of mind . . ."

"Mark . . .?" It was Connie's voice calling from the house; she was at the open window of the downstairs sitting-room. "I thought I heard your voice. Are you coming in? Hello, Arch . . ."

I waved to her, hissing the while at the top of Arch's head. "Don't leave without first talking to me. It's important."

"Okay, guv, if that's what you want." He dropped me a stagey wink. "Mum's the word."

"I've just made some tea," greeted Connie, meeting me in the hall. "Will you stay and have a cup?"

Following her into the sitting-room I avoided Gerald's chair lounging alongside the debauched triffid, and, while she ducked into the kitchen for another cup, stood at the window watching the roses and wondering again about the pink one in the water-glass upstairs on her bedside table.

Joining her on the sofa I cast a surreptitious eye over her as she poured tea. In grey pleated linen skirt, trim white silk blouse and pearls at her throat – no widow's weeds for her, thank God; she was one of the enlightened – she was immaculate again, each white hair in place, cheeks slightly over-powdered perhaps, lips delicately pink tinted and perfect; only the shadows about the eyes and the raw pain within them betrayed her inner distress.

"There are only biscuits, I'm afraid," she murmured passing me a cup of impossibly pale tea. "I haven't really felt up to getting out and about – meeting people." She watched me while I took a genteel sip at my cup, then, gently clearing her throat, tore into the inevitable question: "How are you getting on?"

Despite her previous insistence on knowing the truth no matter what, there was nothing I felt I could bring myself to tell her – like for instance: "Did you know your husband was a killer and was being blackmailed?" or, "By the way, you may be surprised to know that you have a talented and illegitimate step-daughter . . ." She wasn't ready for any of that, nor, if I could help it, would she learn it from me.

With sinking spirits I recalled her panegyric: "He's never stepped out of line, never done anything dishonourable or reprehensible . . ." She needed confirmation not denial.

"Mark . . .?" Her voice broke into my thoughts.

"I heard you," I smiled. "I was just wondering how I *have* been getting on." I paused and took a deep breath. "As a matter of interest, Connie, how long had he been a diabetic?"

She looked surprised. "A long time now; years – fifteen, twenty years. How did you know about that?"

"Sugar in his pockets, tablets and insulin in his bedside-cabinet drawer."

"He didn't like anyone to know about it."

"Nothing to be ashamed of."

"Of course there wasn't. I used to tell him that, so did the doctor. It was under control but only because Dr Nathan kept at him all the time. He was always forgetting his tablets, and, of course, never carried his card with him – they're all supposed to carry cards, you know, saying that they're diabetics, in case of an accident, or a fainting fit in the street." She broke off, frowning at me. "You don't think . . .?"

I shrugged. "The post mortem should tell us. From what little I know about diabetes, excessive exercise, unless balanced by extra food and medications, can be pretty dangerous. In Gerald's case, and at his age, playing King Lear and rehearsing for six weeks, would come under the heading of excessive exercise, wouldn't you say? *Was* he eating more? *Did* he take any extra medicines? Because if he didn't . . ." I left the sentence unfinished.

There was silence between us, then she said, "He was seeing quite a lot of Dr Nathan – they were good friends – so presumably John would have been keeping an eye on him. He certainly wasn't eating any more – if anything he was losing a little weight, but whether or not he was taking extra tablets, I really couldn't say. He never talked about it."

I said, "Suppose, for instance, he couldn't sleep after the excitement of Saturday night and went up there on the tower for a breath of air . . . and suppose the level of his – what do they call it, blood sugar, is it? – if that had fallen he could quite easily have become light-headed and simply lost his balance . . ."

"But he *was* sleeping," she interrupted. "When I went in to say goodnight he was dead to the world, snoring like a grampus, his clothes all over the place; I picked them up, folded them away, but he never stirred. Once he was asleep nothing would wake him."

"Something did," I reminded her quietly. "He got up, dressed and walked out of the house without disturbing you."

"You think he was pretending to be asleep?"

"I think he was a good actor, and even the simplest of us can give a pretty fair imitation of a snore. If you'd known he was awake you'd have sat up and fussed over him, read *Winnie the Pooh* aloud, and made yourself a general nuisance, like wives do." I grinned, then clumsily changed the subject. "While I remember it . . . Your car in the garage; Arch was telling me she's out of commission. Do you know what's wrong with her?"

She shook her head. "Gerald just said she was *kaput* – his word, not mine. She's very ancient, of course, and has been giving us a lot of trouble lately. So he went off and hired a self-drive. Why do you ask?"

I shrugged. "I just wondered if you'd mind me taking a look at her. It's a pity to be without your own transport just now, and I'm one of those idiots who like to think they know all there is to know about cars. I'm what is known as a tinkerer."

She smiled for the first time. "Please tinker away then. I think you'll be wasting your time. I'll give you my keys, or better still take Gerald's, then you can hang on to them. They're upstairs on his dressing-table."

"How long has the car been laid up?"

"Oh, some weeks now. He had to go over to Birmingham for something or other, something to do with the play . . . Oh yes, of course, it was a local radio interview for the BBC. He came home very late and drenched to the skin – bad tempered too, said he'd had to get out and push at one stage. He only just managed to limp home. Poor old Gerry, how he hated mechanical things."

Suddenly, without any warning, the tears came; she scrabbled in her sleeve for a handkerchief and I took her by the shoulders and held her close – a situation I was fast becoming accustomed to. The front of my shirt was getting used to it too.

"Arch," I said, eyeing the lawn-mower, "were you thinking of mowing the lawn?"

"I just done it."

"You wouldn't care to run over it again, I suppose?" As he was drawing breath I went on, "I need noise, Arch. I want to start up the car and don't want her ladyship to hear it."

"No fear o' that – she won't start up."

175

"Bear with me, will you, Arch, please? Just chase it around the garden a couple of circuits, that's all I ask."

He grinned and touched his cap. "Right, Mr Bond."

"And don't call me Mr Bond."

"Right, guv."

As I shut the garage doors behind me and checked the communicating door between house and garage, the clatter of the lawn-mower shattered the stillness; it sounded like a Jumbo-jet clearing its throat; you could have blown a safe and got away with it.

I clambered glumly into the driving seat, inserted the key and switched on. I had expected the engine to purr, rattle or roar into life – whichever it did best. I was disappointed. It did nothing at all. It really was *kaput*. I tried again, a couple of times, but it was as dead as a doornail, not even the grind of a flat battery.

Taking the flashlight, I slipped off the eiderdown and, opening up the bonnet, shoved my head into the works. It wasn't very complicated; he had just disconnected the battery terminals. I reconnected them, switched on and away she went, quite sweetly considering her age.

Shutting her down again, I sat for a second or two worrying about the next move, wondering whether the cops would still be on the look-out for a vehicle involved in a hit-and-run incident several weeks old. It was highly probable that a police directive had been issued to all repair-shops in the neighbourhood itemising the possible nature of damage sustained by the lethal vehicle.

I disconnected the battery terminals again, planted the distributor-head with a dead geranium in a nearby flowerpot, wheeled the Honda out of the garage and locked the doors behind me.

Arch was charging around the back lawn with his motor-mower like a demented charioteer. As he turned into the straight I stood boldly in his path; the machine came to a halt two inches from my toecaps. When he switched off the engine the silence hurt my ears.

"Nearly 'ad you then," he grinned, panting like Pheidippides. "'ow was it? Get 'er going, did you?"

"No sweat." I gave him a smug smile and nodded at the mower. "Where does it live?"

"Round the back in the shed."

"Let's go."

I glanced guiltily up at the house as we moved off. I had left Connie in the front sitting-room and hoped she was there still. Not that it mattered if she caught us sloping off into the undergrowth together, but explanations of clandestine assignations are always a bore and rarely ring true.

The shed in question was a creosoted wooden affair jacked up on a platform of yellow brickwork overlooking a small but functional kitchen-garden.

Jam-packed with garden tools it was completely airless and smelled of hot rubber and paraffin.

Helping him up the steps with the mower, I watched, scarcely able to breathe, while he detached the grass-box and covered the machine with a decrepit army groundsheet – the source of the rubberised oxygen.

Turning away, I collapsed on to the step, closed my eyes against the sun and waited for him to join me. A couple of squirts of compressed air and he was looming over me, an open can of beer in his outstretched hand. I took it gratefully. "Mud in your eye," I said, "and come and sit down if you have a spare moment."

He hunkered up beside me on the step, moulded his schoolcap carefully to his knee and took a long swallow of beer. He smelled of sweat and hair-oil; I edged away a little.

"Arch," I said. "The car . . . there's nothing wrong with it. She's been sabotaged – by your guv'nor."

He stared at me in disbelief. "Why would 'e do that?"

And I told him, as monosyllabically as possible. When I'd finished he was deep in a concentrated study of his wellington boots. I took a drink of warm beer and awaited his reactions.

"It was all in the paper," he said at last in a subdued voice. "Weeks back now, it was. Bloke was 'igh as a kite, they said, so it would've been as much 'is fault as the guv'nor's." He frowned. "'E should 'ave stopped though." Then he brightened a little. "Still, no one saw it actually 'appen 'parently, that's one comfort. They said it was pissing with rain at the time and

177

luckily no one was about. So they 'aven't got nothing on 'im really, 'ave they?"

"Not unless they find the car."

Scratching at his stubbly chin, he nodded thoughtfully. "So what we've got to do . . ."

". . . is get rid of it," I finished smartly. "Or get it repaired by someone who can keep a still tongue in his head."

"Easier said than done, guv."

I gave a dismissive shrug. "There's a price for everything. One more thing, Arch. Apparently there *was* a witness." He blinked at me. "A witness who was asking your guv'nor for ten thousand quid for keeping his mouth shut."

"Not blackmail?"

"Blackmail."

"Did he pay up?"

"If he didn't, we can have a damn good guess as to what his next step will be."

He pursed his lips into a silent whistle. "'E'll 'ave a go at the missus?"

I raised a finger. "On the nose."

Reaching abstractedly into his pocket he produced his cigarette manufacturing machine. I edged away a further couple of inches and watched apprehensively as he selected a paper and poked a grubby and preoccupied finger into a tinful of evil-looking tobacco. "No idea 'oo this bugger is, I suppose?"

"Not yet, no. That's my job. Yours, if you feel so inclined, is to sniff out someone who'll cope with the car. I'll cover expenses. But we'll have to work fast. If he hasn't already been paid he's not going to hang about long."

I watched furtively as the stubby fingers rolled and fumbled the paper and tobacco into a travesty of a cigarette. He said, "First thing is to get that jallopy out o' the garridge and 'idden away before the rozzers get around to it, right?" I nodded. "You can count on me."

He stuck out his tongue and gave his cigarette a long sensual lick; when he offered it to me I shied away from it like a frightened virgin. "I don't," I muttered thankfully and cringed as he boldly set fire to it and engulfed us both in a noisome cloud of thick black smoke.

178

"You'll set fire to your eyebrows one of these days," I choked through the gloom.

"Funny you should say that," he coughed reminiscently. "I did once."

I waited until things had settled down to near normal. "There's one more thing you can do for me," I said tentatively, mentally crossing my fingers. We'd had decision time, now it was hunch-and-crunch time. He was sprawled untidily on the step, head back against the wall, eyes closed, enjoying his shaggy cigarette. "Tell me about Berlin."

His Adam's apple gave a convulsive leap and his eyes snapped open. Slowly he turned his head and watched me with the wariness of a trapped animal. "Berlin?"

I nodded. "Major Rosner and Colonel Brooks. Tell me about them."

"Colonel Brooks?" he muttered huskily, as if he'd never heard of him.

"You remember Colonel Brooks, your commanding officer? Killed shortly after he came back from leave in England."

A pulse was thumping away in his temple. Now he was nodding in time to it. "*That* Colonel Brooks, right, yes, I remember now. A sniper got 'im. They was all about them snipers, even if the war was supposed to be over. Some said it was the Ruskies – they didn't like us much, the Ruskies. They didn't like anybody much."

In the almost awesome silence which followed, Gerald's clock began to give voice above our heads. His head swung a little towards the sound, tilted slightly, as if listening, not to the chimes but to some inner, clairaudient voice. When the last sounds had died away, he gave me an uneasy sidelong glance and draining the rest of his beer in a series of convulsive gulps, crushed the can in his fist and flung it over his shoulder into the hut with a clang.

He nodded. "Them snipers. After dark you 'ad to walk about with your eyes in the back of your 'ead, know what I mean? 'E was shot right through 'is medals."

"You saw it, did you?"

"I 'eard about it."

"Come on, Arch, what really happened?"

"I told you."

He fell silent, his mouth compressed and sullen. He tore at the ill-made cigarette, scattering scraps of paper and tobacco, glowing sparks shooting from the ends of his stubby fingers. "Arch, listen to me." He shook his head and made to rise. I grabbed violently at his thigh and held him down. "You bloody will listen to me, whether you like it or not. As a friend and colleague, Gerald Grantley meant as much to me as he did to you as an officer and guv'nor. I'm not out to destroy his memory but to protect it, no matter what. But I have to know 'no matter what', don't you see that? Only by *knowing* can I avoid messing about with half-truths if and when I have to face his wife with it. Only by knowing about this accident of his, can I be certain of keeping Connie out of it – otherwise she could go steaming off in that car and get herself arrested by the first beady-eyed copper on point-duty. Now, to get back to Major Gerald Rosner and his commanding officer: there's another angle to that story which even you may not know about. A daughter has turned up." He stared up at me, his jaw sagging. "Yes, the daughter your young Major spawned on his CO's wife when he was on leave here in England back in '45. And that daughter is threatening to turn nasty and spill her all to Connie. Whether she will or not, now that Gerald's dead, remains to be seen, but before, and if, she does, *I* want to know all about it – everything. Then, if things turn prickly for Connie, I can at least head her off from the more sordid details."

I fell back exhausted. If he didn't come clean now, he never would. He'd die with his bloody boots on. He hadn't been exactly galvanised into action by my plaintive peroration. I had released his leg long ago but he was still busy massaging it as if I'd done it irreparable damage. Finished with that, he again took up a moody stare at his boots which went on for what seemed like half a century. I was beginning to think I had lost him for ever when he cleared his throat and heaved a loud, put-upon sigh.

"Okay, guv," he muttered in a resigned voice, "if that's what you want . . ." A moment's silence while he collected his thoughts. "Right then . . . Colonel Brooks comes back from leave in England like 'e's 'ad a stroke or something, and first thing I know 'e's stalking into the guv's quarters with murder in 'is eye and chucking me out on my ear. Well, I 'ung about in the 'all, trying to 'ear what was going on. I 'eard the Colonel shouting: 'You dirty little Jew-boy, we'll settle this once and for all.' That was all, then 'e was out again like a dose of salts, shoving me up against the wall like I wasn't there. I went in to see if the guv was all right. 'E was sitting at 'is desk sort of laughing like. "Ow would you like to be my second, Corporal?' 'e says. 'Second what?' I says thinking it was a joke. But no, it wasn't no joke – far from it."

He half swivelled round to face me. "You're not going to believe this, Mr Bond, but that so-and-so 'ad challenged 'im to a duel." He stared at me nodding his head at my show of disbelief. "Straight up. Army revolvers at dawn, sort of thing. 'Cept that it wasn't going to be at dawn but some time during the night. A duel, I ask you! Even the guv thought 'e was bonkers."

He paused for a second, waving his hands vaguely in front of him as if to set the scene.

"Like you said, the guv 'ad been over 'ere on leave 'aving it away with the colonel's missus and the silly cow 'ad got 'erself this bun in the oven, if you get my meaning. Not surprising the CO was all steamed up about it. But 'e couldn't just bash the guv on the nose like anyone else, could 'e? Oh no, that'd be breaking army regulations – superior officer striking subordinate, and all that crap – 'e was a great one for the book – so 'e settles for this duel. Honour and all that. Anyway, the guv says would I go with 'im in case anything 'appened to 'im.

"So there we were, in the middle of the bloody night among all them ruins, cold and wet, miserable as 'ell crawling around in the dark with no one about 'cept jeep patrols to keep us company. We 'ad to keep our 'eads down when they come around."

He was silent for some time. I didn't prompt him. I sat instead communing with myself and doing my best to come to terms with the bizarre events he was describing. A duel yet! An affair of honour . . . in the middle of war ravaged Berlin . . .

Arch continued almost in an undertone. "So, up comes 'is nibs with 'is batman, a corporal like me . . . Corporal Jameson

181

'e was, younger 'n me. It was like one o' them war pictures – two blokes fighting over the same woman. 'Back to back,' says 'e. 'Ten paces, turn and fire, one shot each.' Well, I mean, it would 'ave been funny anywhere else. The guv says as much. 'Let's settle it some other way,' 'e says and the Colonel just slaps 'im right across the face. Well, o' course, that really got the guv's dander up, and the duel's on, back to back with their guns out.

"Well, the corporal starts counting. There's 'ardly any light to see by. I'm watching the guv and see 'im turn. The Colonel fires first and misses and I see the guv taking careful aim – I remember seeing the whites of 'is eyes sort of shining in the dark, and the Colonel just standing there, waiting for it. Bang, and it's all over. I never believed the guv would do it, but 'e did, just like that – bang – in cold blood.

"Me and Jameson goes over to 'ave a look at 'im. 'E's lying there with an 'ole in his chest. Then little old Corporal Jameson loses 'is 'ead and starts bawling at the guv and calling 'im a murderer, then off 'e goes yelling for the patrol . . . mad little bugger . . . mad, stupid little bugger . . ."

He sniffed loudly and scrubbed at his eyes.

"What happened?"

He was having difficulty with his voice. "'E shot 'im, didn't 'e? Shot 'im in the back." He turned, his face drawn, devastated by the memory. "The guv shot 'im down like 'e was a rabbit. Then 'e just drops 'is gun in the mud and walks away like nothing's 'appened. I only stayed long enough to pick up the gun and shove it in my pocket, then I went after 'im." He was silent for a bit. "I 'spect it's the same gun what was under 'is bed – 'e 'ung on to it, I shouldn't wonder."

He made some snuffling noises then creaked slowly to his feet, shook himself down and went into the hut in search of some more beer. I could hear him discreetly blowing his nose.

"I imagine all sorts of official enquiries were made?" I said as he handed me a second beer.

"They didn't go into it much. Wasn't time in them days – too much else to do, everything being shot up like it was. They dug out the bullets, though, 'cos there was this scare about the Ruskies being on the loose, so they wanted to make sure they

182

weren't Russian bullets. Then a rumour went around that the bullets were British, and that was the end of it, nobody never 'eard nothing more." He was staring at the backs of his hands, shaking his head. "I can't ever forget the way he . . . That poor little Jameson sod . . . 'e 'adn't done nothing."

Opening his beer he took a long, grateful drink and wiped his mouth on his sleeve. He gave an involuntary shudder as if suddenly chilled, clearly distressed by the memories he had disturbed. "I never told all that to a living soul before," he muttered in a slightly aggressive tone.

I nodded, opened my beer and saluted him with the can. "I raise my hat to you, Arch."

He also nodded and we drank together.

"Does it clear anything up?"

I shook my head glumly. "If anything, it's muddied the water even more. That's my fault. I asked for it."

He took another lengthy drink, gave a polite burp, tapped his chest a couple of times like a penitent doing his *mea culpas*, and muttered, "Pardon me," in a distracted murmur.

"Arch," I said, "just for the record – why did you stay with him for so long? It's over forty years now. I'd have thought – after all that – well, the way you told it just now, it seemed you hadn't a lot of sympathy for what he did."

He pursed his lips. "I 'adn't. Still 'aven't. But 'e wasn't 'imself, was 'e?" He cocked an eye at me. "You weren't in the war, were you?"

"I wasn't born."

"Count your lucky stars, mate. With all that going on, you start to *think* different, know what I mean? You change, do things you thought you could never do. Like I said, I can't ever forget what 'e did to little Jamie, but I know *why* he did it. If there wasn't going to be no witnesses, 'e 'ad to do it."

"*You* were a witness."

"But I was 'is man, wasn't I? I was more bothered about 'im than I was about the other two. Brooks brought it on 'imself, and Jamie got in the way. I didn't owe 'em anything. With the guv it was different; with 'im it was a question of . . ." He shook his head, looking for a word.

"Loyalty?"

"You could put it like that, I s'pose. Loyalty, why not? I'll settle for that. I was right too. 'E was a great lad."

"So after your demob, what happened?"

He gave a stifled snort. "The day *before* my demob I got run over by a truck, didn't I? One of ours too! I 'ad both me legs up for months. I wasn't always like this, you know, I was four inches taller for one thing. When I come out of the 'ospital 'e says to me, 'Arch,' 'e says, 'why don't you come and work for me?' Well, why not? I thought. I didn't 'ave no one to come back to, no mum or dad, no wife, not even a job. So I said, okay, yes, I'd do that."

"And when did he change his name?"

The abrupt question threw him. "When?" He shrugged. "Soon as 'e was demobbed."

"Did he say why?"

"Look, I was just 'is old corporal, wasn't I, not 'is bosom pal."

"But you guessed there was a reason?"

He hesitated, then shrugged again. "It's only a guess, but it could 'ave been something to do with 'im being a Jew. The day the papers came with 'is new name and that, 'e got tanked up. 'Arch,' 'e says, 'I'm respectable at last. I'm not a Jew any longer, so you'd better drink my 'ealth.' And 'e never mentioned it again – not ever. I reckon 'e'd 'ad just about enough of it. Some people can be right bastards about Jews 'specially at school and in the army. Funny thing is, I never knew 'e was one 'til I 'eard the Colonel shooting 'is mouth off.

"Well, then 'e married the missus and they come up 'ere to live. And 'e kindly set me up in a little place, too, just down the road. 'E didn't want me to 'ave to live in, see, said I'd be better off in a place of my own. It's not much but it's 'ome." He raised his beer can. "And that's the story of my life."

Again we drank to each other.

"Guv," he said, wiping the top of his can with the heel of his hand, "this daughter of 'is . . ."

"What about her?"

"She around?"

When I hesitated, he looked me straight in the eye. "I told *you* everything . . ."

184

"She's around; staying with the Ardens as a matter of fact."
His eyes rounded. "You don't mean . . .?"

I nodded. "Emma Hardcastle."

He continued to hold me with his eyes. "But she's . . ."

"Crippled? Yes. The direct result of her mother being beaten up by her loving husband, your Colonel Brooks, before he steamed back to Berlin to get shot through the medals."

He digested that in silence, letting out his breath slowly like a deflating balloon. I finished my beer and flung the can over my shoulder into the hut. His followed shortly afterwards.

We sat deep in thought for several minutes, then he stirred and stretched himself, burped again and shook his head. "It's what they say, isn't it?"

"What is what they say?"

"All that about being a tangled web . . ."

Chapter Fifteen

Connie was in the front garden standing forlornly among the roses, like Ruth, breast-high amid the alien corn. The tears were there too; a discreet gesture brushed them aside as she became aware of my approach; when she turned to greet me a bright smile was fastened securely into place. "Mark, I thought you had gone."

"I was just having a word with Arch."

"How's the car?"

"Gerald was right. She's *kaput* enough to resist all my puny efforts. But Arch thinks he might know of a little man who could breathe some life into her, so I'll leave the keys with him – they might have to tow her away. Is that in order?"

She was barely listening, turning away and, head bent, was cupping a crimson rose in the palm of her hand. "Isn't that beautiful?" she murmured. "Crimson Glory. We've had a really lovely show this year, and still have, late as it is. Roses were Gerry's pride and joy, you know."

"What was the name of the pink one in his pocket?"

A moment's pause. "The Doctor, I think."

I glanced in the direction of her gaze half expecting to see Dr Nathan on his way, but apart from a Post Office van the road was empty. She caught my thought and smiled over her shoulder. "That's the name of the rose."

"The Doctor? Funny name for a rose."

"Oh, I don't know. There's a Whisky Mac over there, and a Just Joey, a Topsy, a Mrs Sam McGredy . . . it just depends who originally cultivated it. Mark . . ." she changed the subject impulsively. "Is there nothing you can tell me? Have you found out anything at all?"

I shook my head. "Nothing really definite, no. We've got to remember that our suspicions about the possibility of foul play

186

are completely unfounded – except for a deep-rooted belief that Gerald would not have taken his own life. Our killer may not exist; I hope to God he doesn't. At the moment everything points to an accident."

"That's what the police say," she retorted with a little show of impatience.

"Well, don't let's knock it. Let's hang on to it as long as we can. Better that than either of the alternatives – at least your worst fears would be laid to rest."

"I suppose so." She patted my hand affectionately. "Well, I mustn't hold you up. I'm sure you want to get on. But you must promise to tell me everything you find out."

I gave her a foxy smile. "I promise to tell you everything I think you should know."

"That's not quite the same thing."

I kissed her cheek. "That's what you're going to have to settle for, Connie darling. Oh, one other thing – would you mind if I had a quick pry through Gerald's desk before I go?"

"Of course not. It'll be in a terrible mess. Are you looking for anything in particular?"

I gave a noncommital shrug. "I'll know that when I find it. Sure you don't mind?"

"I don't think I mind anything any more."

Turning away, I came face to face with a bushful of pink roses. "Are these Doctors?" I asked, sidestepping them adroitly.

She shook her head. "The Doctors are in the back garden beyond the lawn. They were Gerald's favourites."

Returning to the house I found myself immersed in a reconstruction of Gerald's movements on that last night. His need for stealth would have dictated the use of the lawn – past the rose-bed – to the back gate – rather than the front path which was heavily gravelled and made a noise like Brighton beach. He had probably torn the rose from the bush himself. But why, when it was practically a house-rule that the roses were not to be picked? The very act of breaking so simple yet so dogmatic a rule suggested, to me at least, a spur-of-the-moment gesture – of defiance perhaps, even finality – like the hoisting of his blazer on the flagstaff.

Suppose, for the sake of argument, he had known he was going to his death, what would be more natural than to take along with him something which Connie had called his pride and joy – as a Christian martyr would have taken a cross, or a battle-bound soldier a picture of his nearest and dearest?

I wondered about the other doctor, the human one, Doctor John Nathan. Did the name of the rose have any significance? "I am picking a rose called the Doctor because a doctor is about to knock me off the top of the tower. For Doctor Rose please read Doctor Nathan . . ."

I blew myself an impolite raspberry. In his shoes I wouldn't have bothered about the bloody rose; your average detective wouldn't know the difference between horticulture and pisciculture. I'd have dashed off a sharp note to the local constabulary and left it propped up on the mantelpiece where everyone would see it. Better still, I wouldn't have kept the appointment.

No, the rose would seem to me to be a comforter of sorts, a talisman, something to touch, to linger over, before . . .

The study was airless and smelled closed-up and musty. I padded over to the windows and threw them open. Outside it was pretty airless too.

For a second or two I stood looking out over the lawn towards the great spreading oak and to the roses beyond, pink and red and yellow . . .

A few hours ago the idea of his suicide had been unthinkable; now, in the light of what I had since learned, the cracks in his make-up were beginning to show, like faults in the fabric of a condemned building.

With a four-letter expletive on my lips I turned back into the room.

Desks are depressing affairs at the best of times. If a man doesn't happen to have a personal valet to answer your questions, the next best thing is his desk; all manner of trivia hoarded for no obvious reason will point to hidden traits of character you never even dreamed of. Stationery, Sellotape, address books and sticky labels I could understand, but inoperable ball-point pens, buttons, fuses, a box of farthings, and an old Vick inhaler were something else entirely and told me nothing other than the fact that he had been a picker-up-of-and-holder-on-to-unconsidered-trifles *par excellence*.

With little hope of turning up anything of significance, I picked over the scripts, blew off the dust and placed them in a neat pile. They all looked like the kiss of death to me. I riffled through the bills and receipts beneath the brass paperweight, most of them household accounts — gas, electricity, car-maintenance and so on.

As in his dressing-room, the one bright spot was the mandatory locked drawer. With Gerald's keys in my possession I was into that in no time at all.

The first thing that came to light was his last will and testament. Since it was in an unsealed envelope I took a quick peek at it. Simplicity itself: everything he died possessed of went to Connie; in the event of her pre-decease, to son Richard. No other beneficiaries.

Next came a couple of building society pass-books revealing savings amounting to a little over twenty thousand pounds; a folder containing monthly returns of a personal current account — not a joint account — with the Bank of Scotland, the most recent showing a credit in excess of twelve hundred pounds. So, although he was not wanting a ready penny or two, it was not the sort of fortune one might have expected not only from a knight of the realm but also from one of the most prestigious actors of our time. But then, prestigiousness does not necessarily include financial rewards. You can play Hamlet for peanuts and soap opera for millions. To the best of my knowledge Gerald made only two major movies, both for Andrew Elliot, and he hadn't been exactly the big spender of the year.

However, the contents of one drawer didn't necessarily represent the complete particulars of a man's financial status; there could be investments, bonds, shares, a dabble or two on the Stock Exchange, even Ernie; he could have run a tame stock-broker, rented a deposit box somewhere, crammed with convertible assets like jewellery, diamonds, gold bars and stamp-collections. But one thing was certain: although he had enough ready money to pay off the blackmailer there was no evidence here that he had done so. For apart from various

189

insurance policies covering his life, car, house and house contents, the drawer contained only one other item of interest: a photograph, dog-eared and faded, of a handsome, dark-eyed, middle-aged woman with a forties' hair-do. A bold hand had inscribed *Gerry, Love, Miriam* in the bottom right-hand corner.

I stood it up against the brass paperweight and eyed it solemnly.

Emma had her mother's bones, and mouth, but the eyes in the photograph were more knowing, more predatory than hers. In fact, studying them closely, I would be hard pressed to decide who the front runner would have been in a matter of seduction, Gerald or Miriam.

A strangely disturbing portrait, there was an innate frowstiness about the sitter not altogether due to the out-moded clothes or the unattractive hair style. If it were a true likeness, then Gerald would have been some ten or fifteen years younger than she. In uniform, tall, handsome and excessively masculine he must have been quite a catch for the lonely wife of an absent and estranged company commander. How feasible was it, I wondered, that he would have set his cap at a woman fifteen years his senior and looking as she did, without some little encouragement from her?

A moment's hesitation, then I stowed away the photo in my wallet. Unless Emma demanded whatever satisfaction she thought she could get, Connie could live on without knowing that Miriam had ever existed.

Before leaving the office I collected the bullets I had deposited in the Venetian box and slipped them into a pocket, wondering again about the missing gun – a Smith & Wesson .38 according to Arch. I was convinced that it had been removed from its box only recently and in good working order. If it had lain untouched since it had killed a colonel and murdered a corporal in the ruins of Berlin forty years back, the leather wrapping would have been dry and hard and the smell of the oil stale.

Wandering across the lawn I prowled among the rose-beds until I ran down the Doctors – even found the broken stem of the one Gerald had taken. It gave me an odd sensation to stand where he had stood two nights ago, perhaps only a few minutes before he had plunged to his death. What had been in his mind, pausing here in the scented darkness, touching the rose, smelling it and uncharacteristically snapping it from its stem, before moving on through the sleeping village to climb the tower?

To meet his murderer? Willingly? By appointment?

Or to take his own life?

I found myself confronted by the rear gate.

Arch's voice behind me: "You all right, guv?"

"Fine, Arch, fine," I said without turning. "Just having some bad thoughts, that's all."

"Guv, I been thinking . . ." I turned to watch him leaning on a spade, thought disfiguring his crumpled features. "About the motor-car. There's a little bloke I know over in Shipston . . ."

"I knew there must be," I interrupted him with a bland smile, removing the car-keys from Gerald's key-ring. "So long as he doesn't open his big mouth. A rash word from him and her ladyship's up the spout."

"So will 'e be, mate, take my word for it," he growled, clenching a grimy fist.

I unclenched it for him and dropped the keys into the open palm. "If she asks for them, you've lost them, swallowed them."

The clock struck the half. I made for the back gate. "It'll be worth your while, Arch," I promised over my shoulder. "His too, if he pulls it off and makes a good job of it."

Grantley's main street was busier than I'd seen it before with late shoppers, school children and commuters coming home to roost. I dodged athletically between their cars. Residents in doorways paused in mid-sentence to watch me pass, wondering who I was and what I was doing in their village. The shops were closing, shutters going up. I glanced at the church clock; just gone five thirty.

I was hot and sweaty, my jeans were too tight and my shirt clung to my naked skin like a wet plastic mackintosh. I needed a shower, a drink and somewhere to put my feet up, so I pushed my way into the church to find neither shower nor drink but plenty of places to sit and freeze. Poor God, what dismal places they build for him to live in; stone, plaster and black and white tiles; they even block up the windows with coloured glass so he can't even look out over his trees and flowers and skies to see that they are good.

I stretched out my legs, closed my eyes and listened to my body freezing over.

A shadow passed between me and the east window. I opened an eye.

"Mr Savage." The Reverend E. Chancey Bun was smiling down at me. "How fortuitous. You must have been led here." I struggled to my feet. "No please, don't get up. Unless . . . yes, on second thoughts . . . have you a moment? Yes? Good, then let's find a warmer spot. I need to talk to you."

He led me along various echoing passages, through an empty schoolroom, across an open court, into a compact residence I guessed to be the vicarage, and finally into a small but comfortable book-lined study complete with filing-cabinets and a modest desk piled with more books.

"We shall be undisturbed here," he said homing in on what looked like an early radiogram but turned out to be a drinks-cabinet which lit up when he raised the lid. I half expected it to play the 'Hallelujah Chorus'.

"A little sherry?" he enquired, his spectacles glinting archly. "The sun is almost over the yard-arm."

"Thank you."

"I do hope I wasn't interrupting anything out there?" A generous glass of golden liquid changed hands. "It occurred to me that you might have been . . ."

I shook my head. "I'm afraid not. I came in to cool down."

"And did, rather fast, I imagine? These old buildings are so impractical. Please sit. That's nice and comfortable and you can look out into the garden."

I took the chair he indicated and through a pair of open French windows watched a couple of blue tits nibbling nuts from a feeder suspended from a stone bird-bath. The little garden was high-walled, paved and compact, with rambler roses climbing a trellis.

He raised his glass. "God bless you," he said and took himself off to the desk where he cleared a space and sat frowning, fiddling disconsolately with his collar.

192

I watched him expectantly. "Yes," he nodded, catching my eye. "I have lured you here for a purpose." He cleared his throat, took another drink and spent an unconscionable time mopping at his lips with a handkerchief. "I've thought a great deal about our conversation of yesterday and have decided, in the light of Sir Gerald's tragic death, to – confide in you. Needless to say, I'm not very happy to do so, but since you were a friend of his and not of the immediate family . . ." He broke off for a second, tugging at his collar. "Gerald came to see me a fortnight ago on, let me see . . ." He leafed through a desk diary. "Yes, here it is . . . 23rd August to be exact, asking for – and needing, believe me – some comforting words on the question of death and what, if anything, lies beyond the grave. It appeared that . . ." He broke off for a second shaking his head mournfully, "It appeared that a few days before, he had learned from a specialist in Birmingham that he could look forward to only a few more months of active life, after which . . ." he raised his shoulders in a silent and helpless gesture, "an indefinite period of slow deterioration . . ."

I sat stunned, staring sightlessly at the birds in the garden, seeing only that great oak of a man, hearing his voice ringing again in my ears until, through the confusion, the little vicar's voice surfaced once more. ". . . probably an inoperable cancer. I don't really know. Doctor Nathan could probably tell you more, though I doubt if he will. Gerald swore us both to silence and in betraying his trust I feel I have betrayed myself, though, of course, I could not have foreseen the circumstances which would tempt me to do so. His only care was Lady Constance. She'd know soon enough, he said, and when the time came he'd be the one to tell her and no one else." He paused, frowning, then turned his head and looked at me directly for the first time. "He also said: 'Maybe she'll never need to know.' "

Each of us held the other's eyes for a moment or two of silence. I said, "Which might mean . . ."

He nodded. "Exactly. I'm afraid I didn't fully realise the significance of the remark until – after the event."

Rising, he moved heavily to the window where he stood with his back to me staring out into the garden. "I have simply been guilty of not telling the whole truth," came his voice over a flutter of wings which had greeted his appearance. "Sergeant Hunter's questions were not all that astute; I was able to avoid the issue."

Turning back into the room he retrieved his glass and perched on the edge of the desk. He was wearing odd socks; I wondered whether I should mention it; I asked instead, "Did he say whether or not you would be asked to attend the inquest?"

"There was no mention of it. I can't see that I'd be necessary at the hearing, except, perhaps, as caretaker of the premises, ostensibly in charge of two keys to the tower."

I shifted in my seat. "*A propos*, your own key was not missing, by any chance, for any part of that night, was it?"

He shrugged. "There's no way of knowing. It could have been, I suppose. Why do you ask?"

I told him about Connie's problem. "You see, if Gerald used his own key and took it up there with him, I would have expected it to be found in his pocket; as far as I know, it wasn't. So we have to assume that he threw it away or left it in the lock. On Connie's first visit to the tower she swears there was no key in the lock. Later, when I returned with her the key was there. How do we account for that, do you think?"

After a moment he said, "Gerald and I had an arrangement about the keys. When he was ensconced up there I asked him always to lock the door from the inside and take the key with him, so that he wouldn't be disturbed by the odd passer-by who might be tempted to take a bird's eye view of the countryside – or fans, of course, who knew he liked to work up there. Now, should there be *bona fide* visitors or tourists who wanted to view the tower, I could let myself in and warn him – that's why he had to remove his own key, so that I could use mine. It sounds complicated but it isn't really."

I pondered for a second. "What you're saying is that it would have been almost a reflex action for Gerald to lock the door behind him and pocket the key?" He nodded. "So, on Saturday night, why was the door open with no key in the lock, and half an hour later, still open but with the key in place?"

We looked blankly at each other.

He said at last, "Connie could have been mistaken?"

194

I nodded slowly. "Possibly. It was dark; she was in a state of near panic."

"You see," said the little vicar, thinking aloud, "if Gerald let himself in, changed the key to the inside, but failed, for some reason or other, to close the door properly, when Connie arrived the key wouldn't be visible from the outside. She opens the door, calls up to him and when there's no reply, goes running out again leaving the door wide open with the key visible but on the inside." He looked at me in some triumph, head on one side, bright and perky as a bird. "What do you say to that?"

I smiled slowly. "I'd say you've been reading too much Dorothy L. Sayers."

He chuckled. "It holds water though, doesn't it?"

"It's possible. Connie certainly wasn't thinking all that straight at the time. Yes, it's possible."

He drained his glass and replaced it carefully on the desk. "In which case . . ."

A silence closed down over us. "In which case," I said at last, "a third person needn't necessarily have been involved."

The little vicar stared unhappily at his odd socks. "Oh dear," he whispered distressfully. "Oh dear . . ." He blinked up at me. "It's a terrible thing for me to have to say, but I would almost sooner he had been struck down by an adversary, than for him to have taken his own life. I'm talking about the state of his immortal soul, of course."

"I doubt whether he was all that concerned about his immortal soul."

"Ah, but he was, Mr Savage, believe me, he was. That's why he confided in me in the first place. When a man reaches a certain age, no matter what beliefs he may or may not have held during his lifetime, there comes a moment when he is face to face with the one and only certainty of existence – his own death. Is it an end or is it a beginning? Sooner or later every thinking man must ask that question of himself. When Gerald was faced with what was tantamount to a death sentence he came to me for the answer. And I failed him. You see, the Church's most important asset, stock in trade if you like, is faith, pure and simple, the be all and end all of our sales service.

Without it the Christian teaching is a ship without a rudder. Faith cannot be taught or bought. It has to grow inside you and become part of you. Gerald, I fear, expected too much of me." He sighed. "A parson's lot is not a happy one, Mr Savage." He hesitated, then smiled across at me, a roguish glint in his eye. "That concludes my sermon for the day, you'll be delighted to hear – in the name of the Father, the Son and the Holy Ghost... Another small noggin, perhaps?"

I glanced at my watch. "I have to get back to Stratford, but while I'm here in Grantley I wouldn't mind having a quick word with Dr Nathan if he'll see me. Perhaps you could tell me where to find him."

He too consulted his watch. "He'll soon be in surgery, but you could probably catch him if you went right now."

He took me to his front door and pointed out a black and white house a hundred yards away. "But don't expect too much of him – he might not wish to discuss Gerald's affairs before the inquest ... ethics and all that."

I held out a hand. "I'm grateful for your thoughts – if not for your sermon. Having listened to it I realise, I'm afraid, that I'm a dyed-in-the-wool and never-to-be-saved sinner."

"Don't be afraid, Mr Savage," he smiled massaging my hand with confidence. "When you're ready to admit that and mean it, you're halfway there – so beware!"

I turned at the gate and smiled as he stood at his front door waggling his fingers at me.

I leaned on the bell of the black and white house. Dr Nathan himself opened the door and seemed pleased to see me. "I've a few minutes before surgery," he nodded when I asked him for a moment of his time.

He led the way into a comfortable and well-appointed consulting room and parked me in the patient's chair. "Now what can I do for you, Mr Savage?"

He didn't look quite so pleased when I told him what I had come about. He shuffled the papers on his desk unnecessarily, frowned at me and cleared his throat.

"How do you know about this?" he asked, then noting my hesitation, "Well, never mind, it'll all come out at the inquest.

196

Connie doesn't know, does she?" I shook my head. "I'll have to break it to her before the inquest. She can't have it sprung on her in public." He leaned back in his chair and ran his hands through his hair. "Poor old Gerald . . . I shall miss him. He was a great lad. Quite a trial too in his own small way. You knew he was diabetic?" I nodded. "Connie and I seemed to spend the best part of our lives reminding him about his jabs. He could remember all those lines on the stage but not his jabs. However, diabetes is not our problem.

"Some time back he began having some nasty dizzy spells. My first thought was that he was not eating properly – if you're diabetic, you've got to eat regularly. He was losing a bit of weight too, not much but significant, I thought. So I sent him for some barium X-rays and the best oncologist in Birmingham diagnosed cancer of the stomach which had spread to his liver – too far advanced to be operable. And that was it. I must say, considering it was a death sentence, he was magnificent. He swore me to secrecy. Whatever happened, Connie was to know nothing until he had to take to his bed. Then he settled down to live with it." He brooded for a moment. "At least I thought he had."

"And now you don't."

He eyed me soberly. "It doesn't matter what I think. I'll be bold enough to predict the coroner's verdict: death by misadventure – and I'd prefer to go along with that."

"But the post mortem must have revealed the cancer."

"Of course it did, but that doesn't mean he took his life, if that's what you're suggesting. A coroner has to have irrefutable proof before he commits himself to a verdict of suicide. The PM also revealed a hypoglycemic condition: low blood sugar and too much insulin. He appeared not to have eaten properly on Saturday – there was little or no food residue in the stomach – also evidence of alcohol. In addition, the energy expended on that performance of *Lear*, to say nothing of the build-up of rehearsals over six weeks, would have been excessive for a man half his age, let alone a diabetic of sixty-eight. Even the exercise of climbing that tower could have been too much under the circumstances – and led directly to a comatose state which could easily have resulted in the fall to his death." He broke off and closed his eyes wearily. "Death by misadventure, Mr Savage," he murmured quietly. "Let's settle for that, shall we? There's no proof to the contrary." He opened his eyes and narrowed them at me. "Or is there?"

I made my face a blank. "If there is, I don't think I'd want to find it." I allowed a second or two to pass. "How long had he known all this?"

"Two, three weeks, thereabouts. The diagnosis was only really confirmed some time last month."

"By this specialist, or whatever you called him, in Birmingham?"

He was rooting around among his papers and drew from them a leather bound desk-diary. "I have the exact date here somewhere, I think." He riffled through the pages. "Yes, here you are: '14th August, 11 am. GG to Charles B.' That answer your question?"

Chapter Sixteen

Business at the Dirty Duck – or the White Swan depending upon which direction you approached its sign-board – was booming. The compact little terrace looking out over the river was groaning beneath a horde of steaming bodies, mostly actors taking in liquid refreshment before humping themselves across the road to the theatre for the evening performance – *Romeo and Juliet* if all was going well over there.

Actors are the most inquisitive people in the world and as I parked the Honda and unscrewed my helmet I was aware of the sudden hiatus in the general roar of upraised theatrical voices, as curious heads craned over the balustrade to see who I was – if anybody.

As I climbed the short flight of steps I felt like Sydney Carton mounting the guillotine; any minute now there'd be a clamorous roar as my head fell off; then they'd all go back to their knitting.

I shoved my way through the sea of faces, looking at none of them but conscious of a rising mutter of mild interest as certain of their number remembered who I was and passed on the information to interested neighbours.

Inside it was like a scene from a Marx Brothers' movie. If you fainted you'd have to wait until somebody left before you could fall down. I peered vainly through the smoke for a glimpse of George the Red and his ferrety friend, Jack; they were both so small that they could have been trodden underfoot without anyone noticing. Somebody pinched me painfully on the right buttock. Sonia of course, seated at a small table with a hundred and fifty other people, most of them bearded and none of them her husband. Next to her, without a beard, was the gypsy-looking Megan somebody who had played Goneril in *Lear*.

199

Sonia drew me down to her by the front of my T-shirt and planted a wet kiss on my chin. "Mark darling, come and join us," she crooned sexily; she was slightly high. "This is my lovely Ex, everybody," she told the rest of the company. "Mark Sutherland that was."

I nodded unhappily at the bovine faces staring across at me and did my best to unshackle my shirt. I met Goneril's eyes: they were friendly and sympathetic, as was her smile.

"I'll get a drink first," I muttered straightening up and unhooking Sonia's clutching fingers one by one.

At the bar I stumbled up against George and Jack keeping a couple of low profiles in a shadowy corner. George was effusive in his greeting, Jack less so, and I bought them each a pint, myself an orange juice.

Memories and pleasantries were exchanged for a couple of minutes, George becoming slightly hysterical as he related to Jack the story of how, one day during rehearsals of this flying sequence we had done together, he had left me dangling twenty feet above stage level while he went off to lunch. I remembered it well.

Jack allowed his face to crack open for a split second, a wary cockle peering out of its shell, then snapped it shut again.

"George," I said, turning him slightly towards the bar and lowering my voice. "Give me a moment will you? This morning on the stage I just happened to overhear you and Jack talking about an upset between old man Grantley and Paul Braidy before the show on Saturday night. Is that right?"

He nodded. "They 'ad an almighty barney going on and that's a fact."

"Know what it was about?"

"Jack 'eard more'n I did. 'Ere, Jack . . ." Jack bent in towards us. When George had told him about my troubles he took a lengthy swig at his beer and wiped his mouth with the back of his hand. "They was just shouting at each other, that's all. Well, more 'issing, like, than shouting, 'cos the curtain 'ad just gone up. 'E said 'e'd tear 'im limb from limb and Fart-face said 'e 'adn't got a leg to stand on. Nearly knocked me over they did. I was standing right in the doorway, see? When 'is cue come the guv'nor just shoved 'im out of the way and says something like, 'Get out of my sight and stay out.'" He pulled himself up, frowning painfully. "Come to think of it . . ."

"What?"

"There *was* something else . . . just before I got 'it with the door. 'E was saying something about newspapers . . . that's it . . . 'in all the newspapers' 'e said."

"Who said?"

"'Im, Fart-face."

"Lucy O'Grady," translated George for my benefit.

"*What* 'in all the newspapers'?" I urged.

He screwed up his face. "They was 'alf in and 'alf out of the door, see, so I didn't 'ear the first bit . . . or did I? I can't quite . . . wait a sec . . . *Something* in all the newspapers. I remember thinking just before they sent me flying that they was talking about the press being in front of 'ouse, it being the first night and that." He stopped abruptly, his eyes widening; he raised a finger and stood for a moment with his mouth half open. "Exposed!" he said softly; I leaned in to hear. "'Exposed in all the newspapers.'"

"To which Grantley replied, 'I'll tear you limb from limb'?"

Jack nodded. "And 'e said, 'You 'aven't got a leg to stand on.'"

The noise around us seemed to rise up and hit me between the ears as I gave up concentrating on his voice and turned away, leaning over the bar to stare fixedly into my orange juice. One by one the pieces were coming together. Arch's tangled web was beginning to disintegrate.

"That answer your question?" asked George.

"It's helped."

He leaned in closer. "Read in the papers that you're now a private dick, that right?"

I gave a shrug. "It's a living."

"What, sort of 'Umpty Go-cart sort of thing?"

"Sort of." I nodded at their glasses. "How about the other half?"

"Blimey no," muttered George. "I'm on the swill already. We got work to do." He crossed his eyes at his wristwatch. "Christ yes, come on Jack. Nappy Pants'll be over 'ere in a minute stamping 'is foot at us." He drained his glass and waited with restrained patience while Jack gulped away at his. "You up 'ere for long?" he asked me.

I shook my head. "Back to the smoke tomorrow."

"All the best then." He crushed the bones in my hand until my eyes watered. "See you. Tara . . ."

As I watched them forging through the crowd, I noticed that others too were on the move. The clock said it was six forty-five – over the road the curtain was due to rise at seven-thirty.

Sonia and Megan were still at their table. Reluctantly I girded my loins and wandered over. She saw me coming, reached out and trapped my left thigh, wrapping her arm about it like a boa-constrictor on the make, her elbow nudging suggestively at my crotch. "Come and join us, hunk," she invited.

My arrival was the cue for everyone else to get up and go. I felt like the one who brought the news of the plague to the island. Beards waggled, heads nodded, teeth smiled and they departed in droves leaving the table empty except for Sonia, Megan, and the only beardless male among them, a young man who, according to Sonia's introduction, went by the name of David Ravel.

The pearl had dropped into my lap.

"Sorry about that general exodus," Sonia apologised. "Nothing to do with you. They've been threatening to go for the past half-hour, coarse lot. We've all got to go in a minute anyway."

I was aware of David Ravel's eyes upon me – wide and blue, lashes sweeping his cheeks like palm-fronds: he was almost a platinum blond, his skin pink and smooth. As a girl he would have been stunning, as a boy he was worrying.

"So what have you been up to since I saw you last?" asked Sonia with no interest at all and scrabbling industriously in her handbag. I knew exactly what she was looking for: a nail-file. She was the nail-file queen and used to drive me mad sawing and picking away at her nails.

"This and that," I told her.

"That's what you said on Saturday."

"Nothing's changed since Saturday."

She discovered her nail-file and set to work on her already

202

immaculate nails; it was a *tic* with her. "That's not what the papers say. They said you were a private detective."

"I was a private detective long before Saturday."

"It's true then, is it?"

"I dabble." As I glanced across at David Ravel he dropped his eyes uncomfortably, almost guiltily, the slightest shadow of a frown gathering on his smooth brow.

"But how exciting," exclaimed Megan. "A private eye yet!" She leaned across Sonia in her excitement. "Tell us all!"

"For God's sake, Meg, we've got to go. We haven't got time to listen to his life story." That was Sonia, ever interested in what the other half did. This time, however, I was grateful for the interruption. The last thing I needed at that moment was an autobiographical trip down memory lane. What I did want before the party broke up was some information.

I smiled winningly at Megan. "It's all pretty dull and boring really – most of it what the cops call leg-work. You just wander around and ask questions. Sometimes you get the answers, sometimes you don't. At the end of a very long day you get paid for it – usually. It's just a job, like yours, only not quite so glamorous."

"Give us a 'for instance'," pressed Megan.

"Well, for instance . . ." I searched deviously around for a "for instance". "Take poor old Gerald's death. Suppose there was some doubt about the way he died and I got called in to sort it out. I'd follow up all the leads I could find – all the people he knew, met, talked to, quarrelled with, threatened – and build up a sort of behaviour pattern right up until the actual moment of his death. Then there'd be the various attitudes of those same people *after* his death – and the beneficiaries in his will, and so on and so forth." I eyed Sonia's finger-nails. "Sorry, Son, I didn't mean to bring it so near to home."

She gave a preoccupied grunt and surveyed her right index finger critically. "It's okay. If you were to tell me that somebody had shoved him off that tower quite deliberately, it wouldn't surprise me one little bit. There have been times when I could cheerfully have done it myself. Richard too, even if he was his father."

"To say nothing of Paul Braidy," put in Megan. "He and

Gerald were always yelling at each other. It was like the Wars of the Roses, it went on for ever. Even on Saturday – a first night, for Pete's sake! – they were at it! We tried thumping the wall but it didn't do any good."

"About the play, was it?" I asked casually.

"What else? We just wanted them to shut up." She looked at the boy opposite. "Dave could probably tell you."

He looked startled and seemed to come out of a coma.

"Dave is Paul's friend," explained Megan rather archly and giving me a glassy-eyed look dripping with ulterior messages.

David Ravel shook his head. "I haven't really seen much of him lately, but I know they were always at each other's throats." He looked at his watch. "I think I ought to be going."

He was deathly pale and clearly rattled. I didn't want him frightened off; now that I'd found him I wanted to hold on to him. I could think of only one way of doing it: beneath the table I pressed my knee gently against his. It was a long shot and a cruel one but it had the desired effect. Our eyes met and held for a second longer than was necessary.

"Do you have to work too?" I asked.

Flustered, he shook his head doubtfully. "I'm not an actor. I just . . ."

"Dave works in a male boutique," supplied Megan. "And good luck to him, say I. If only I could do something like that – anything but act! But there's nothing else I *can* do – and according to the esteemed Paul Braidy I can't even do that."

"According to him, dear, no one can act," put in Sonia tartly. She blew on her nails. "What an overweening, self-satisfied, tight-bottomed, patronising, dehydrated little squirt he is, isn't he?" She slid her nail-file into its plastic sheath. "And having got that off my chest, I shall now sally forth and give my monumentally boring Lady Montague to the world." She packed her bag and got up to go. "Coming, Meg? 'Bye guys."

Meg levered herself out from behind the table as I got up to let her through. "I don't suppose you'll be coming over to see it?" I shook my head. "Pity. Sonia's Lady M may be boring but you should see my Mrs Capulet – it's an experience all on its own." She looked up at me appealingly. "You wouldn't be looking for a lady Doctor Watson, I suppose?"

I grinned. "I couldn't afford you."

"I'd do it for nothing, man," she growled. She gave me a sly wink. "Don't do anything I wouldn't do." She waved a hand at us and followed Sonia.

I stood for a second looking down at David Ravel's bright head low over the table as he turned a beer mat over and over in his hands, watching it intently as if expecting it to give up some hidden secret. He wasn't happy. He wasn't a platinum blond either; a bird's eye view revealed dark threads among the silver.

"Another drink?"

He shook his head. "No thanks. I've . . ." He cleared his throat and fell silent.

I sat down again and watched his slender fingers fiddling with the mat.

"Have you anywhere we can go?" he asked at last in a gruff undertone.

The vision of an assignation of consenting males at Bull Street brought me to the verge of hysteria: Enter Barbara Sterling, rattling keys: Hello boys, how's it coming?

I shook my head. "I'm only passing through," I told him, hoping he wouldn't suggest the churchyard.

Another moment of silence then he cleared his throat again. "How about my place?"

I nodded. "Fine."

"We'll have to get a bus."

I removed the beer mat from his grasp. "Not necessary," I told him, "I have wheels."

The waiting Honda threw him into a state of near dementia. The spare helmet made him look like something from outer space, all legs and arms and much too tall. When we were all set and I told him to hang on, he did so with no little enthusiasm, his hot hands sliding voluptuously inside my T-shirt with the speed of light. I hope he enjoyed it. I was sweating like a pig.

His "place" was about four feet square with a bed in it and a huge walnut wardrobe which leaned in at a desperate angle second only to that of the tower of Pisa. I eyed it nervously, shying away from it at my first encounter, but was reassured by the seventy-odd suitcases piled on top of it, thus wedging it firmly against the ceiling. The bed was unmade and sir's clothes were strewn everywhere like opening day at the sales.

"It's not much," he apologised. I watched him as he locked the door, closed the curtains, straightened the bed-linen and shoved an unfinished bowl of cornflakes into a drawer. "It's only temporary 'til I can find something better."

He was as nervous as I was. Nevertheless he stripped off his shirt and shoes and unbuckled his belt. About his neck hung a variety of metal charms on silver chains; even in the half-darkness I identified a cross, a swastika, a shield of David, a St Christopher, a cross of Lorraine and an Egyptian ankh. He was prepared for everything. When he moved he tinkled like a Buddhist temple.

He perched on the edge of the bed and undid the top button of his jeans. If I was going to come out of this with any semblance of self-respect, now was the time to speak – before he got to his zip.

"Dave . . ."

"Were you really married to Sonia?" he asked in a sudden rush.

I nodded. "Yes, I was. And, Dave, I have to tell you that I'm here under false pretences. I'm sorry. I needed to talk to you in private – just talk."

I should have been chagrined at his obvious lack of disappointment. In fact there was little or no reaction from him at all; he just sat there staring down at his shirt for a second, then carefully began to fold it into a small and unsightly ball. "Would you like a cup of tea?" he asked.

I shook my head. "I want to talk to you about Paul."

The muscles in his jaw twitched and he shot me a slightly hostile look from beneath his eyelashes. "What about him?"

I took a breath. "I think you already know most of it."

Ambling over to the window I drew open the curtains; the room might look better in the dark but he didn't; I couldn't see what was going on behind his eyes. I went back and stood over him like Judgment Day.

"What would you say, Dave, if I told you he was responsible for Gerald Grantley's death?"

He swallowed hard. "Gerald Grantley committed suicide."

"Did he? Who told you that?"

"Everybody knows it."

"I don't. Nobody told me." I took a turn up and down the room in front of him; he watched my feet with a mesmeric stare. "All right then," I went on. "Let's talk about the accident back in August."

"Accident?" he interrupted too quickly. "What accident?"

"He and Gerald – coming back from Birmingham one night in the rain. I can't believe he didn't mention it to you – you being so close, I mean." He was frowning now, biting at his lower lip. I gave an indifferent shrug. "Please don't worry about it, it's not all that important – simply a question of insurance, that's all. He wasn't hurt, was he?"

"No, I'm sure he wasn't." If he could have bitten his tongue out he would have done, but, having committed himself, he added with a distant, sour sort of smile. "I do seem to remember something about it, now I come to think of it. It was quite a long time ago . . ."

I nodded. "Back in August." I allowed a moment to go by. "How long have you two been together, by the way – you and Braidy?"

The question threw him even more. "What's that got to do with it?"

"How long? Since he first came to Stratford? Six weeks, eight, ten weeks?" He shot me a sullen look but said nothing. "You don't really know him all that well, do you – his background, I mean?" His collection of dingle-dangles gave an uneasy tinkle. "What did he do, offer you money?" I pushed him back as he attempted to rise. "Okay, that was below the belt. But even you must admit that he doesn't have a whole lot going for him. I mean, he's not exactly the Body Beautiful, is he? Or is he? Maybe he is and I can't see it. But someone like you could do a whole heap better if you worked at it, don't you think?"

"Paul's okay," he muttered uncertainly.

"So why are you now living here on your own in this God-forsaken hole? I understood you were nicely shacked up together. What happened? Did he chuck you out on your ear when you wouldn't play ball with him about the accident?"

207

He flared with sudden petulance. "Why do you keep going on about that bloody accident? Get out of here, will you?" He lurched to his feet, shoving me aside as he made for the door. "It's none of your business."

"Oh, but it is," I said quietly. "Blackmail *is* my business."

He pulled up short of the door and stood with his back to me for a long moment.

"Did he ask you to record that tape for him?"

He turned slowly, his face quite white.

"Tape?" The word was barely audible.

"What was he offering in return? A small cut of the proceeds? Ten grand is a whole lot of money." I watched a bead of sweat trickle down his forehead. "Don't cover for him, Dave; don't be an idiot. What do you think is going to happen when I hand that tape over to the fuzz? It won't matter a damn, you know, whether your voice is on it or not. By not coming clean you're an accomplice – and as guilty as he is. Have you any idea what sort of sentence blackmail carries?"

He was wagging his head from side to side. "I don't know what the hell you're talking about. What tape, for God's sake, what tape?"

I reached into my hip pocket. "This tape," I told him quietly.

He was suddenly very still. I heard him take a shuddering breath and saw the flicker of panic in his eyes. Misreading the signals I moved in a couple of paces to prevent him reaching the door. But retreat was not what he had in mind. With hands outstretched he was lunging towards me, thrusting me back against the wardrobe which buckled alarmingly as I crashed into it with a violence which juddered my teeth. The heavens rained heavy objects, one of which – a suitcase I believe it was – hit me hard on the head, half stunning me and bringing me to my knees. Rolling instinctively to face the enemy I found myself staring up at the slowly collapsing wardrobe which flapped open its doors invitingly as it lumbered down on top of me with all the predatory intent of a man-eating shark.

Engulfed in a welter of suffocating clothes and further unidentifiable flying objects, I caught a glimpse of what looked like an entire edition of the *Encyclopaedia Britannica* hurtling in my direction; as I threw up an arm to protect my face, something else, more successful than the suitcase, dealt me the *coup de grâce* and I disappeared, senseless, into the dark maw of the wardrobe.

A few minutes later – or was it an hour? – I opened my eyes to the unnerving probability that I had lost my sight. Everywhere was dark as the grave. I lay for a while doing my best to assess any damage which might have befallen me, conscious only of a light-headedness which threatened to overcome me and send me into an unseemly fit of giggles. *The Night the Wardrobe Fell on Savage* sort of thing. Roger Howells would have himself a ball.

I flexed a few muscles and moved a couple of limbs – arms – which appeared intact; legs, on the other hand, were pinned irrevocably to the floor. I initiated a rolling, heaving motion; all around me creaked and groaned alarmingly. I felt like Boris Karloff stirring in his mummy-case – a wild fancy which increased as I set about extricating myself from other people's sweaty garments. The irresponsible cackling I could hear was coming from my own lips. I pulled myself together.

By dint of raising that hideous great lump of furniture and supporting it bodily at arms' length above my face, I managed to release my legs and wriggle out from beneath it; when eventually my arms gave out and I rolled free, the awesome reverberations as it crashed to the floor rocked the building to its foundations. I lay panting and sweating, wondering vaguely at the studied lack of interest from the neighbours; nobody tapping urgently at the door: "Excuse me, is everything all right? I thought I heard something fall . . ."

Feeling every minute of my age, I eased myself into a sitting position and, after a short rest, on to my knees. Needless to say I was alone; my pretty young cock bird had flown, taking with him, I was prepared to wager, the evidence – one tape. I cast a desultory glance or two about me, but my neck muscles weren't responding all that well. I was beyond caring anyway. I was one huge bruise and didn't have to be told what the salty taste in my mouth was. Blood splattered over my jeans. I was bleeding to death.

In the distant corner of the room a sleazy-looking wash-basin was surmounted by a medicine-cupbord with a mirror for a door. I shambled over to it and viewed the damage. The bruise on my right temple was about the size of a large poached egg and increasing every minute; the gash on my left cheek was no bigger than a church door but it would serve; if it continued to bleed like that I'd be needing a blood transfusion by nightfall.

Snatching some tissues from a handy box I clamped them over the wound and sorted through the contents of the cupboard: a bottle of colourless iodine and a couple of tired-looking strips of Elastoplast. The iodine brought tears to my eyes while the plasters partially ensured I wouldn't go on bleeding all over my shirt front.

In a half-hearted attempt to turn up the missing tape, I contrived to shove the felled wardrobe to one side – and there it was, nestling beneath a fallen anorak. I tucked it away in my pocket for future reference.

There was no doubt in my mind that Braidy himself had made that recording. Aside from Dave Ravel, who else could he have trusted? And no matter what that young man had said, I was fairly certain he knew every detail of the accident. If he did, then only Braidy could have told him, and not in the course of idle conversation either. He was far too culpable in the eyes of the law to risk admitting involvement in a hit-and-run incident unless there were something to be gained by it. My guess was that he had done his best to persuade Dave to tape the message, offering as recompense the smallest possible slice of the profits; Dave had refused and got himself thrown out into the street with the never-darken-my-doors routine hurled after him.

So now what? I squatted on the edge of his bed to review the situation. Braidy had been next on my list; I had intended to get his address from Dave, but as things had fallen out I hadn't had time to ask him. Barbara would know, of course, so I decided to call in at the theatre to see if she were still around.

She was, and as I stood at the stage-door waiting for her to appear, I listened with growing concern to the clash of arms and various alarms and excursions emanating from the stage. With the introduction of fire-arms and a cast of thousands, the Montague and Capulet street-brawl sounded like a replay of the battle of the Somme.

"Sounds like the end of the world in there," I greeted Barbara as she clattered down the stairs.

"It practically is. Hello, man." Then she stopped and stared wide-eyed at the ovoid contusion on my head. "Wow!" she whispered. "Whatever happened to you?"

"I was eaten by a wardrobe."

"And your cheek too – you're all cut about. Have you been beaten up?"

I quietened her with a firm hand and led her out to the Honda.

The sun was low as we bubbled through the town to Bull Street. She too managed to insinuate her hands under my T-shirt but she was bolder than Dave and much more to the point, with the result that by the time we reached her Victorian hide-out, my management of the Honda was almost as sketchy as that of my self-control.

We loitered just inside her front door for a long and rewarding bear-hug, moved by degrees down the passage, shed clothing like autumn leaves, and ended up under the shower.

She then clucked over me like an old mother hen, bathing my head and changing the dressing on my cheek while I filled in the time by telling her how I came to be in such a state of disrepair.

We then took ourselves off to the Mayflower to see what the Chinese could do about feeding us.

It was good to relax over a leisurely meal. I remember thinking that she was the perfect companion and wondered why the hell I had let her go so many years before.

"What's your cooking like?" I asked.

"Pretty lousy."

"House-management?"

"Non-existent."

"And you're devoted to all that Victoriana rubbish?"

"Why?"

I shrugged. "I was just looking for somewhere to hang my hat."

Even in candlelight I saw the surge of blood to her cheeks.

"I could go to cookery classes," she murmured, reaching across the table and touching my hand with the tips of her fingers. "And Victoriana isn't exactly a way of life, is it?"

211

I trapped her fingers in mine. "Prince Albert probably thought it was."

We giggled, shook ourselves down and I told her the rest of what had been happening since we last saw each other. She listened intently and when I paused for breath, sat in gloomy silence staring at the remains of her banana fritter, her head bowed between her hands. I poured her some Jasmine tea.

She spoke at last. "Our Gerald seems to have been something of a whited sepulchre."

I shrugged. "Not much more so than the rest of us."

There was a pause. "Have *you* ever shot someone in the back?"

"I've never been to war."

"Or fathered a child on someone else's wife?" I was silent. "Have you ever knocked someone down and left him to die in the gutter?"

"Shut up, Ba, please."

"Which reminds me . . ." She ferreted around in her handbag and produced a folded paper. "This is the Stratford Herald, dated 15th August. I called in this afternoon and made a copy."

She spread the typewritten sheet before me. *Hit-and-Run Fatality* ran the headline.

The body of sixty-four-year-old Stanley Verdun was discovered early this morning on the verge of the B4102, half a mile south of Earlswood. Multiple injuries, consistent with being hit by a moving vehicle were the cause of death, though it is believed that death occurred some time after the injuries had been sustained.

Mr Verdun, of no fixed abode, was last seen leaving the Bourne public house at ten fifteen last night, where he had been refused further drinks owing to the fact that, in the opinion of Mr Bob Inskill the landlord, 'he'd already had several too many.'

The police are treating the incident as a case of hit-and-run, and believe it to have occurred between eleven o'clock last night and one thirty this morning. Anyone who witnessed the accident or can supply information regarding the identity of the vehicle responsible, is asked to communicate with . . .

"Bastards," I muttered. "If they'd bothered to stop they might have saved his life."

She was frowning at me in the dim light. "They?"

"What?"

"You said 'they'."

"Gerald wasn't alone."

"How do you know that?"

"I gathered as much from Dave – even if I did put the words into his mouth. But he only confirmed what I had already guessed. It was raining that night. There were muddy foot-prints all over the car's floor mats and the ash-tray was crammed with cigarette butts. Camel cigarette butts. If Gerald did smoke I doubt if he'd have smoked Camels. Did he smoke?"

"Not that I know of."

"Paul Braidy admitted to Dave that he'd been in an accident."

"Paul Braidy?"

"The blackmailer. It was he who recorded that tape." She gave a little gasp. "I thought you'd like that. So the black-mailer wasn't a passing pedestrian at all; he was sitting right next to the driver. The last time Gerald used that car was when he drove to Birmingham to do a radio interview. As company manager you must know something about that surely?"

She nodded. "Back in August some time. I arranged it. He and Paul were on it together."

"There you are then. Gerald probably offered him a lift back."

"That doesn't sound right."

I shrugged. "Maybe they were on better terms then. Does Braidy drive?"

"He doesn't have a car up here."

"Gerald could have had an attack of magnanimity; after all, it was pissing with rain. This report's dated 15th August so the accident happened the night before – the fourteenth. That be about right for the broadcast?"

213

"Easy enough to check."

"No need. Tomorrow morning I shall be paying our Mr Braidy a visit. Have you got his address?"

"I have back home."

"I want to know if Gerald paid him his ten grand, and if he did, I, personally, will see to it that he pays back every last penny into Gerald's estate. And that's a promise."

I lapsed into a well-earned silence while she replenished our cups and mulled over all that she'd just been told.

Finally she gave a weary sigh and leaned back in her chair. "What?" I asked.

"I was just thinking, maybe Emma Hardcastle's nearer the truth than we like to think – the head of a satyr, sly, rapacious. Maybe she's the only one who really saw through the make-up."

"Do you believe that?"

She made a face. "Her Gerald wasn't the one I knew, that's all. The Fates ganged up on him, shoved him into a corner, it happens to all of us sometimes." .

"There's more to come. But it's classified." I finished my tea and sat for a second examining the inside of the cup. "Gerald had only a few months more to live."

It was like hitting her between the eyes.

"And he was told about it," I added quietly, "by a consultant in Birmingham on the morning of 14th August. Are you surprised he got drunk and had an accident?" I gave her a run-down of the doctor's views. "It'll influence the coroner's verdict, of course, but you do see what it means, don't you? It brings the possibility of suicide a step nearer."

"Suicide," she repeated, a statement rather than a question.

"As you say, the Fates ganged up on him."

We sat in silence for an age.

"So now you believe he killed himself?" she said at last.

I gave a unhappy shrug. "The odds are getting shorter."

She shook her head. "Poor Connie."

"The alternative would have been worse. Can you imagine what it would be like, watching a man like that rotting away in front of you, and knowing there was nothing you could do about it? I can understand why he did it – *if* he did it – but, in his

214

shoes, I think I'd have chosen an easier way – spiked my insulin or whatever . . ."

"*Why* so violent, I wonder?"

"Self-flagellation, probably. It *had* to hurt, didn't it? Exorcism, laying ghosts to rest, and all that, I don't know. But if you're going to knock yourself off, I guess you have the right to choose your *modus operandi* – the punishment to fit the crime, so to speak."

The longest silence yet closed down over us. When she spoke again, her voice was gentle but insistent. "Why don't we go home, Mark?"

Chapter Seventeen

Paul Braidy lived in a mansion only slightly smaller than Blenheim Palace – a fitting residence for so lustrous a representative of the English Theatre – the only drawback being that the house was sub-divided into thirty-two self-contained, furnished flatlets.

P. Braidy, said an awesome array of bell-pushes, lived in number 13, so I pushed number 27 and waited until a female squawk came out of the wall at my elbow. "Recorded Delivery for Spraggs," I answered, squinting at the name beside the bell.

"Eeow!" said the squawk. "Bring it up will you, there's a dear man." A buzzer sounded and I shoved open the door.

I just hoped he was in, that's all. With my luck he'd probably gone on a trip around the world and wouldn't be back until this time next year.

As I followed the arrows and numbers along echoing, once elegant passages and hallways and up a couple of cheaply carpeted grand staircases, I held Barbara Sterling's ancient portable tape-recorder to my ear and pressed the *Play* button. She'd warned that it was unreliable but at the moment it seemed to be behaving itself. I pressed *Rewind*.

Apart from the depressing state of disrepair the place also appeared to be deserted, the blank-faced, numbered doors firmly shut, no sound of radios or the comforting chatter of voices coming from the rooms beyond.

Number 13 was at the rear of the house on the second floor. I knocked at it with my knuckles, discreetly, so as not to raise the hopes of number 27 waiting for her recorded delivery. No reply. I knocked again, louder, and called "Paul" through the keyhole. Still nothing. I tried the door; locked. He was out, gone on his trip around the world.

"Are you the postman?" A female, halfway up the next flight

216

of stairs, was peering down at me. Mrs Spraggs, frail and pale, with a bird's nest on her head.

"No, madam."

"Funny, the postman just rang with a delivery for me. He seems to have got lost." She narrowed her eyes at me suspiciously, pulling nervously at the sash of her dun-coloured dressing-gown. "Can I help you, young man?"

"No, I don't think so, unless you can tell me the whereabouts of Mr Braidy who lives here. I'm a friend of his. I think he must be out."

"No, he's not. He's out there on the lawn, taking the sun. I saw him only a moment ago." She leaned over the balustrade twisting her neck at an absurd angle to peer through a lofty window overlooking the rear of the house. "Yes, there he is, down by the river."

I followed her pointing finger. The supine body stretched out on a blue lilo could have been anybody but I took her word for it; to date I had been fortunate enough to be spared the sight of Paul Braidy in the near nude; it wasn't one I looked forward to.

I touched my forelock and turned to the head of the stairs. The querulous voice followed me. "If you see the postman will you tell him number 27 is waiting. The name is Spraggs – Evelyn Spraggs."

I waved a cheery hand at her. Come in number 27, your time is up.

Although it was not yet mid-morning the heat of the sun was already intense; its rays prickled my skin as I left the house by a rear exit. The river sparkled before me. A wide stretch of well cared-for lawn formed part of its bank where the recumbent figure on the lilo lay within a yard of the water's edge. No one else was in sight. Stripping off my shirt I wrapped it around the tape-recorder and padded towards my prey.

Paul Braidy, resplendent in a pair of well-packed orange beach trunks and a scarlet sweat-band, was not a pretty sight. Tufts of black hair sprouted at all points centering eventually upon his chest and shoulders so alarmingly that, for an irresponsible moment, I found myself wondering whether he'd stuck them on with spirit-gum. A tube of Ambre Solaire sun-tan cream lay on the grass beside the lilo, but so far appeared to have had little effect, his skin bearing the leaden hue of suet-pudding. Alongside the tube was a carton of Camel cigarettes and a lighter.

I stood between him and the sun and when he opened his eyes, side-stepped neatly, thus giving him the full benefit of the sun's rays. It's small things like that which make life worth living. He threw up an arm and blinked around it, grunting his irritation.

"Hi, Paul," I greeted him cheerily.

His eyes were watering. "Who is it?"

"Barbara Sterling's step-father."

Heaving himself on to an elbow he wiped his face with a forearm and narrowed his eyes beneath a shading hand. "What the hell are you doing here?" he demanded. "And don't give me that bunk about Barbara Sterling's step-father either. I know exactly who you are and what you do. How did you get in here and what do you want?"

"Number 27 let me in and I want you."

He struggled into a sitting position, the lilo giving his equilibrium a bit of bother. If you want to disconcert a suspect, interview him when he's squatting on a half-inflated lilo. He drew a towel from beneath him and wiped his face and shoulders. "What's all this about?"

"A few words in private with you, that's all."

"You have them," he answered grandly, like the Pope granting an audience, then spoiled it by adding, "You do realise you're trespassing, I suppose?"

"I'm sorry, sir. I'll make an appointment next time."

"There won't be a next time."

I nodded. "That's for sure." The underlying finality of the remark brought a furtive look of disquiet to the eyes. He paled a little and bounced awkwardly on his lilo. "For Christ's sake, get on with it." He made a hurried grab at his cigarettes and lit one, exhaling the smoke in small gusts.

I sat beside him on the grass, unveiled the tape-recorder and, taking my time, placed it carefully between us, smiling at him benignly. "A little light relief first," I said and pressed *Play*.

I watched him turn from pale to ashen in about two seconds

flat; his face tried to drain away but never got past his Adam's apple which bobbed convulsively as he did his best to swallow it. The fingers holding the cigarette trembled. When he was reduced to a fairly palpable pulp, I switched off the machine. "Sorry it's not a better recording – someone must have been running a bath at the time. Is that how you did it, by the way, against a running tap?"

After a considerable struggle with his controls he trotted out the predictable response: "I don't know what you're talking about."

"Oh, come on, Mr Braidy, we don't have to go through all that, do we? You know and I know, and very soon the whole of England will know what I'm talking about. Blackmail is the word. Extortion by menaces – and, incidentally, the end of your career. Now, if you're sitting comfortably, let us, as you say, get on with it. You were driving back from Birmingham with Gerald Grantley on the night of 14th August last and knocked down and fatally wounded a pedestrian by the name of Stanley Verdun. You failed to stop and Verdun died of his injuries. So the charge will be manslaughter."

"I wasn't driving!" he protested in a sudden panic-stricken splutter. "I don't drive."

"You should have stopped, though, shouldn't you?"

"He wouldn't stop."

"Then you should have persuaded him. There was a handbrake between you, for God's sake, you should have used it. However, that's not the point at issue. Having manfully overcome whatever conscience you may have felt regarding your failure to save a man's life, you then decided to use the incident as a means of improving your personal income to the tune of ten thousand smackers. So that'll be manslaughter *and* blackmail."

As he did his best to clamber to his feet, I leaned over and poked a strategic pair of rigid fingers behind his left knee. "Sit down when I'm talking to you," I told him mildly. He made a pancake landing on the glowing end of his cigarette. "Oh, hard luck, sir." I threw over his pack. "Have another."

"You think yourself bloody funny, don't you?" he exploded.

"And you'd do well to grab me while I'm in the funny vein,

Mr Braidy," I informed him grimly. "I usually prefer violence. Now, tell me about the money."

"What money?"

"The ten grand you extorted from Gerald Grantley."

He stared at me in silence for a moment, a sneer gathering on his lips. "If you think that old sod parted with a penny piece you're not as clever as you think you are. There wasn't any money, and what's more I didn't expect any . . . not really."

"You mean it was a try-on?"

"Something like that. So what? It might have worked."

I watched in silence as he lit another cigarette and gulped the smoke deep into his lungs. "He out-smarted me and I don't mind admitting it," he muttered half to himself, adding with a sour snigger, "Canny old bastard." He shook his head in a gesture of almost wry appreciation. "When I rang him to give him instructions about where to leave the money, he just swore at me and told me to go to hell; said he'd contacted the cops and they knew all about it. The pay-off line was that he hadn't yet told them that I had been in the car with him." He gave a snorting laugh. "See what I mean? A real old bastard. I must have given myself away somehow. Maybe I won't take up acting, after all. I did all the right things too: disguised the voice, stuck a handkerchief in the phone – it's all in the blackmailer's book of rules, but he was there before me."

"When did you ring him?"

"Last week, just before the dress-rehearsal. I suppose I hoped it would throw him. It did too; it was one of the worst performances I've ever seen." He sniggered again. "But he put the fear of God into me. I didn't know what to do. Any minute I thought he was going to bring it up in front of everybody, but he just ignored me, looked through me like I wasn't there and didn't listen to a word I said as usual. It was weird, man, really weird."

He broke off to light another cigarette from the half-smoked butt of the last.

He was weird too. I sat watching him, wondering why he was telling me all this. I know I'd asked him to, but I hadn't expected a blow by blow confession; it was always encouraging to have to resort to thumbscrews somewhere along the line.

Then, of course, I realised he was actually enjoying it. He had almost brought off a coup and the fact that it had been aborted had, in his own mind, turned the whole affair into a practical joke which had misfired – like a defused, unexploded bomb. Now he could talk about it, kick it around; now he was in the clear and a dangerous protagonist dead.

Stanley Verdun, a harmless drunk, was dead too.

Braidy was speaking again.

"On the first night I went round to see everybody before the show and was damn fool enough to include him. He went for me like a mad bull, frightened the life out of me – and dressed up like that he looked like bloody Moses with the Ten Commandments. I denied everything, of course, but he wasn't having it. But he knew it was deadlock; like I said, he couldn't expose me without exposing himself. And, of course, he hadn't been on to the fuzz at all – if he had, they'd have had him inside before he was off the phone."

"How did the accident happen?"

He ground his cigarette into the grass. "The guy was tight as a tick, wasn't he? And Grantley wasn't much better either. He'd been up in Birmingham all day on some business of his own. We were pre-recording a chat-show for the Beeb that night, so we met up at the studios. He looked as if he'd been on the booze all day. When it was all over he offered me a lift back, God knows why. I didn't much fancy the idea, but it was such a filthy night, pissing down, and I hadn't even got a coat, so I said okay. Wish to God I hadn't now. He was all over the place. Then this guy came out of nowhere, weaving about in the headlights and coming straight for us. There wasn't much Grantley could do; he jammed on the brakes and skidded right into the bugger, head on. The guy hung on to the mirror and the car just picked him up and dragged him along, then dropped him. Much later on we stopped because the mirror had been bent and Grantley got out to straighten it. I watched him banging away at it in the rain like a maniac. Then he was sick as a pig in the gutter."

He drew heavily on his cigarette. "When we finally got back he said something about us both being in the shit together, and that if the fuzz got on to it, *King Lear* would be off for good. It would have been too. And that's all there was to it. Later I got this idea of getting back at him. It was worth a try but it didn't work, did it?" He added with a sudden flare of malice, "That old bastard stood for everything I loathe most in the theatre."

"The feeling was mutual."

"God, he was a miserable sod to work with. Everything I did, right from the beginning, was undermined by him. And he got the rest of the company on his side too – they were like a lot of sodding puppets on strings."

My fingers began to itch. "Has it ever occurred to you that you, too, might be a miserable sod to work with? That just once, you could be wrong? That the reason you lost the company was because they rumbled the fact that you couldn't direct pussy out of a paper bag?"

He shambled suddenly and awkwardly to his feet. "Why don't you just piss off?"

"Oh, grow up, for Christ's sake," I said wearily pulling my shirt over my head. "Go away and learn something from the people who've spent a lifetime in the business before blasting off half-baked ideas which prove your ignorance of the theatre and the people in it. Give yourself ten years, little man, and try again."

He was wobbling uncertainly on his lilo, white with rage. As I rose calmly to my feet, I saw him register the tape-recorder still on the ground between us; I read in his eyes his intention to trample on it. I lunged forward, caught at his raised foot, twisted it and brought him smartly down on to his front. Picking him up bodily by the seat of his shorts and his sweaty head-band, I carried him, wriggling and bawling, down to the water's edge and flung him as far as I could into the river.

"Cool off!" I shouted after him.

I stood for a second watching until he came up for air, spluttering and spewing out great mouthfuls of the Avon, then, retrieving the recorder, I waved a hand at him, turned on my heel and made off towards the house.

The white face of Evelyn Spraggs hung disembodied at a third floor window. I gave her a wave too.

Chapter Eighteen

"Was he telling the truth, do you think?" asked Barbara, trenchering away at her chicken salad. "About the money, I mean."

"I'm sure of it. He was pretty fed up."

"So what are you going to do about it?"

"Nothing. It never happened."

"So he gets away with it?"

I shrugged. "He might have learned something."

"How to behave like a human being, you mean?"

"We must hope for something better than that."

She smirked at me over her raised fork. "Cynicism, Mark Savage, does not become you."

Having left Paul Braidy wallowing in the Avon, I had decided to winkle Barbara out of her office for a quick lunch and a gossip in the theatre's Riverside Restaurant.

"So what's next on the menu?" she asked.

"Apple pie and ice-cream."

"On *your* menu?"

"Ring Mitch."

"Your office?"

I nodded. "She'll think I've died."

"Doesn't she know where you are?"

"I was last heard of at the Swan's Nest, from whence, you may remember, I was kidnapped and carried off to an address in Bull Street."

"The telephone number of which she is ignorant?"

"Well put."

"You can use my phone upstairs."

I stared down at the crowded river. "And then I'll have to go."

She was silent for a time, then, "You're finished here?"

"One or two loose ends I'd like to tie up, but they won't take long. I should be away this afternoon." I touched her hand. "But back for the inquest."

"When?"

"Thursday, Friday, I don't know."

"Is that going to be tricky?"

"I'm not going to enjoy it."

"Will you tell the whole truth?"

"No." I paused. "But whether withholding the truth will make any difference to the verdict remains to be seen."

"And what's *your* verdict?"

I hesitated, miserably twisting at the stem of my wineglass. "He took his own life," I muttered at last. The words seemed to create a void inside me.

"No doubts?"

I pondered for a moment. "I guess he'd had just about enough."

"Will you tell Connie that?"

Again I hesitated. "Whatever I tell her, she'll have to live with the official verdict. At least there's no indication of foul play – or if there is, I've missed it. That's what she most feared. In the light of medical findings, suicide would seem almost acceptable – even, probably, to Connie. He'll lose none of his stature because of it. Everyone except the Catholics will sympathise. As for the rest of it, in the shoes of the devil's advocate, I would be unprepared to recommend canonisation." I gave a wry smile. "*Saint* Gerald is just not on, I'm afraid. Would you like some apple pie?"

Her office on the second floor, a converted dressing-room, contained more junk and rubbish than an ordinary, normal householder could accumulate in a decade.

"I inherited it," she protested when I pointed it out. "It's for posterity – handed down from generation to generation. If anyone bothered to look they'd probably find the original manuscripts at the bottom of that lot, written in the Bard's own hand on period toilet-paper. Incidentally," she added, clearing a space for me at the desk, "have you ever wondered what they used for toilet-paper in those days?"

"I can't honestly say that I have," I told her. "Nor do I think I want to know."

224

I dialled my office number. She perched in a corner on a pile of boxes. "I'm going to sit here and listen," she said as I looked at her enquiringly. She was in pink slacks, a black, yellow and white striped blouse and reminded me of a liquorice allsort.

"Mitch?"

"Mark! Where are you?" Mitch's voice wailed over the phone like an air-raid siren. "I've been trying to get you. What happened? You checked out of the Swan's Nest on Sunday, they said, and nothing, not a word from you since, no address, no phone number, nothing . . ."

"Mitch," I said. "You've been pony-trekking in Wales, yes?"

"Yes."

"And you got back to the office today, yes?"

"Yes."

"Then I've been missing for about four hours."

She had read about Gerald's demise and was deeply distressed by it. I filled her in with the vaguest details and said I'd tell her the rest when we met.

"I've been trying to get you," she said, "because there's a package here for you marked *Strictly Personal and Urgent*. I didn't want to open it in case it was 'naughty' personal if you know what I mean."

"Where's it from?"

"According to the postmark, Stratford-upon-Avon."

A strange sense of foreboding crawled over me. I gave Barbara a preoccupied frown. "Open it, will you, Mitch?"

"Hang on." A moment later. "It's from Gerald Grantley," she said in a mystified voice.

I felt the blood drain from my face. I sat carefully on Barbara's office chair. "Read it out to me."

After a moment's silence she said: "Mark, are you sure? He has marked it personal . . ."

"Read it, Mitch."

More silence then, "Okay, here it is. 'My dear boy, When this comes to your hand I shall have committed the two most dastardly crimes in the ecclesiastical canon – murder and self-slaughter . . .'"

She broke off. I could hear the rustle of paper and sensed her eyes skimming over the next few lines. "Go on," I muttered irritably.

"'Please don't doubt the soundness of my mind; I'm perfectly lucid, I assure you, and in full possession of my faculties. The gun lies in front of me here on the desk as I write and when the time comes – as it will soon – I shall use it without fear or conscience and certainly without regret.'"

Again she hesitated. "Mark, don't you think it would be better if . . ."

"Get on with it, Mitch, please."

She continued huskily. "'The cloud-cuckoo-land which some believe lies beyond the grave worries me not at all, since I am of the opinion that no such scarey twilight-zone exists. Only *you* will judge me – you and dear Connie, my friends and enemies – most of you with little sympathy I fear – but that's something I have to learn to die with. I can only say "Sorry" to you all and leave it at that. *None of you stands in my shoes.*' That's underlined," said Mitch on her own account.

"'Wouldn't it be fitting,'" she went on, "'if each one of us were permitted to take into the darkness with us one erring and undesirable individual – thus ridding the world of the machinations of such a one? Would that not benefit mankind? But then, "use every man after his deserts and who shall 'scape whipping?" eh? Few of us, alas, would reach maturity. Anyway, for better or for worse, it's a theory I, for one, mean to put into practice. I shan't be going alone into the shadows.

"'Well, enough of all that. It's late and I haven't a lot of time. Mark, dear boy, I need to ask you a last couple of favours. Enclosed you'll find some bearer-bonds. I would like you to pass them on to Emma Hardcastle, the sculptress, who is staying with the Ardens just down the road – Connie will know. There'll be no difficulty in converting them. She and I parted company under somewhat strained circumstances and I'd like to try to make it up to her. I can be an irascible old cuss at times.'"

I heard her turn the page.

"'The second favour takes the form of a challenge. You're a detective, see if you can find out the reasons behind all this hullabaloo, and when you've done so, as I'm sure you will, pass them on to Connie; then, and only then, give her the enclosed

226

envelope. In recompense for which I would like you to accept one of the bonds here enclosed – with good grace! It has all the elements of Hamlet seeking out the murderer of his father, don't you think?

" 'So glad you liked old Lear – I quite enjoyed it too, in my own small way – twenty-two calls they tell me. Not bad, eh, for a beginner? Ho ho!

" 'Think of me only as you knew me – fellow artist and friend. If there is a God, may he rain blessings upon you. If, by the same token, I discover that a God really exists, then you'd better pray for me – hard.

" 'Good night, dear sweet Prince . . . G.' "

There was a long silence. I felt the pricking of tears behind my eyes and could hear Mitch's in her voice – tough and practical though she was. At last I cleared my throat. "Thanks, Mitch . . . sorry to have burdened you with that."

After a short silence during which I could sense her pulling herself together, she said, "What do you want me to do? Send it on to you?"

"No – er – just a minute, hang on . . ." I sat for an indecisive moment. "On second thoughts, yes, send the whole lot on by Datapost so that I get it first thing in the morning." I gave her the Bull Street address. "Then I can cope with it before I come back."

"Right."

"Thanks, Mitch, you're a treasure, thanks a lot."

I hung up and stared at the receiver for a long time in silence. I could sense Barbara's unrest; I looked across at her. She met my eyes. "Trouble?"

I shook my head dumbly, finding it difficult to wrestle with my emotions. "A letter from Gerald," I muttered more brusquely than I intended.

She came to me and pressed my face against her gaily coloured blouse. I wrapped my arms about her and remained there for a long time, feeling her warmth and thinking of Gerald.

"But who did he kill?" I whispered at last, releasing her gently and staring blankly into her concerned eyes. "He says he – took someone into the darkness with him . . ."

227

I broke away and moved restlessly to the window and back, giving her the gist of the letter as I roamed the tiny office. Then I stood for a second, staring glumly at my feet. "But suppose it all went wrong, and it didn't work out as he'd planned – the best laid schemes of mice and men and all that. Gerald planned for two bodies and only one turned up. Why? There's only one answer to that: the other walked away."

"He didn't say who he was going to kill?"

"Someone erring and undesirable."

She made a face. "That's all of us, isn't it? We're all erring and undesirable to someone."

"But who particularly to Gerald?"

At the same moment we each read the identical name in the other's eyes. I made for the door. "I should have bloody drowned him when I had the chance," I muttered.

"Where are you going?"

"Where do you think?" I banged out into the corridor, my footsteps echoing in the confined space like Gerald's damn clock clacking away the seconds of his lifetime.

Nearing the end of the corridor I caught sight of a lithe figure in jeans and trainers climbing to an upper floor.

Dave Ravel.

What was he doing in the theatre? He had no status here, no function. Unless he and Braidy had made it up . . .

I followed him quietly as he climbed the stairs to the upper floor and into the corridor immediately above the one I had just left.

"Is that the lot?" I heard him ask as he pushed open the second door along.

I snucked up a couple of steps beyond.

"I'll bring the rest," came Braidy's voice. "Tell the driver I'll be down in a minute."

Seconds later the boy reappeared carrying a small suitcase, a couple of coats and a pair of boots. I watched him out of sight, then strolled nonchalantly into the room, closed the door quietly behind me and leaned up against it in the casual way so beloved of movie directors the world over.

Paul Braidy, with his back to me, was hunched over a littered desk, sorting through various papers, some of which he flung into a waste-bin, transferring others to an open canvas hold-all which stood on a corner of the desk.

"You off then?" I enquired in my silkiest of silky voices.

He wheeled around with a stifled exclamation. His hair was still wet and there was a wild, vacant sort of look in his eyes. A couple of seconds later he had recovered himself. One way and another he was quite an actor. He had me fooled right out of my Y-fronts.

"What the hell are you doing here?" he snarled unpleasantly, turning his back on me and going on with what he was doing. "Thought I'd seen the last of you."

"That's not very kind. I was just checking on your health. Heard you fell in the river – thought you might have done yourself a nasty."

"Very funny."

"Wasn't meant to be."

"Look." He half turned as he stuffed a couple of books into the hold-all. "Would you just go away? I have a car waiting and I'm in a hurry."

"Doing a bunk, are you? I don't blame you. In your shoes I would too."

He gave a patient sigh. "Mr Savage, I'm tired of your performance. I've said everything I intend to say to you, so would you kindly mind your own business and leave others to mind theirs?"

"That's what I am doing. Unfortunately, my business happens to be yours too."

He moved over to a high shelf, reaching up to collect a couple of video tapes; his hand, trembling visibly, muffed the movement and sent one of the tapes clattering to the floor. As he stooped to recover it, I said, "If I were you, Mr Braidy, I'd send that car away. You won't be using it."

Righting himself slowly and almost painfully as if he were an arthritic, he turned towards me, his face ashen and shiny with sweat, eyes curdled in a mixture of fear and malice.

From the corridor behind me came the soft scuff of feet and the door was shoved open against my back. I peered around the edge of it. "Hello, Dave, thought it might be you. Do me a favour, will you? Trot down to the car, unload it, tell the driver

229

to take it away, and sorry he's been troubled and all that. Mr Braidy won't be going anywhere after all."

Puzzled blue eyes tried to peer over my shoulder; I edged open the door a fraction to allow him a glimpse of the view. "Tell him, Mr Braidy."

I watched the eyes widen with disbelief, saw the jaw slacken and drop in dismay. Turning my head to see what was worrrying him I found myself staring stupidly into the black muzzle of the biggest revolver I had ever seen. I suppose it was no bigger than your ordinary standard Smith & Wesson .38, but in the puny fist of Paul Braidy it took on the importance of an anti-tank weapon.

I regarded it fixedly for a long moment before raising my eyes to meet the manic glare behind it.

"Come in and shut the door, Dave," whispered Braidy hoarsely.

I made just enough room for Dave to slide through, which he did with a marked lack of enthusiasm, then closed the door. "Over here, Dave."

The boy padded a couple of steps towards him, hesitated, then pulled up between us, settling for no-man's-land.

"I wouldn't stand there if I were you, Dave," I warned him. "If we join battle you might well get hurt."

Eyeing the gun nervously he glanced uncertainly at each of us, then took a couple of cautious steps back, standing at last with his back to the wall, still unprepared to take sides.

"All right, Mr Braidy," I said, lounging back against the door. "Now what do we do?"

Unrehearsed in a situation brought about by his own panic, he was now in the unenviable position of initiating the next move – since it was he who was holding the gun.

"Get away from the door," he ordered in a spindly sort of voice, waving the weapon at me.

I shook my head. "No."

"I've got the gun," he reminded me.

"True. The question is, what are you going to do with it? You've been pretty clever up till now, I'll give you that. Except for one thing. They say a murderer always makes one mistake, and you're no exception. That gun is your mistake.

How did you happen to come by Gerald Grantley's gun, I wonder?"

He grabbed at the hold-all on the desk behind him and moved a step towards me, brandishing the revolver with a wild show of bravura.

Again I shook my head, folded my arms and went on leaning against the door hoping that my . pounding heart wasn't showing through my shirt front. I didn't care much about the way his sweaty trigger-finger was trembling but there wasn't a lot I could do about it. If I tried a lunge at him I had no doubt that his panic would drill a hole through me. I could, of course, move out of the way and let him go – there was always another day – but I couldn't honestly see myself doing that – not until I'd had a few more quiet words with him.

"You haven't answered my question," I reminded him. "How do you come to be in possession of Gerald Grantley's revolver?"

One step more and I'd have had him – and he knew it. Some crazy instinct warned him that to come any closer would spell disaster for him, as surely as I knew that a fractional move on my part and they'd be setting me up in tomorrow's obituary columns.

"You see what I mean, Dave?" I said flicking a lazy eye at the young Greek god plastered against the wall, his eyes glazed with fright. "You never really knew him, did you? I really think you should get out of here while you can. Let him go, Braidy. It's our quarrel, not his."

"He'll stay where he is," snapped Braidy moving back a pace, his eyes never leaving mine. When I unfolded my arms, my last moment was only a breath away: he crouched suddenly, snapping the gun up towards my face, the knuckle of his finger white with tension. I doubt if I'd ever been closer to my end.

It was a ridiculous situation, the three of us crowded together in that overheated, claustrophobic box-room of an office – even the walls seemed to be sweating.

"Put the gun down, Braidy," I said again. "Let's talk about it, for God's sake. Even if you kill me it's not going to do you any good. How far do you think you'd get? And would it be

231

worth it? One killing is enough. A good lawyer might even get you off the hook. But two . . . they'd stash you away for at least twenty years, and then where would your precious career be?"

He stood uncertainly for a second, then dropping his hold-all with a sigh, smoothed his long black hair, stranding it across his glistening brow; his eyes, deep in their dark sockets, glittered with malevolence; he breathed shallowly in sharp uneven bursts – everything about him trembled as if the build-up of tension would finally burst through the pallid skin and destroy him.

"He tried to kill me," he whispered hoarsely. "The bastard was going to kill me."

"He set you up, didn't he?" The mouth twitched convulsively as I intervened, his eyes narrowing. His tongue flicked out to lick at his dry lips. " 'Come up to the tower on Saturday night and I'll give you your ten thousand to keep you quiet.' That's what he said, isn't it? And you fell for it."

"I told him to get lost."

"But you went all the same. And there he was, waiting for you, ready to shoot the guts out of you. What did you do, fall on your knees and grovel, beg for mercy?"

Maybe I wouldn't survive the afternoon; maybe he wouldn't either. I glanced across at Dave; he hadn't moved a muscle and was still propping up the wall like a stone carving, blue eyes on stalks and his mouth half open.

My irresponsible outburst was greeted not with the expected stream of invective but with a strangely subdued and intro-verted line of self-congratulatory satisfaction – as if he had floated off into a dream-world of his own.

"I fought him, didn't I?" he whispered, a twisted half-smile on his lips. "Twice my size and I fought him. I'd climbed all those steps, too, *and* walked all the way from Stratford. It was dark. I couldn't see him at first, then he was there, in his shirt-sleeves, hauling something up the flag-pole. His jacket, he said it was – he'd flipped see? – flying it at half-mast, he said, because he'd decided to do away with himself and thought it'd be appropriate. But he wanted to settle accounts with me first – didn't want to leave any unpaid debts behind him. Then he showed me the gun – he'd had it behind his back. 'So I've decided to take you with me,' he said. 'We'll be company for each other.' He thought that was very funny."

He wiped his forehead with the back of his hand and gave me a mocking smirk. "And, just like you, Mr Savage, he was expecting me to cringe and slobber. You remind me of him, you know – a lot – leaning up against that door so smug and sure of yourself. He was just like that too, half drunk, off his guard. Know what I did? I put my head down and ran at him before he could even get the gun up; I butted him in the stomach. He never knew what hit him. He went back against the battlements and I just – " he raised two fingers of his left hand like a priest giving a blessing, " – pushed him, quite gently, and over he went . . . backwards. It was a great moment. And do you know what? I didn't feel a thing – no remorse, no regret, nothing. I just looked over the edge, and there he was – sprawled like a dead starfish."

There was a long pause. He licked voluptuously at his lips again. The smile of remembered triumph smeared over his sweaty face made me want to vomit. I glanced briefly at Dave. He was staring at Braidy as if he were something nasty looking out from under a stone; he felt my eyes on him and we exchanged a look.

Braidy gave a jeering little chuckle. "Dave told me about your visit. I hear a wardrobe fell on you. Tough! And now you're trying the same tactics on me, are you?"

I summoned up a sour smile. "Small chance of that."

"Right, man, small chance." He patted the gun complacently.

"As a matter of interest, how *did* you get hold of that gun?" I asked.

"He dropped it when I butted him. The key too – the key to the tower." He drew in his shoulders and wriggled a little, as if he were hugging himself. "That's all there was to it – except that old Connie suddenly turned up and began bawling up the stairs. Luckily for her she decided to stay where she was. I watched her go, then went down and locked the place up. But, see? I remembered that a dead man couldn't lock doors after him, so I opened it up again and left the key in the lock." He gave à little crow of laughter. "See? I had all my wits about me. The perfect crime."

I smiled back. "Except for the gun. You should have thrown the gun in the river." I shook my head and clucked my tongue at him. "And the following day you gave the performance of your career. I take my hat off to you – you convinced me. I never guessed any of it. May I ask you one question?"

"Be my guest" He waved an expansive hand, enjoying every minute of what I hoped would be a short-lived preening session.

"When did Grantley make this date with you – to meet him up there on the tower?"

"Saturday, during the show, in the first interval. I went backstage to give the cast some notes and he called me into his room. He was like my long-lost brother – full of apologies for the brawl we'd had earlier, even offered me a drink – real smarmy he was. Said he'd decided to 'meet my demands' – *his* words, pompous old fart – but I'd have to go to Grantley to collect. Well, the top of a bloody church tower at four o'clock in the morning sounded pretty naff, but what the hell? – ten grand was ten grand. Later, after the scene at the party, I wondered if he'd go back on it, but I went anyway." He gave a wet giggle. "Glad I did now, otherwise he'd still be around, wouldn't he, making everybody's life a misery?"

I was about to launch myself at him and to hell with the gun, when the telephone on the desk gave voice and frightened the life out of all of us. Braidy jumped visibly and glowered at me as if it were my fault. The gun remained levelled at my chest.

"Answer it, Dave."

Dave pushed himself unwillingly from his wall and picked up the phone. We listened to a lot of squawking from the other end. "It's the car," said Dave, an unsteady hand over the mouthpiece. "The driver can't wait any longer. He's got another booking."

"Two minutes, tell him," snapped Braidy. "I'll be with him in two minutes."

"You're not going anywhere," I said loudly.

"Do as I tell you, Dave," Braidy shouted, snatching at the telephone, momentarily turning the gun on Dave.

It was the moment I had been waiting for. I hurled myself across the room; he saw me coming, as did Dave who grappled awkwardly at the gun while Braidy's attention was divided.

The shot almost blew away my ear-drums. Through the stupifying impact of it I heard a strangled shout of pain and the shattering of glass; a picture toppled from the wall with a great crash; acrid blue smoke enveloped us. The three of us were inextricably locked together in a struggling heap for what seemed an endless space of time.

Then I registered Dave's blue eyes, full of pain, slowly glazing over, his mouth opening and shutting convulsively as he struggled for breath; he began sliding slowly backwards from the desk. I grabbed at the front of his shirt; it was warm and wet with blood and slid stickily from my grasp; the eyes were closing even as he crashed to the floor.

I rounded on Braidy, but he had already wriggled himself free and was halfway to the door. "You've killed him, you bastard," I shouted, lunging after him. He had the door open and, turning, raised the gun. I was flat on the deck before he could squeeze the trigger. The bullet zipped over my head and smashed through the window beyond.

Through the echoing roar I was aware of a confusion of voices, the sound of running feet and Braidy shouting as he raced down the corridor. Another shot reverberated through the building followed by the angry whine of an endless ricochet. A woman screamed.

Scrambling to my feet, I made for the corridor, which was thick with smoke and loud with the babble of voices; white startled faces turned towards me as I erupted from the room.

I ploughed through them, shoving them roughly aside shouting as I went, "See to Dave – he's been shot . . ."

At the corner I came face to face with Barbara wide-eyed with alarm. I seized her by the shoulders. "Braidy's gone berserk. He's shot Dave. Get an ambulance. Call the cops." She nodded automatically as I left her and raced on. "Be careful," she called after me.

Although the theatre was thankfully pretty deserted at that hour in the afternoon, there were enough administrative staff caught in various stages of confusion to chart the progress of the fugitive Braidy. The bedworthy lady stage-door keeper was poised on the terrace, shading her eyes, staring after him as he leapt down the steps, pausing only to kick out at something on the pavement. "What's happening?" she yelled shrilly as I shot past her in pursuit. "Are they making a film?"

It was a pile of luggage he'd kicked at, lying on the pavement; the cab driver had been as good as his word.

A crocodile of uniformed schoolgirls queuing on the steps of the museum scattered like chaff as Braidy swept through them like an ill-omened wind, taking a couple with him and up-ending several more. Felled schoolgirls, yelling and shrieking at the tops of their voices, seemed to be everywhere as I bore down upon them. It was like a nightmare sequence from St Trinian's. Their outraged female guardian, pint-sized and magnificent in straw hat and glasses askew, stood foursquare in my path and belaboured me with her handbag as, leaping over several of her more hapless charges, I passed through shouting apologies.

The road ahead was empty. I pulled up abruptly. The gravelly sound of a concrete-mixer in operation drew my attention to the building site adjacent to the museum where they were putting up the new Swan Theatre.

Two safety-helmeted workmen standing at the door of a site-office were staring across the littered yard shouting something inaudible above the juddering mixer. Following their gaze I was in time to see what I took to be Braidy's heels disappearing through a hole in a shaky-looking wall.

As I chased after him the concrete-mixer ground to a halt. "Oi!" yelled one of the tin-hats behind me. "Where d'you think you're going? You got a pass?"

I was through the hole and stood for a panting second, blinded by the sudden darkness. I could hear him scrambling ahead somewhere, falling and cursing, whimpering in his distress. Silhouetted against the daylight I was an easy shot should he decide to resort to target practice; I ducked to one side, stumbled against a stack of bricks which collapsed beneath my weight taking me with it. Muttering angrily to myself I lay there for a second listening. There was plenty of noise in the offing, drilling and hammering and voices raised in song, but none of it as close as the sounds I'd picked up a

236

moment before. He was either holding his breath or he'd put a wall between us.

As my eyes became accustomed to the gloom I could make out a mortar-trough miraculously avoided in my fall, and beyond it stood a six-foot wall of concrete blocks above which glowed a pallid suffusion of light.

Picking my way through vast quantities of mud and rubble I found a break in the wall, the only path Braidy could have taken. Again I listened for any extraneous sounds, but other than the customary racket expected of a building site, and the rudimentary vocalising of a latter-day Caruso yodelling his way through *O Sole Mio*, there was nothing.

On the far side of the wall was a mucky-looking concrete staircase littered with battered buckets and empty cement bags. The light came from a bare electric bulb suspended from an overhanging plank. My feet gritted on sand as I climbed.

Now, suddenly, the auditorium of the projected theatre yawned before me, little more than a three-tiered shell and reminiscent, in its present state, of one of the lower reaches of Dante's *Inferno*.

Instead of a floor there was a seemingly bottomless pit seething with a sweating army of yellow-helmeted workmen digging and delving, sawing and hammering; the ear-splitting clamour of a battery of pneumatic-drills and the intermittent screaming of a bandsaw only helped to confirm my fanciful vision of demonic chaos.

My spirits sank as I stared disconsolately about me. The chances of rooting him out in the midst of all that seemed negligible.

Above me rose two further tiers, forming the "wooden O" of Shakespeare's theatre, and because the roof was already in position, the only light was shed by a succession of naked bulbs strung on sagging cables.

Through choking clouds of dust and a labyrinth of scaffolding, I peered into the shifting shadows for the sight of a head without a safety helmet. He could be anywhere, watching me at this very moment, snucked down behind any one of a dozen vantage points.

I moved upwards to the next gallery and stood in despair,

237

surveying once more the chaos below, peering again into the darkness of the balustraded upper tier. In a place like this he could remain invisible until the theatre opened and the audience tramped in.

I was turning away when something on the upper gallery caught the corner of my eye. It was simply a patch of shadow, nothing more, but more intense than the shadows around it. Why it should have attracted my attention I had no idea, unless it had moved a split second before my eye had lighted on it.

I drew back into the gloom, my eyes never leaving the spot for an instant, and waited.

And waited.

I grew impatient and was on the point of giving up when it moved, slowly, warily edging out into the dim light. No helmet, only a round, black head hunched on narrow shoulders. There was only one round black head like that. Now I could see his eyes glowing oddly beneath the dark fall of hair; I could make out the sweat glistening on his face, the teeth bared as he drew deep and painful breaths.

I faded into the background, turned and slid silently upwards. A couple of workmen carrying buckets passed me on the stairs. "Where's your 'at, mate?' one of them enquired but didn't wait for an answer.

Up there, beneath the inverted funnel-like roof, the echoes were even more pronounced; acoustically, the building was as sensitive as a whispering gallery.

Crouching behind a stack of timber I edged forward until he sidled into my eye-line. Gun in hand, he was standing perfectly still; only his eyes moved as he quartered the building for a glimpse of pursuit. His chest was heaving. Above the almighty welter of sound I couldn't hear his breathing, but I guessed he was pretty spent. He was hardly the type to have kept himself physically in shape; jogging and daily press-ups weren't exactly his bag; getting up in the morning and brushing his teeth was probably all the exercise he ever took.

There was also fear in his breathing; I could almost smell it. His head turned in my direction; I ducked instinctively but the light was so bad I needn't have bothered. I took another look. Now he was moving away from me, hugging the wall, a shadow among shadows, every now and again the gun glinting in his hand.

Rising to my feet I fell in noiselessly behind him, moving swiftly to overtake him. Nobody could afford to have him on the loose again.

I don't know what happened to make him turn; the slightest sound perhaps; the inbuilt instinct of the hunted out-manoeuvring the hunter. A couple of yards separated us when he swung about, gun at the ready, facing me. *Now* I could hear his breath, see the panic, smell the fear sweating out of him.

"Come any closer and I'll kill you." The hoarse, trembling whisper bordered on hysteria. "I swear I will . . . I'll kill you . . ."

I didn't doubt it for a moment. "Don't be an idiot," I told him, rooting myself firmly to the floor. "You'll only make matters worse for yourself."

He was staring at me wildly, tears beginning to well up into his eyes, the gun, shaking though it was, homed in on my chest.

He was speaking again, inaudible above the racket.

I held a hand to my ear. "What?"

"Dave," he repeated. "Is Dave all right?"

I shrugged. "You probably just winged him. You'll see . . . Come on now, be sensible and give me the gun."

I stretched out a hand and took a tentative step forward. He backed away, stumbling slightly and righting himself, one hand on the wooden balustrade.

"I don't want to shoot you but I swear I will if I have to. I don't care now, one way or the other . . . not about you, me or anything." His voice went up a couple of notches. "You can all go to hell for all I care. Just let me get out of here. For Jesus Christ's sake, leave me alone to work things out for myself – in my own way."

With a sudden jolt in the stomach I became aware of a workman looming up behind him – a burly figure in overalls and a yellow safety-helmet.

"What's going on there?" he demanded in a loud voice.

"Go away!" I yelled at him.

Braidy pivoted, the gun roared and the man buckled grabbing wildly at his stomach, his eyes wide and startled.

Before he struck the ground I had hurled myself at Braidy's ankles bringing him down with an almighty crash. He kicked a foot free and drove it down on to my head like a pile-driver. I heard myself cry out and released my hold on him. For a second I lay stunned, giving myself up to the sheer agony of it, vaguely aware that he was crawling on all fours, reaching for the fallen gun – aware too that at the sound of the shot all other noises had abated.

Reaching for the balustrade, I dragged myself up on to my knees, resting my head against it. Down below, work had come to a standstill, the men peering upwards, hands shading their eyes, faces white, mouths agape.

"What the hell was that?" said a plaintive voice. "Sounded like a shot."

I hauled myself to my feet. Braidy was squatting against the wall, swaying slightly, his eyes wide with fright, the gun, clasped possessively in both hands, trained on my face. Between us lay the wounded man, groaning and half-conscious, blood oozing thickly between the fingers clutching at his stomach.

Risking the shaking black muzzle, I drew a deep breath. "There's a wounded man up here," I shouted. "Send someone up with a doctor – and get an ambulance."

Braidy started up, shrieking like a madman. "I'll shoot the first one who moves."

"Don't be a damn fool," I bawled back at him. "Drop the fucking gun!"

From below there came a concentrated roar of voices as the stunned army of workmen began to take in what was happening.

Braidy stood for a second irresolute, shaking, tears streaming down his face. I saw his waterlogged eyes shift and widen as they caught sight of something behind me. I twisted my head. The two men I had passed on the stairs were moving slowly towards us. Braidy was whimpering with fear. A huge coloured man was closing in on him from the other side.

I think the next few seconds were the most terrible I have ever lived through. Paul Braidy, trapped with nowhere to go, trembling so violently that he found it almost impossible to remain upright, gave a great lonely cry and before the sound had died away, he had thrust the muzzle of the gun into his mouth and squeezed the trigger.

His blood and brains splattered my face. The bullet thudded into the wall behind him, the plasterwork splintering, blossoming suddenly like a flower, red and shining. He fell back against it, hung there for a second almost wearily, then, as his knees began to buckle, stumbled forward slowly, already dead, pitching finally onto the balustrade, the back of his head wet and black and hideously gaping.

Swallowing the bile rising in my throat, I scrubbed maniacally at my face with my forearm.

That last cry was echoed by those below, horrified as the slack figure folded itself almost neatly over the wooden balustrade and hung there like a vanquished puppet in a Punch and Judy show.

There followed a silence so complete, beating so hard against the ear-drums that it hurt.

The dead hand holding the gun relaxed, the fingers loosened, the heavy weapon slid from between them and fell a hundred feet to the ground below. The men around it drew back into a tight and silent circle, watching it as if it were a deadly reptile.

Chapter Nineteen

It had been a bad day, and what was left of it was over-shadowed by a king-size headache the like of which I couldn't remember – and I can remember quite a few in my time.

A placid, pale-faced doctor in black came to have a look at it, parted my hair and made various soundings with his knuckles as if he were trying to get in. He frowned at my various contusions of the previous day, hummed wordlessly over the gash on my cheek, and, curiosity getting the better of him, asked what I did for a living.

When I told him not a lot, he seemed satisfied and nodded wisely all the way to the door. "Aspirin and rest," he advised. "Nothing like it. Take care of that head, it's the only one you've got."

Then a fully paid-up member of the CID turned up – an inspector – rotund, bald and jolly-looking, bearing no resemblance whatsoever to a policeman. He was closely shadowed by the narrow and ubiquitous Sergeant Hunter who introduced me as an imposter, declaring that I had given false information to the police by telling him I was an actor when all the time I was a private investigator.

When they'd finished with me my head had grown consider-ably larger. I could recollect little of what I had told them, remembering only that there had been no mention of the hit-and-run incident and the resultant attempt at blackmail.

They departed with a solemn promise to call again and would I please not take off for foreign climes without first consulting them. "In addition," added the lean Hunter hovering in the doorway, "you are required to attend the inquest on the late Sir Gerald Grantley at the coroner's court at eleven o'clock on Thursday morning."

"Which," put in the Inspector glumly, "may well be

postponed until the evidence you have given regarding this present case can be sifted and studied. You'll be hearing further from us, I shouldn't wonder."

I hid my head in my hands as they creaked out and left me alone. Uneasy people to live with, the fuzz; a dance card for the Policeman's Ball would read like the cast of *Titus Andronicus*.

All this went on in the tiny wooden shed they laughingly called the site-office where, shortly after their departure, Barbara Sterling found me, wretchedly hunched on a high stool staring at an architect's plan of the new Swan Theatre and wondering how the hell anyone could ever begin to make any sense of it.

She scooped me up in her arms and carried me off to her office where she sat me at her desk and produced a none-too-opportune bottle of Courvoisier. Almost immediately the well-known Savage stiff upper lip finally and irrevocably crumpled.

Every distressful detail of Paul Braidy's final moments was permanently engraved on the retina of my mind's eye and continued to flicker through my bruised brain like a recurrent nightmare on a film-loop. In time, I supposed, the colours would fade, the edges blur, the wound heal over, but the scar would remain. For ever.

"Tell me about Dave," I said reviving a little after my second brandy. "Is he really not dead?"

"He was lucky." She perched on the edge of the desk beside me. "The bullet went right through his shoulder – knocked a picture off the wall. They say he'll be all right. They carted him off to the Krankenhaus."

"Silly little sod," I growled. "He oughtn't to be allowed out on his own." I watched her replenishing my glass. "And you oughtn't to be doing that either. I haven't touched brandy since my troubles. You'll have a raving lunatic on your hands."

"But are you feeling any better?"

I closed my eyes and held my head in both hands. "The doctor said this was the only head I had. I have news for him: I've got two. I'm all right, I guess – frail but otherwise okay." I gave a snort. "All I did was to come up here to see a play, and what did I get? Murder, suicide, hit-and-run and blackmail;

243

I've been swallowed by a wardrobe and had my brains kicked in. Maybe I should settle for the simple life, after all. Hey diddle-de-dee, an actor's life for me." I peered up at her. "On the other hand, of course, there's always you."

The blood rose to her cheeks. "Not always," she reminded me. "You're going away again."

"I've got to stay for the inquest on Thursday, and if there's any truth in what that Inspector says, probably longer. I may even have to move my wigwam up here." I took her hand. "Ba, listen . . ."

She gripped my hand tightly. "I know . . . I know what you're going to say, but . . ." She hesitated. "Don't you think we ought to let it ride a bit? We're both working – me up here and you in London. If we rush things we might mess it all up again – like we did before, and I for one wouldn't want that – not again." She lowered her eyes. "I think I love you, Mark. I think I always have – ever since the geyser set fire to your hair, in Henley Street over the fish-shop."

When she laughed, a tear splashed on to the back of my hand, she got off the desk, knelt beside me, head against my chest, and wrapped her arms about me. I held her close.

That was the moment Roger Howells chose to look in.

"Go away, Roger, will you, there's a good lad?" I murmured mildly looking at his startled reflection in the mirror.

Datapost thundered at the front door next morning while we were still lolling about in bed. I lay like a dead seal while Barbara fumbled an uncertain passage to the ground floor, said good morning to the postman and reappeared some ten minutes later bearing a redolent pot of coffee; the package from Mitch she deposited gently on my dozing chest.

Aspirin and a bottle of sparkling Italian wine taken medicinally the night before had marginally cleared my head and I heaved myself into another day with considerable hope for the future.

While Barbara read aloud from the morning newspaper the report on the untimely demise of the late Paul Braidy, I imbibed black coffee before shambling down to the bathroom to shower, shave and consider my wounds. The bruise on my

244

temple, diminished in size, had taken on a rich and clearly permanent purple hue; the top of my head where Braidy had stepped on it felt as if it were scheduled to break loose at any moment, while the scar on my cheek, quietly impressive, was reminiscent of sabre duelling in Heidelberg.

Not until we sat at breakfast did I find the strength of mind and purpose to rip open Gerald's letter and peruse his last words.

Like an army in battle order, the thick black characters marched upright and resolute across the page, with no hint of distress, indecision or regret, only an implacable determination to finish with things as they were, once and for all, leaving no room for argument or reasonable doubt. Violence was there too: the underlining of the phrase: *None of you stands in my shoes*, was scored so deeply that the pen all but penetrated the paper. Violence was a natural adjunct to a state of mind poised on the brink of murder and self-destruction. What I didn't understand was the almost childlike challenge flung at me as an investigator to unravel the whys and wherefores of his actions. If he had succeeded in his original intention as he fully expected to do – the killing of Paul Braidy and his own suicide – he could have depended upon the full co-operation of the police force to do all that. Maybe it was merely a sly theatrical gesture, an oblique thrust at my less than honourable profession. My eye lighted upon the folded bearer bonds on the table before me. Maybe it was a canny excuse for giving me a hand-out. I unfolded the bonds – six of them, each for a thousand pounds. Five for Emma, one for me. A thousand pounds. I could almost hear him laughing.

I folded the bonds about the envelope addressed to Connie, pushed the letter over to Barbara and sat watching her as she read it.

When she'd finished, she laid it on the table and smoothed it with the back of her hand. "There's something almost macabre about it," she murmured. "A voice from the dead. Do you think he was a bit unhinged?"

I shook my head. "Not Gerald. Not in any way. He just wanted to rid the world – his world – of Paul Braidy. He had two grievances against him; attempted blackmail and his utter

245

incompetence in the theatre. And of the two, I'd be willing to bet that the second was the besetting sin. To Gerald he was an imposter and an iconoclast, destroying everything he believed the theatre stood for – though I must say, I could never see Braidy becoming a talent dangerous enough to topple the theatre – unlike some I could mention; some I could quite happily gun down myself in cold blood."

"But you wouldn't?"

"No I wouldn't. They're not worth it."

"But Gerald did. That's the difference. And I think his marbles were a bit loose." She leaned in and raised the corner of one of the bonds. Her lips pursed in a silent whistle. "A thousand pounds. Will you accept it, do you think . . . with good grace?"

I frowned at my plate for a second. "Yes," I said eventually. "He left it to me in his will."

Lizzie Arden, in picture hat and outsize sunglasses was crouched over a bamboo table in the middle of the lawn slaving away at a jigsaw puzzle; above her, a multi-coloured plastic umbrella filtering the sun's rays, turned her into a multi-coloured semblance of a stained-glass window.

The sight of my bruises gave her quite a turn. "Dear boy, your face! What *have* you done to it?"

"I fell off the bike."

She clicked her tongue. "I'd have thought you far too intelligent to ride one of those things. What's wrong with a nice comfortable car?"

"Tin boxes on wheels," I told her. "Lizzie, I'm sorry to burst in on you like this, but I was wondering if Emma was around?"

"She's in the summer-house, working. Funnily enough she was asking about you only this morning. But don't be beastly to her." She showed her large teeth and slapped my hand. "And don't you dare go off without saying goodbye to me."

Emma was sitting motionless on the high stool with her back to the door. When I knocked she made no move. I drew alongside her, staring at the moulded head of Gerald Grantley. It seemed to stare straight back at me, shrewd eyes, quizzically humorous. The meanness and the shut-away arrogance which had before repulsed me were gone; honesty and genius were there instead; it was the urbane face of a man of the people in the prime of his life.

I gave her a sidelong glance. She was perched primly on the stool, feet and knees together, hands, clasped in her lap, holding a modelling tool.

"Well?" she said, conscious of my look. "Does that satisfy you?" The tone was that of a school mistress addressing a backward child; the coldness of it both disturbed and angered me.

"You aren't here to satisfy me," I retorted. "But since you ask, I think it's very fine."

It was the truth, but not the whole truth.

She had whitewashed him, canonised him; he was now too good to be true, a Renaissance Christ incapable of human failings. Whether or not this was evident to me because of what I now knew of Gerald, I had no way of judging. For some reason, best known to herself, she had withdrawn her own admittedly blinkered conception, but instead of the grudging compromise one might have expected, had backed down completely and presented the sort of image which would be palatable to all. By so doing she had betrayed her own talent.

"It's yours if you want it," she said abruptly. "A gift. I'll have it cast, let you know when it's ready."

I was quite taken aback, only half believing her. I said lightly, "That's the best offer I've had today, but I don't see how I could possibly accept, much as I'd treasure it. If you are in the giving vein, shouldn't you, perhaps, let Connie have it — his wife?"

"What you do with it afterwards is your concern," she said stubbornly, adding with impatience, "Take it, for God's sake, otherwise I shall destroy it." She raised the modelling tool threateningly.

"I'll take it," I said hastily. "And thank you."

"Good." She looked up at me for the first time, her eyes widening a little as she registered my battle scars. I thought I caught the slightest glint of amusement in them but she made no comment.

Reaching into my shirt pocket I produced the photo of her mother. "In exchange, there's something here you might like to have. I found it among Gerald's things."

247

She took it and held it, balanced wonderingly on the palm of her hand. It was a long time before she spoke. "He'd kept it all these years," she whispered solemnly, then, "May I really have it?"

"That was the idea." I took out the envelope into which I had sealed the bonds. "There's one other thing. Gerald left instructions that you were to have this – with his thanks and regards."

Placing the photograph upright against the head of her father, she took the envelope, stared at it blankly for a second, then stood it unopened alongside the photograph. As I hovered awkwardly for a further couple of seconds she said in an uncompromising sort of voice, "There's something else you could do for me, Mr Savage, if you will?"

"Ask."

"Sit for me – some time – would you?" She sounded almost gruff.

For a second I felt ridiculously embarrassed and said lightly, "You'd have to tie me down."

"I'll do that if I have to." She turned her head to look up at me, the slightest of smiles twitching at the corners of her mouth. "Will you think about it?"

"Sure I will. But if I do," I nodded at the head on the stand, "no compromises."

She laughed for the first time. "Bruises and all, I promise."

Arch was sitting on the doorstep of the Grantley cottage, drinking tea and fanning himself with his cap.

"'Ullo," he greeted me, narrowing his eyes slyly at my scars. "What 'appened to you then? Run up against a door, did you?"

Ignoring the remark, I joined him on the step. He shot a couple of furtive glances about him and leaned in close. "The car, guv . . . I talked to young Sidney in Shipston and 'e'll give 'er a new wing and a paint job – and not a word to no one."

"Can you trust him?"

"'E owes me," he said darkly and closed one eye.

I reached for my wallet and gave him an office card. "Tell him to send the bill to that address. And if he utters a word to anyone, I'll kill him. Tell him I'm Mafia." I pointed to my bruises. "The man who did this is already dead."

"Don't you worry none," he nodded, not believing a word of it, "Sid's as honest as the day is long."

"Sounds like it." I shoved a tenner into his hand. "Buy yourself a Guinness."

He returned the note, poking it into my shirt pocket. "I ain't in it for the money. I'm doing it for the guv'nor and 'is missus."

I was about to ask him the whereabouts of Connie when he beat me to it. "'Er's round the back in the garden if you want 'er."

I patted him on the head and with leaden feet tramped through the quiet house to what threatened to be the most painful interview of my life.

How much should I tell her? How much *could* I tell her?

Despite my affection and admiration for her husband as a friend and artist, I knew him now to have been a flawed and tarnished human being. He had cuckolded a brother-officer, got his wife with child, killed him in a highly improbable duel, murdered in cold blood the only witness capable of exposing him and then turned his back on the woman and the child she bore him. Years later, in a drunken stupor, he had run down and killed an innocent pedestrian and, for the advancement of his personal career, had deliberately withheld the information from the law. Threatened with blackmail he had then planned a cold-blooded murder, to be followed by the taking of his own life – a desperate remedy embarked upon, not, it must be said, in a state of remorse for the killing, but to save himself from a lingering and far more painful death.

But this time, the Furies had not spared him. "And if there *is* a God, Gerald," I whispered to myself, "I'd better start praying for you."

Connie sat beneath the great oak tree looking lost and frail. Game though she was, the spirit seemed to have gone out of her; the sadness locked into the pale eyes was there to stay.

There was no smile of welcome as I approached, awkward and unprepared for the task before me. I stooped to kiss the cool, powdered cheek. "Connie," I murmured.

In the tree above our heads the wet whistling of a blackbird served only to deepen my uneasiness.

"The doctor was just here," she said in a scarcely audible voice.

"Ah . . ." I stood awkwardly for a moment.

"He said you knew about Gerald." I gave a shrug and a nod. "How?" I was silent. "Did he tell you himself – Gerald, I mean? Please sit down."

I was groping around for some sort of explanation when she added, "Did you really believe he might have killed himself?"

"It was always on the cards, wasn't it?"

She nodded a couple of times, vague and preoccupied. Except for the blackbird there was a long and intense silence. I glanced at her surreptitiously. She was picking at a loose thread in her dress. "Why do you think he didn't tell me?"

"Because I'm sure he didn't want to distress you."

"Distress?" The word was almost shrill. "I was his wife. I'd lived with him for forty years. Surely I had a right to know."

"You had," I mumbled. "I agree."

She turned her head slowly and peered at me through shrewd narrowed eyes. "What happened to your face?"

"Oh, I – er – got into a brawl . . ."

She continued to stare at me, then laid a gentle hand on my knee. "There's something more, isn't there?"

I took a deep breath, said nothing and shook my head instead.

She took my hand in hers. "Mark, please. If it's something about Gerald, I want to know. You gave me a promise, remember?"

Turning towards her I took her other hand, holding them both tightly in mine. "You'll know soon enough anyway. Connie . . . he didn't kill himself." Her eyes seemed to lose focus. "He was going to but didn't."

"Then . . .?"

"Paul Braidy killed him."

She stared at me blankly, her hands now loose in mine.

Slowly, deliberately and using as few words as possible, I told her all, spelling it out carefully as if I were talking to a child. She had married him, she had told me an age ago, for better or for worse; she had known the best, she'd said. Now she learned the worst.

Was it cruel to tell her? I don't know. She'd find out most of it anyway during the next few days, when the motives for Braidy's suicide were revealed. Better she should hear it from a friend rather than from the police and the newspapers. It was no good pretending that Braidy had just gone berserk, even though it were partially true, for there had been little sanity behind the muzzle of that gun when he had exposed to me the pride he'd felt in the destruction of the man he had hated.

But the initial decision to kill lay at Gerald's door, not Braidy's. He would have blown Braidy away with less compunction and compassion than he would have stamped on a cockroach. Braidy had just been quicker off the mark, that was all, and had lived to see a few more days.

When I had finished, Connie sat motionless, her body sagging, hands still and limp in her lap. It was a long time before she spoke; when she did it was merely to whisper, "Thank you, Mark."

A thin wind rustled through the trees; she looked up at the sky. "A cloud . . . look." Her voice seemed to come from a great distance. "Perhaps it will rain at last." I don't think she knew she'd said it.

A squirrel loped across the lawn, pausing every now and again to scratch at the parched grass.

"Why on earth didn't he tell me?" she murmured half to herself, straightening up slowly and smoothing a careful hand over her skirt.

"You'd have told him to go to the police, which was the last thing he wanted. He saw himself being arrested on the spot, shut away, *King Lear* down the drain for ever. *Lear* was the only thing that mattered to him – and to Braidy if it comes to that. So they were sort of – locked together in their own guilt, so to speak, until Braidy thought of a way to profit by it."

"Gerald didn't pay him anything?" I shook my head. She closed her eyes, seeming to draw the silence about her like a cloak as she sat for a long time motionless except for a slight twitching of the fingers. "Oh Gerald, Gerald," she whispered, shaking her head, "what a fool thing to do . . ."

251

I stared hard at the backs of my hands wondering whether it was time for me to go. When I raised my head again she was looking at me. "They'll drag him through the mud for this."

I said slowly and with care, "Gerald is dead, Paul Braidy is dead and Stanley Verdun, the hit-and-run victim, is dead. Verdun was a vagrant it seems, with no fixed abode and no living relatives. When I gave my statement to the police yesterday there was no mention of the accident. The two cases don't relate. Gerald died because he tried to kill Braidy, but Braidy, in self-defence, let us say, killed Gerald instead. Later, Braidy went off his head and blew his brains out. Case closed, finished, and no connection with a hit-and-run incident that happened several weeks ago in another part of the forest."

She frowned. "So why, then, should Gerald and Braidy have met up there at all at four o'clock in the morning? *We* know it because Gerald was being blackmailed. But what about the police? What explanation could they produce for that meeting?"

I shrugged. "None at all. Both the protagonists are dead, taking the reason with them. It's common knowledge they hated each other; in the eyes of the law that could well be enough. They could have decided to have it out, once and for all – pistols at dawn sort of thing."

She shook her head. "But that poor innocent man . . . left to die . . ."

"He was drunk."

"So was Gerald," she reminded me gently. She gave an exasperated little sigh. "I hope he's thoroughly ashamed of himself – getting us all into this pickle. Why couldn't he have . . .?" She shook her head abruptly "Silly man . . . oh, what a silly man."

She brooded to herself for a moment longer then suddenly touched my knees lightly, her despondent manner lifting a little, almost as if her outburst had opened up a new train of thought. "Your mentioning pistols at dawn just now has reminded me of something that once happened to Gerald – years ago now. It's funny how you remember things at the most inopportune moments. Gerald was involved in a duel once – he

252

actually fought a duel – he really did. It's much too long ago now to go into details, but the outcome of that duel, believe it or not, is now living just down the road with Lizzie Arden. You've met her, I think, Emma Hardcastle?" I nodded. "Well, Emma Hardcastle is my step-daughter. There, what do you think of that? I haven't even met her yet, but I shall when all this is over. And the extraordinary thing is that neither Gerald nor I knew of her existence until a few weeks ago when she suddenly faced him with it. He came back here looking as if he'd seen a ghost."

I stared at her almost with disbelief. "Is that when he told you about the duel?"

"Oh Lord no, I knew about that years ago, long before we were even married. That's what I mean, you see, about him always being so open with me. It must have taken a lot of courage to tell me about that. He could so easily have lost me. That's how he's always been with me – open and honest. But now, suddenly, there's this." She gripped my arm hard. "He must have been so appalled by what he'd done – so ashamed. He couldn't even bring himself to tell me." She frowned down at her hands, clenched tightly now in her lap, the knuckles showing white. "If only he had . . . confided in me. I'm sure I could have helped. But he went away full of guilt and left no word . . ."

I put my arm about her narrow shoulders and hugged her to me. "But he did, Connie, he did. That's one of the reasons I'm here – he did leave word."

I took the letter from my pocket and laid it gently on her lap. For what seemed to be an eternity she stared at it wordlessly. Her hands trembled as she took it up, smoothed it, stroking it delicately as if it were made of gossamer. She touched her name lightly with her finger-tips, then looked up at me, doing her best to blink away the tears welling into her eyes.

I cleared my throat and got to my feet. "I'll go and leave you to it. See you again very soon."

Reaching up she took my face between her hands and kissed me on the lips. "God bless you, Mark dear," she whispered. "I can never thank you enough." She touched the scar on my cheek. "And look after that."

I moved away across the lawn, glancing back over my shoulder as I entered the house. She hadn't opened her letter, but was sitting there, holding it in both hands, just staring at it.

We sat hugging our knees on the river bank watching a lone pair of swans glide regally up river, the water around them burnished with the glow of the setting sun.

"A single pair," she murmured half to herself, "where there used to be dozens. It's funny, isn't it? The Avon doesn't seem to make sense without its swans."

The lights were on in the theatre. She peered at her wristwatch. "I'll have to go in a minute."

"What is it tonight?"

"*Troilus.* Want to come?"

I shook my head. "I've had enough of theatres for one week."

A flock of starlings twittered over our heads.

The nightmare part of my mind snapped open suddenly like a shutter: I heard the thundering echo of a gunshot, saw a plain wall deluged with gouts of blood, heard the wet sound of it as it splattered against the fresh plaster . . .

"When does the new one open?" I heard myself ask.

"The Swan? Next year some time, they hope."

. . . a shadowy body, already dead. Stalking grotesquely downwards . . .

I shut my eyes tight. "It's a place I shall avoid."

. . . a phantom folding itself neatly, by numbers, like a glove-puppet, over a wooden balustrade . . .

"Jesus Christ!" I whispered hoarsely.

She reached for my hand and held it crushingly in hers. When she spoke it was in a matter-of-fact voice. "When do you have to go back?"

I damned the phantom back to hell and forced open my eyes. "Tomorrow's inquest is postponed and they want me to stick around for further questioning. Then, of course, there's Gerald's funeral. Mustn't forget dear Gerald's funeral, must we?" I blinked up at the brazen orb of the sun. "Do you know something? I don't want to go to the bloody thing."

"You must." She folded her hand firmly but gently over mine. "If only for Connie's sake."

254

I nodded silently, then said with a sudden flare of petulance, "I just hope to God his letter gave her some comfort, that's all! What a bastard thing to do, leaving her like that without a word." I turned on her suddenly, unreasonably, "Would *you* do a thing like that?"

"Come on, Mark . . . how do I know what I'd do under those circumstances? How do any of us know? We're not in his shoes."

"That's what he said in his letter," I muttered.

"He also said," she pointed out quietly, "that you should remember him as a friend. Forget the rest, darling Mark, forget it. It's not for us to judge him. Remember him as Lear, remember only the best of him – and he did have a lot of the best going for him, didn't he? Come on now . . ." She got to her feet and held out a hand to me. "Put it all away; it's done, finished. You're not going to change anything by brooding over it – that's just a waste of time and energy."

She drew me to my feet and we moved slowly across the gardens mingling with those bound for the theatre. Her quiet practicality steadied me; her hand became a sheet anchor.

"So," I said pulling myself together, piece by piece, relatively calm again. "Can I stay on for a bit in your li'l ol' Victorian hideaway? Please."

"Welcome is on the doormat," she nodded.

"Tomorrow morning at eleven," I went on, "I have an 'in depth' interview with Sister Annabel."

"God help you."

"Tomorrow afternoon, I shall visit the young and beautiful Dave Ravel on his bed of pain."

"God help *him*."

"And tomorrow evening," I went on, "I shall drool over you ever so slightly more than I did today."

I couldn't see that well-known suffusion of blood to her cheeks but I knew it was there.

"I shall look forward to that," she whispered softly. "Good old tomorrow."

I felt suddenly light-headed and raised our hands triumphantly above our heads. " 'And all our yesterdays have lighted fools the way to dusty death,' " I proclaimed loudly to the world

255

at large, smiling winningly at several earnest Shakespearean heads turned enquiringly in our direction. "'Life's but a walking shadow,'" I told them, "'. . . A tale told by an idiot, full of sound and fury . . .'" I turned to look at Barbara, "'Signifying . . .?'"

"'. . . nothing,'" she finished with a satisfied smirk.

And together, hand in hand, we walked into the sunset.